The Sea Around Them

Trobador Publishing
Wakefield, MA 01880
www.normanggautreau.com

ISBN 978-0-9856885-2-3

Cover photograph by Darryn Schneider

The author gratefully acknowledges the expertise of Bill Richard
who lent a great deal of advice on the characteristics and flying of
a Lockheed Electra 10A as well as some of the lexicon of aviation in
the late 30s and early 40s.

By the same author

Sea Room
Island of First Light
Iniquity
Francesca Allegri

The Sea Around Them

A novel

Norman G. Gautreau

Trobador
Publishing

Contents

We live in an old chaos of the sun,
Or old dependency of day and night,
Or island solitude, unsponsored, free,
Of that wide water, inescapable...
Sweet berries ripen in the wilderness;
And, in the isolation of the sky,
At evening, casual flocks of pigeons make
Ambiguous undulations as they sink,
Downward to darkness, on extended wings.

—Wallace Stevens

Part

July, 1941

A Brew *of* Storms

THROUGH LINGERING WINTERS and brief summers, the surrounding sea claims sovereignty, isolating the tiny archipelago of Saint Pierre and Miquelon. Here, the Baffin Current carries freezing waters, sometimes icebergs, around the southern tip of Newfoundland to seal off the islands in winter. And in summer the cold waters, still carrying a rumor of arctic ice, merge with warmer waters to enshroud the islands in fog. At all times these islands are subject to the cadence of seawater respirating at its shores, sloshing on the pebbled beaches, wheezing among the rocks. Land life here is not numerous; whatever is alive is cherished and invites comment.

Whether by ice or by fog, or by its vastness and its brew of storms, the sea ensures the utter seclusion of the islands.

And their loneliness.

He woke from another unsettled sleep to hear a mockery of bird calls, an audacity of life on the bleak island. He heard the rash, gasping burps of the cormorants, the deep growls of the razorbills, the rasping of the snipes, and the shrieking *kyie kyie* of the gulls squawking the sun up. More brazen still was what he heard close by his window—the twitter of a bobolink. All a raucous antiphony—the caterwauling of a tuning orchestra—and he, left out, a violin locked in its case whose strings nevertheless vibrated with a shy sympathy. A hopeful sympathy?

It was like this every July on Saint Pierre, a burgeoning of life that summoned him like a wanton siren. And though his soul and his body responded as would a reckless lover, his mind and his memories told him it was a hoax, an undisciplined reflex.

Like love in a time of war; like peace of mind.

Like forgiveness.

It was an aberration in the vastness of the sea and it always occurred before the snows of the last winter melted and as the winds of the next winter brewed anew in the Arctic. Despite the awakening of life, the Baffin Current flowed unceasingly, bringing the bite of Arctic waters to the surrounding sea. In truth, winter was always present—in the air, on the ground, or in the soul's memory. Life here was born from a womb of ice.

It hadn't always seemed so bleak to him. There once was a time when he enjoyed the awakening earth, the sounds of life, the smell of the fermenting land in estrus. But that was before he was forced to burrow into the earth like a rat as shells sundered it, raining death with each blast, parts of bodies, dismembered trees. Drizzling blood. It was before death overwhelmed life, before sediments of fear and grief and guilt settled inside him.

It was before he died at Verdun.

To him, life was like a lover who abandoned him but for whom he still yearned. When he was young and that love affair was still unseasoned, he'd run the hills and fields and streets with his brother, impressing the girls and delighting in the life that dared unveil itself in so stark a place—like a temptress, her red dress unbuttoned, lying open on a bed of ice. But his brother was lost in a storm at sea and while he locked himself away in grief, all the girls got taken.

Soon after, he lost his parents in a house fire and he was alone in the world. He could have found a different girl, started a new family, but instead he went to war and when he returned he no longer felt fit to be with women. He feared the intimacy of life with a woman would germinate that seed of rage that hunkered within him like something snarling. It had been his misfortune to be pulled back from the front lines before he could give full vent to the rage, before he could leave it in no-man's-land, before he could kill every last German he faced, before he could kill the entire French officer staff that had squandered his humanity in the trenches.

He had been pulled from the battle before he could find his own bodily death. And so he had died anyway.

And then he returned to Saint Pierre, awash in seawater.

He rose from his bed and went toward the window. A wedge of sunlight shouldered through the gap in the curtains and puddled on the worn linoleum floor. It deciphered the radiating cracks where the coal stove had settled into the floor and it irradiated the dust balls that rose and drifted after him, spiraling, as he passed. The sunlight filtered through an empty whisky bottle on the sill, laying a murky prism on the linoleum, and it illuminated the desiccated carcasses of wasps scattered across the floor.

He paused, staring at the light as he would a shy seductress. He was a small, wiry man who often had a two or three day growth of stubble and whose forehead was as furrowed as the land in the north of the island. And in his eyes, sadness. Often, currents of memory rose to the surface bringing an upwelling of dross that clouded them.

He pulled back the tattered curtains. A sudden flittering, seen in the corner of his eye, told him he'd scared off the bobolink. He was mildly surprised to see no fog, a frequent presence at this time of year. The bloated sun shone as angry as the gaze of a forgotten God. It was a curdled sky, clouds resting heavy like sleepy, well-fed cats.

A pair of large, winged shadows swooped across the field, undulating over the ridges and ruts of the gravel road. Wistfully, he watched the two birds fly over the Cormier farm, their bounding flights and deep wing strokes identifying them as petrels. Shortly after, a flock of sea gulls overflew the farm. They were all heading for the ferment of the pebbled beaches and the racks of drying fish. There seemed more seabirds of late, undoubtedly because of the overabundance of fish.

Ever since the Nazi invasion of France the previous year, the trawlers had been unable to ship the fish to the mother country and the men could think of nothing else but to spread the fish out, dry them, preserve them. And wait. The ferment of fish smell was thick enough to congeal over the land.

In the distance he heard a cacophony of barking; the island dogs were also scarfing up scraps.

Jérôme Sabot closed the curtains, noting how they were starting to shred again so soon after Adrienne had patched them.

Sweet Adrienne.

He thought of breakfast; it was merely a life-sustaining reflex.

The birds and all such signs of life invariably made him wonder how it was possible in a land scraped almost to the bone by a glacial flensing knife and scoured by centuries of salt-laden winds, a land of ragged rocks, a land where stunted trees marched across the hills like reduced men shuffling to the front.

For a long time after the Great War he had managed to suppress memories of it. He had even, for a time, stopped talking to Antoine's coat; it had hung on its peg in the storm vestibule, limp, mute—back to being just a coat. Only in summer would the memories appear again, first as eddies, then as whirlpools, or like toothaches endured most of the time below the surface of awareness, but that erupted occasionally into unbearable pain.

It was the contrast between present life and past war that did it.

But this new war of the Nazis had made forgetfulness impossible and the memories had come flooding back like a cold current from the Arctic persuading him that death still reigned in the world.

Like all men who have suffered greatly, he didn't like the lucky or fainthearted ones, the men who knew nothing of the Great War, what it did to human beings. In particular, he didn't like his neighbors Claude Cormier and Marcel Morel, both of whom evaded the war and didn't have one tenth of his knowledge of the way the world can be, but who strutted and brayed about the island like prosperous men-in-full, men who never had to suffer, men who never had to live in the clutch of death, men who never had to burrow into the earth, men who had an opinion about everything and were right about nothing, men who had never been diminished by combat. He liked nothing better than to show these two men up for who they were, not only because Claude Cormier liked to kill when he had no idea what real killing was, not only because Marcel Morel presumed himself worthy of sleeping in Antoine's bed with Antoine's wife, but also because of the way they treated his only true friends in Saint Pierre and Miquelon—Adrienne, Gabriel, and Marie-Lisette.

His lips formed a mischievous grin as he thought of the plan he'd hatched the previous night over a bottle of whiskey with Gabriel. He took a cigarette from the pack in the small bureau near his bed, packed it against the back of his hand, and lit it. He let twin streams of smoke curl from his grinning lips to his nostrils, then turned to the trench coat hanging in the storm vestibule, and said, "I have them this time, Antoine. For sure I have them."

The trench coat, hanging limply from its peg, remained silent.

Jérôme continued. "You remember Claude Cormier, don't you, the idiot who didn't have the guts to join up with us when we went over to fight the Boche?" He paused and gazed at the coat. The grin on his face faltered. He held the cigarette tightly between thumb and forefinger as though crushing a fly.

... as the reserve column approaches the front lines, explosions rip the air, spew earth into the sky. In the distance, dead trees spin through the buckling air. A smell of cordite settles over the reduced men. Palls of smoke. Another smell. Sickening. A stench of decay coming from the trenches ahead of them.

Antoine says, "I'm scared to death."

"Me, too," answers Jérôme.

He shook his head to expel the memory. He sucked on his cigarette and as he did, a hesitant grin returned to his lips. He rose from the kitchen chair, walked over to the small window again, peered out. "As soon as your Gabriel gets here, Antoine, we go into action," he said. "Poor Gabriel." He glanced over his shoulder at the still silent trench coat and let out a devious chuckle. "We're gonna turn Claude's new calf into a zebra. What do you think of that? You remember how ignorant and superstitious he is? This will make him crazy, then I will have him." He paused, shook his head, and added, "What that man does to poor Adrienne ... it's ... it's unforgivable."

He crossed the small kitchen to the iron sink, careful to avoid the section of linoleum that had split and curled up from the plywood underfloor. He held a pitcher under the spigot of the red pump and worked the curved handle. The pump wheezed like an obese man as he primed it through several strokes before it gushed water into the pitcher. Carrying it carefully, he moved about the kitchen watering his begonias and cyclamen.

A trail of tiny puddles followed him along the linoleum floor. He placed the pitcher back on the table, peered out the window again and slapped at the buzz of a fly that was bothering his nose. "Ah, there's Gabriel. He's become a fine young man, Antoine, truly. You would be proud of your son. We must forgive him his ... his difficulties. It comes from living with that idiot, Marcel Morel. I don't understand why your Sylvie married him. I can only guess she was lonely and figured that Gabriel needed a man around the house. Well, don't worry. My zebra plan will show Marcel up for the fool he is, too. I've got it all worked out. I'll get both of them."

At that moment a knock came on the door. Jérôme opened it to find Gabriel Morel standing in the tiny, enclosed porch called a tambour, a feature of houses on Saint Pierre, a kind of mud room where people could remove wet clothes and boots before entering the house proper.

"Who are you talking to, Monsieur Sabot?" he asked in a mellifluous voice. He was a man of twenty-three who had the arrested mind of a seven-year-old. He was short and stocky with sloping eyes and a forehead too big for his small, friendly face. His body was lost in clothes several sizes too big for him—the result of his mother's expectation (hope?) that he would yet grow. But his voice was man-sized, a pulpy baritone that could also effortlessly rise to a sweet tenor and descend to a basso profundo. Some aunt had given him a record of Enrico Caruso singing selected arias and he had learned them all by heart. Jérôme often heard him from across the field singing a cappella, softening the air that was otherwise filled with the harsh cries of seabirds.

"Nobody," Jérôme replied as he slipped into an overcoat. "Let's get going. This is going to make great fools of Claude Cormier and your stepfather." Jérôme's eyes sparkled with mirth.

"I hate Monsieur Morel. He's a shithead!"

"Yes, yes. I know."

"He beats me."

Jérôme frowned. The cloudiness returned to his eyes for an instant. "Well, we'll show him for the fool he is."

Gabriel gave a delighted laugh. "He's the real idiot!"

"Yes, he is. And Monsieur Cormier, too. Come, let's get the paint."

"I'm good."

"Yes, Gabriel, you're good."

"Not an idiot."

"No, not an idiot." Jérôme tousled Gabriel's hair. Gabriel of the sweet voice. Gabriel whose mind was often muddled but who sang like an angel. How often Jérôme had heard him, even through the storm-sashed windows, singing along with the great one. Gabriel had learned every word of every aria without understanding a one.

But he always seemed to get the emotion right. Softening the arctic air, silencing the raucous nonsense of the seabirds.

"Let's get the paint now," said Jérôme.

They crossed the small yard behind the house. It was ridged and rutted with spring mud that had been baked dry by the July sun. Jérôme entered the shack.

Piled against the far wall were cans of paint, two barrels of gasoline, a few barrels of rum, and containers of grease—all salvaged by Jérôme from ships that had gone aground on the Dune of Miquelon. In addition, there were several cases of the moonshine they called miquelon or whiskey-blanc that Jérôme frequently smuggled into Newfoundland or Prince Edward Island.

And at the far wall was a full-sized, wooden profile of a grazing zebra mounted on a stake. It leaned against the cases of whisky.

Gabriel examined the wooden zebra closely. "Do you really think this will fool them, Monsieur Sabot?"

Jérôme gave a dismissive wave. "They'll only see it from a distance. Besides, They're as dumb as can be. They'll be fooled alright." He reached for a can of black paint and a brush. "Okay, we're ready. As soon as Claude and Madame Cormier leave for town we'll do it. We'll go back toward *The Mountain* before heading for Claude's barn. That way, Claude's mother won't see us from the house."

"But how do you know they're going into town?"

"Because Adrienne told me."

"You call her Adrienne?"

"Madame Cormier, I mean." Jérôme saw Gabriel staring at him, a question on his arrested mind. But Gabriel said nothing and Jérôme felt no need to explain.

2
Dreams of Flight

ADRIENNE CORMIER AVOIDED the mirror as she dressed. She didn't need to gaze at her reflection to know the shadows under her eyes were deepening and fine lines were beginning to radiate from the corners of her eyes even though she was not yet thirty-five. She glanced at the empty jar of facial cream. Monsieur Pichot at the shop in Saint Pierre had said there would be no more cream until *Le Celte* arrived from France. For Adrienne, the little ship had always relieved, at least for a time, her island loneliness. There would be fashion magazines, news of Paris, and, most of all, facial cream. But now, with the war and German submarines prowling the sea, who knew if *Le Celte* would ever make it through? The ship might even now be resting on the bottom of the Atlantic with her cargo of kid gloves, perfumes, cosmetics, clothing, liqueurs, catalogues, books, magazines ...

... and facial cream.

Adrienne slipped a cotton dress over her shoulders and let it fall past her slender hips. She pulled the dress away from her belly, testing the fit. There was still room; perhaps her greatest fear would not come true after all. Only the doctor would be able to tell for sure. She held her hand over her belly. If she, indeed, was pregnant (the thought made her shiver) when would she begin to feel something? When would she start to show?

And what then? Dear God, what then?

"Ain't you ready yet?" Claude called from the kitchen. "I ain't got all day." His gruff voice passed over her like the *poudrin* that each winter drove ice crystals into every miniscule gap in clapboard siding, every tiny opening of clothing, every crack of dry skin.

Hurriedly, she slipped the stereopticon, in which she had been viewing scenes of Paris, into its hiding place in the lower drawer of the bureau. It was where she kept her underwear, a place Claude never went. She had just closed the drawer when her mother-in-law, Claudette, appeared at the door. "Hurry up, Adrienne, my boy is waiting. Why are you always so slow?"

"I'm ready, Maman." Adrienne glanced at her mother-in-law then quickly averted her eyes. She hated to gaze upon that wrinkled countenance, that face she had never seen crack a smile.

"Well it's about time."

Adrienne followed Claudette into the kitchen. Her husband was standing by the door, coat on, frowning. He was a huge man, wild black hair and a black beard framing a broad face. His dark eyes scowled under heavy eyebrows. "You're gonna take up my whole day with your damned doctor's appointment," he said.

"It won't take that long."

"It better not."

As they went outside, Claudette said, "You see to it that my boy don't spend his time drinking at the café. He's got work to do."

Claude walked with long, angry strides to the driver's side of the old truck. Adrienne eased herself into the passenger seat. Claude started the engine, cursed when it sputtered before catching, then let the clutch fly. The truck lurched forward, spewing dirt from its rear wheels, then settled into the ruts on the road to the town of Saint Pierre.

As the truck bounced along with squeals from its springs, Adrienne wondered what she would do if the doctor confirmed her fears. Could she escape Claude?

From her perch at the crest of the hill the Saint Pierrais called *The Mountain*, Marie-Lisette Morel gazed down at the town and its harbor. For once, the fog had stayed well out to sea and she could see clear to the horizon. The coruscating seawater winked at her, millions of tiny flashes that freckled her eyeglasses with brilliant reflections. She scanned the sea for a hint of *Le Celte* and saw nothing but emptiness—no sign, among the waves, of the little gray freighter that, three times a year before the war, had relieved the isolation of the archipelago by bringing goods from the mother country. Marie-Lisette wondered if the Nazi authorities over in occupied France would ever allow *Le Celte* to sail.

Two dogs, resembling Labradors with broad, massive heads and small, dark eyes, stirred in their harnesses. They were hitched to the cart she'd used to gather faggots of dwarf spruce for the stove. She patted their noses to shush them. "Lie there for a while. I'm going to read a little before we go back."

She pulled out a worn copy of *Southern Mail* by Antoine de Saint-Exupéry and settled against a boulder to read. Near her, some sweet berries were ripening in this wilderness of rock and scrub pine. She inhaled their scent. For her, these summer months were always a miracle, filled as they were with berries and birds and butterflies after the long winter. How could anyone not feel an exquisite pleasure at the fragrance of things growing, the sounds of the birds, the radiant colors?

Poor Monsieur Sabot!

The thought of her friend made her eyes soft. She had tried often to bring more light into his life but he seemed forever cheerless. She remembered one time when, from this very spot, she and Jérôme Sabot had gazed at the horizon. She had said, "See that glow in the sky? For me, that means hope. Perhaps *Le Celte* will come."

"I see only a reflection of the ice," he'd replied.

"Oh, but Monsieur Sabot, can't you believe it signifies we'll soon be seeing the freighter?"

"It's nothing but an illusion, I tell you. They call it 'iceblink.' You should never allow yourself to imagine that the sea ever offers hope."

"But the sea is our lives. We fish the sea for food."

"Because we're forced to. We've made an unholy alliance with the sea because we have no choice, no way out. It's still a place where creatures survive by eating other creatures."

Whatever pain troubled him, it ran as deep as the sea. She guessed it had something to do with the last war, but exactly what she couldn't fathom. Perhaps one day he would trust her enough to tell her. She shook her head sadly.

At seventeen, Marie-Lisette had already developed the alluring body of a woman. She was slim with small breasts and narrow hips. Her dark hair was cut short, pixyish, and her eyeglasses magnified nut-brown eyes. Several of the young men who couldn't resist looking at her said she was a gamine, but not in the impudent sense. She'd already devoured *Southern Mail* three times, reading it, smelling it, hefting it, but she couldn't get enough. Besides, there weren't many books available on Saint Pierre—at least not ones she would find interesting and challenging. She prayed *Le Celte* would show up soon with a shipment of books for the library, perhaps a new Saint-Exupéry, or more books by Collette, or the writer she had recently heard about, André Malraux.

She knew that months ago Madame LeClair at the library had requested an especially large quantity of new books because everybody knew the war was coming and there was no telling how long it would last. But Madame LeClair had been too late. The war had suddenly exploded on them before *Le Celte* could arrive. Marie-Lisette could only hope that this year would be different.

She opened the book and started to read from the beginning. It was one of her favorite sections because it offered wonderful descriptions of Jacques Bernis flying his France-America mail-plane over the deserts of North Africa and the cities of South America, elbowing his way with ease through storms. The exotic names stirred excitement in her—Toulouse, Alicante, Port-Etienne, Dakar, Casablanca, Buenos Aires, Santiago. She imagined herself sitting in the cockpit of a plane, revving the engine as the wheels strained against the chocks, then lifting off from Saint Pierre's little airstrip into the vast isolation of sky.

As she gains altitude, she circles the tiny archipelago. Below her, Saint Pierre shrinks and everything appears as children's toys—the buildings, the boats in the harbor, the roads, the neighboring island of Île aux Marins. She banks the plane to fly over the northern part of Saint Pierre. Here, the land rises beneath her, barren slopes with stunted trees and mossy muskeag furrowed by many deep gullies. To the northeast, the southern tip of Newfoundland reveals itself, and as she continues her turn toward the west, Langlade appears now with its undulating land networked by rivers and streams and stands of fir, spruce, and pine. Moments later, the five-mile-long isthmus, people call "the dune," that connects Langlade to Grande Miquelon, slides beneath her. Still, she is gaining altitude.

With the dune stretching like taffy pulled to its thinning breaking point between them, the two main islands appear as one cell in mitosis. Now she is overflying Grande Miquelon, its rolling hills covered with purple iris. From this altitude, she can't see the more than six hundred submerged shipwrecks choking the archipelago like a garrote, but she knows they are there, flash frozen in their abdication to the sea and to eternity. And she knows they speak of the loneliness of the islands just as much as the vastness of ocean that now stretches out beneath her. It is a scene of great isolation and she turns the plane away from it to head for ...

for Toulouse ... Dakar ... Casablanca ... Buenos Aires.

Marie-Lisette sighed and closed the book. Nothing but dreams. She was convinced there was no escape from this island; that she was doomed never to see France—if there was a France after this war. A sadness settled inside her like undigested porridge. As she stood, the two dogs rose and gazed at her expectantly.

"Alright, my little ones, we'll go home now." She started to lead them down *The Mountain.*

She walked with liquid steps on the spongy ground ahead of the dogs and the bouncing cart. In the distance, she saw Claude Cormier's truck pull away from his tiny dairy farm, and head for Saint Pierre. Soon after, she saw two figures emerge from Monsieur Sabot's place and stand, apparently watching the same truck.

As they waited for the Cormier truck to disappear from view, Gabriel asked Jérôme, "Do you think *Le Celte* will come soon?"

"I don't know, Gabriel. There's a war on."

"You were in the war with my father."

A darkness came over Jérôme. His eyes clouded. "It was a different war."

He thought of the little freighter. Everybody on Saint Pierre and Miquelon prayed for her arrival—everyone except him. As far as he was concerned, the less he heard from France, the better. In the more than twenty years since the Great War, his fear that news from France would expose him had diminished. But it still lurked inside him, a tiny knot of anxiety, and every time *Le Celte* was due to appear on the horizon, the fear would swell like a chronic infection that flared up from time to time.

Because some reporter or scholar might write an article about the battle of Verdun, or one of his fellow soldiers—someone who knew him and Antoine—might write a memoir. And there it would all be.

The Cormier truck, one short-circuited tail light blinking, disappeared around a bend leaving only a swirling vortex of dust and the faint memory trace of the blinking light.

Jérôme dismissed the thought of *Le Celte*. "Okay, Gabriel, time to move."

Carrying a liberally thinned can of black paint, a brush, a length of rope, and a comb—Jérôme's zebra-making kit—they walked a short distance up the slope before turning toward the back of the Cormier farm. The ground under them was spongy with thawed icewater that oozed from the earth. Soon they arrived at the barn and eased the door open. A band of sunlight shouldered in with them through the open door. Flecks of incandescent dust swarmed in the fusty air. Three cows and a calf, locked in stalls, lifted their heads toward them. Jérôme opened the stall that housed the calf with its mother. "You pull the calf out while I hold back the mother," he said.

Gabriel grabbed the rope that was already attached to the calf and tugged. The calf struggled, stiff-legged, trying not to be separated from its mother, but it was too weak to resist Gabriel's pull.

Jérôme slammed the stall gate shut. The cow gave a low moan and rocked back and forth causing her udder to sway. She flicked her tail at a swarm of flies.

"Tie the calf over there, out of reach of the mother."

Gabriel hitched the calf to a rail on the other side of the barn. Its big black eyes gazed at its mother. It moaned pitifully.

"Stop your complaining, silly calf," said Jérôme. "It's not every calf who gets to become a zebra." Jérôme dipped the brush into the black paint, lifted the short hairs of the calf, and dabbed a small amount of the ink-like paint on the underside of the hairs. "The trick is to make it look like real stripes that are just beginning to come out," he said. "It wouldn't do to just slap paint on the top. Even Claude Cormier and your stepfather ain't too stupid to see through that."

"My step father's the real idiot."

"Yes, he is."

"Not me."

"Yes."

Working carefully but hastily, Jérôme painted as many broad faint lines as he thought would give a passing resemblance to a zebra's stripes just beginning to emerge. When he finished, he stood, surveyed his work, and said, "Now let's go plant the wooden zebra up on *The Mountain*."

Taking the paint and brush with them, they eased out of the barn, slid the door closed with a groan, and headed back to Jérôme's shack by the same route they had come. After returning the paint and brush, they gathered up the wooden zebra and a hammer and started up *The Mountain*, avoiding the flatter areas where the water had pooled ankle deep. When they reached a stand of scrub pine, Jérôme said, "Here, this is a good spot." He placed the wooden zebra upright and jammed the pointed stake to which it was affixed into the ground. Gabriel took the hammer and drove the stake deep so the zebra would stand on its own.

Jérôme walked a few paces away and examined their work. "Perfect. The fools will believe it for sure."

"Especially my stepfather. He's the one who's an idiot."

"Right. Now here's what you do. Go back to the Cormier farm and untie the calf. Put it back with its mother. But make sure the paint is dry first. And don't forget to comb it out; that's the *coup de maître*, the master stroke. Then run to your stepfather and tell him you've seen a zebra. Make him come out to the road and look up here."

"What will you do?"

"I'll hide up here in case your stepfather decides to climb up to take a closer look. If he does, I'll hide the zebra and go down by a different path so he doesn't see me," Jérôme said, nodding toward the south. "He'll think the zebra just ran off."

Jérôme watched Gabriel loping down the hill, splashing meltwater with every step, and settled back to wait. He looked out over Saint Pierre and the harbor toward the horizon, half-afraid of seeing a column of smoke that might signal *Le Celte's* arrival. But there was nothing on the water except for a few motor dories, fishing trawlers and, hugging the shore, the rotting wrecks of several schooners. Otherwise the sea was empty.

The sun shone aslant on the waves producing countless tiny flashes. Waves of liquid light curled towards the shore and spilled onto the pebbled beach. The town itself showed her prettiest face, buildings lathered in buttery, morning light, windows reflecting the bright sea. It was vastly different from her usual appearance—the buildings plunging into a thick impenetrable curtain where the sea submitted to the fog, or streets sliding down crusted snow to an ice-rimmed harbor.

To his left, a casual flock of sea pigeons undulated in the air before sinking downward into the darkness of a gully. A dog barked in the distance and was instantly answered by several others. Soon there was a cacophony of barking dogs that lasted for a few minutes before they lapsed into silence again, a silence that never lasted long on Saint Pierre.

He waited a long time, all the while regretting that he'd sent Gabriel instead of going himself. He should have let Gabriel do the waiting. Times alone with nothing to do were the dangerous times for Jérôme. It was then that thoughts of the war easily stirred in him, disturbing the hot embers of memory hunkering deep within him.

.... the incessant shelling turning up massive clods of earth and bone ... a headless man rolling into the trench, blood pumping from the stump of his neck ... another man with flaps of bloody skin hanging from what seconds before was the right side of his face ... a horse in no-man's-land, a white horse, its side ripped open, its legs twitching frantically ...

"I'm afraid," says Antoine, "I'm so afraid."

"I'm afraid, too," replies Jérôme.

Familiar tears welled in Jérôme's eyes. "It's been over twenty years," he said aloud to the barren hill, to the overarching sky. "Why can't you leave me alone?"

Though most of the war years had faded from his memory, certain scenes came back to him repeatedly in vivid detail. They were like knots on a string, separated by periods of nothingness. And at the end was that final scene, the one he'd so far been able to keep hidden behind the others, the one that showed itself only obliquely, the one he was quick to force from his thoughts whenever it threatened to appear.

He rose and paced the sodden ground the way one walks about vainly and aimlessly to ease a toothache. He peered down the slope for some sign of Gabriel and his stepfather. "What's taking them so long?"

The flock of sea pigeons rose up again out of the dark gully. They traced parabolas and spirals against the limitless sky.

"I did what I did and that's all there is," Jérôme muttered to himself.

He returned to the zebra and tested to be sure it was planted firmly. Again, he gazed down the hill. Where were they?

Passion and 3 Permafrost

WHEN ADRIENNE ENTERED Doctor Tréguy's office, he was bent over his famous gramophone, gingerly dropping the needle on a record. The needle skated from the outer edge to the inner with a high-pitched skirl. "It's ruined," he murmured.

"What's ruined, Doctor Tréguy?" Adrienne asked.

"Oh, hello, Adrienne," the doctor said, looking over his shoulder. "It's Chopin's Second Piano Concerto. Arthur Rubinstein. Such beautiful music. But I'm afraid I've ruined it by playing it too often."

"Can you replace it?"

Doctor Tréguy sighed. "No, I'm afraid not. Since the war started it's nearly impossible to get vinyls. They've halted production. Something about the lack of shellac for the vinyl after the Japanese invaded Southeast Asia."

"I'm sorry."

"Oh, well, not to worry. We all suffer from the war," he said, coming toward her. But for you, Adrienne, I have wonderful news. You're going to have a baby."

Adrienne smiled. There was no point in letting on to the doctor that the news, even if expected, sent waves of panic through her. But she feared that her smile must have appeared fainthearted, for Doctor Tréguy frowned. He sat next to her on the worn divan, peering at her over eyeglasses that were propped on the end of his nose. He was a handsome man, flecks of gray sprinkled through his short brown hair. "You did know that, didn't you? Most women do."

"Yes ... yes ... I suppose. It's just ... startling ... to have it confirmed."

"I imagine Claude will be delighted. You two have been married a long time."

"Yes, delighted." Again, a faint smile. She averted her gaze, staring at the books resting behind the glass doors of a bookcase lining one entire wall of the tiny office. She studied the items arranged helter-skelter on the top of the bookcase—a framed sepia-toned picture of an old, kindly looking woman (his mother?); another of a group of World War I soldiers; a metronome in a scarred wooden case; a small bronze statue of a horse cocooned in a green patina. Outside the surprisingly open window—windows were seldom left open in the harsh climate of Saint Pierre—she heard the familiar, constant blare of car horns. It seemed an avocation of drivers in Saint Pierre, which had no traffic lights, to lean on their horns. She heard the familiar cry of Monsieur Bertiz, the Basque man who delivered Claude's milk to customers in town.

She tried not to think of Claude. "How far along am I?" she asked.

"It's hard to say at this stage, but I suspect about four months."

It was just as she had known. She remembered the previous March. An image came to her of him lying on top of her, shy, releasing himself with a grunt; their mingled tears afterwards; their embarrassment; the strange sense of worry that seemed to emanate from him along with the tenderness.

"How often should I see you?" she asked the doctor. She hoped he would specify frequent visits—anything to get away from the farm, from Claude.

"For now, once a month. As your time comes nearer, I'll see you more frequently."

"Can I ask you, Doctor Treguy, not to mention this to anybody?"

"Certainly; It's a matter of doctor-patient confidentiality."

"Thank you. I want Claude to hear it from me, personally."

"Of course."

"But not until it's absolutely necessary."

"You'll delay telling him?"

"I don't want him to worry."

Doctor Treguy gave a look of bemusement but said nothing more.

When she emerged onto the Rue Maître Georges Lefèvre, she saw a group of women gathered around Monsieur Bertiz. The women carried an assortment of empty wine and whiskey bottles for Monsieur Bertiz to fill with milk. The women chatted as they waited in line. Soon, she knew, they would be chatting about her; the gossips would have a field day. She felt a tingling, a heat on the skin of her neck, a foreshadowing of the shame that was sure to come. She passed her hand over her belly and looked up the street where she saw Claude's truck parked in front of the Café Joinville. She sighed and started toward the truck. Its corroded fenders saddened her, which was odd because all the trucks on Saint Pierre had corroded fenders from hauling salt fish during season.

But there was something different about the decay of Claude's truck. Perhaps it was that it mirrored the erosion of their marriage.

They had started out, like any young couple, imagining their marriage would be different—unlike others they saw that had settled into states of resignation if not bitterness. Claude, especially, was determined to avoid the kind of marriage his mother and father had which led, ultimately, to his father running off with another woman. And at first he was attentive and caring; for a while, it seemed like it would work. But, inevitably, their marriage changed, and they were not among the lucky ones for whom change meant growth and the formation of a new, vibrant relationship. Instead, they had grown tired and bitter.

Adrienne blamed herself for not being more understanding of Claude's weaknesses, especially his desperate need for an ideal marriage. But what could she do? Matched against Claude's impossible expectations, she was unable to ward off the disappointments and mistrust that inevitably crept into their relationship, especially after Claude's mother came to live with them. Things got progressively worse and Claude started to blame her, Adrienne, for his unhappiness.

After a while, he stopped making love to her, probably because he feared more disappointment. And just as his love for her waned, his penchant for violence increased. She assumed it was his way of dealing with the heartache.

Usually, the violent behavior was directed at the birds he endlessly hunted—most often the snipe—but sometimes, when he was drunk, the violence was aimed at her. Was it any wonder, she thought, that she found herself susceptible to the attentions of another man—a situation, of course, that was the *coup de grâce* to their marriage—or that after that first infidelity, a second was easier? Of course, she could leave Claude, but that would be a difficult thing to do on a small island where everybody knows everybody. Where would she go? What man would trust her? If the war wasn't on, she might be able to escape to France, but with the Nazis and the Vichy in power, escape was impossible.

When she reached the truck, she considered peeking into the café to catch Claude's attention, but decided against it. Instead, she climbed into the passenger seat to wait for him to finish his pernod. He usually had only one during the day and he didn't like to hang around and chat with the other men.

Her dress, clinging to the fabric of the seat, slid up her thighs. They felt moist and sticky against the hot material. She raised her hips and tugged the dress down over her knees.

She sucked in her breath when she saw a familiar figure strolling across the Quai de la Roncière toward the Hotel Lalanne. Jean-Luc Lavedan, one of the fishermen from the fleet of trawlers that had become marooned in Saint Pierre at the beginning of the war, had captivated her with his stride from the moment she'd first seen him. She slid forward in the seat to lower herself, hoping he wouldn't notice her. The dress rode up her thighs again. It wouldn't do for Claude to see her talking in familiar tones to a man as young, as handsome, as Jean-Luc. She would never be free to come into Saint Pierre alone again.

But it was too late. Jean-Luc saw her and his face brightened. He started to walk toward the truck and her heart sank. Bunching the hem of her dress in her fist to pull it down over her knees, she shook her head frantically, trying to warn him. But he kept coming.

Then, just as suddenly, Jean-Luc stopped. For a moment, Adrienne was confused until the door on the driver's side flew open with a rusty squeal. Claude piled his huge frame into the truck. "Okay, let's go," he said. He turned the key in the ignition and the truck sputtered to life.

Jean-Luc lowered his beret on his forehead, gave a slight nod, and continued toward the Hotel Lalanne. Adrienne took a deep breath.

As they drove back to the farm under a blazing sun, the inside of the truck became stiflingly hot. Adrienne found it difficult to breathe. She rolled the window down. Claude broke the silence only once to ask, "Well, what did the doctor say?"

At first, Adrienne didn't answer. She wondered if the alibi she had constructed would really work.

"Well?" demanded Claude.

"Oh ... oh, nothing. Just a mild upset of the stomach."

"Didn't I tell you?"

As the truck lurched along the rough road, Adrienne tried not to think of her plight, but it was useless. Sooner or later, Claude would learn she was pregnant and she could only imagine what would happen then; he was so unpredictable in his violence. Unlike Monsieur Sabot, whose pain had given birth to a certain gentleness, a sad tenderness, Claude's pain at losing his father when he was a small boy, and his disappointment in his own marriage, had led only to a spitefulness that was always simmering, ready to erupt. She had seen it too often to ever feel secure in her home.

When she saw the farm draw nearer, she became breathless as though her heart were pressing against her lungs. She wanted to cry. The house had become a prison in which she was in solitary confinement. No, worse than solitary—she was forced to live with Claude and his mother. And now things would inevitably become much more difficult. Would it be Claude or his mother to first notice her swelling belly? Undoubtedly, it would be his mother. But what difference would that make? She would tell her son the moment she knew. And then he would figure the rest out for himself.

Marie-Lisette's hand sidled between her legs like a cat returning from a night outdoors. It felt cool under the warmth of the duvet in the dark room.

I am Geneviève with my lover, the handsome pilot Jacques Bernis and he is pleasuring my body. If I move to lower my head to his chest, will I feel his respiration rising and falling like a wave, with the restlessness of an ocean crossing as it says in the book?

Marie-Lisette squeezed her eyes shut and tried to imagine it. But it was difficult. The pilot's face kept dissolving into other images: her father glaring angrily at her; her mother with a look of sad disappointment; her teacher, Sister Claire-Gertrude, rushing toward her, black habit flowing, waving a reproachful finger; Raymond Pineau, his pimpled, grunting face red with exertion.

The fragile vision of Genevieve and Jacques Bernis was completely shattered, replaced by the memory of that one time with Raymond Pineau.

It had been during the Bastille Day celebrations the previous year. Marie-Lisette found herself alone with Raymond in a dark corner of the frigo, the huge warehouse through which millions of cases of whiskey had passed in the great days of smuggling and where countless fish were now kept on ice. The mingled smell of fish and leftover traces of spilled whiskey created a heady broth of odor, slightly sickening.

When he kissed her awkwardly, she was surprised to feel herself respond. But it was only because the kiss made her think of Jacques Bernis. And when Raymond shoved a bumbling hand over her breast, she was too startled to resist and he seemed to take it as an invitation. She felt his clumsy hand snake between her thighs and grasp her through the heavy wool of her skirt. She gasped. "No, Raymond, don't," she cried breathlessly.

"But, Marie-Lisette … it's …."

"What?"

"I don't know … It's …."

"It's not right," she said. But at the same time, curiosity was churning inside her … persistent … demanding.

"What's wrong?"

She heard herself saying, "It's not the right place. It's too cold here and it smells awful."

Even as the words left her mouth, she was horrified. Undoubtedly, Raymond would read her words as an invitation and try to find the right place, a place where he could do whatever he wanted. She wondered if that wasn't, after all, what she'd intended. Was she *that* curious? Raymond, who was clumsy and couldn't say the right things? Raymond, who smelled like fish? She imagined Sister Claire-Gertrude watching her, eyes wide with disbelief and fury. Indeed, she imagined all of the sisters of St. Joseph of Cluny glaring at her. But, if anything, it only made her more curious.

Raymond embraced her with obvious gratitude and murmured, "Oh, Marie-Lisette …." He pressed his body against her, pinning her hard against the cold wall of the building. Her skirt snagged on the rough surface.

She gasped when she felt a hardness press against her thigh, knowing intuitively what it was. She should have been shocked, but instead she felt only a new, even greater, flush of excitement. He kissed her again and she returned the kiss with a shy fervor. Finally, marshalling her sense of propriety, she broke away and said, "Not here." She un-snagged her skirt and smoothed it over her hips.

"But where can we go?"

"Let's just walk."

"Walk?" His voice was tremulous.

"Yes, walk."

"Walk?"

They walked along the Boulevard Constant Colmay and turned toward the Quai de Pêche. In the distance, she heard the muted celebrations—muted because France had fallen the previous month and nobody felt much like the usual singing and dancing of Bastille Day. A rude wind off the cold water ruffled her hair. She thought: I'm sixteen and most of the other girls my age have already .... Fervently, she wished she could talk with one of them now, but she had no real friends because, as she'd so often heard them say, she was always lost in her books.

When they turned behind a building at the end of the quay, Raymond leaned back against a wall, shielding them from the intrusive moonlight, and drew her to him. He kissed her passionately and murmured, "Oh, Marie-Lisette ...." He spun her around so it was now her back against the wall.

Marie-Lisette tried to draw away from him, but he held her tightly. She stared over his shoulder, past the corner of the building at the band of milk-white moonlight rippling in the harbor. She felt as though the breath was being squeezed from her lungs. Even so, gradually she began responding with the same hesitant curiosity as before. Raymond reached awkwardly between them and for the second time that night—and the second time in her life—a man's hand clutched her between the legs. She shivered. A frisson of excitement and fear.

Raymond fumbled furiously between their bodies as though a moment's hesitation would invite her to change her mind. She wished he would be less hurried. She wished he would say something.

She wished he didn't smell like fish.

Raymond lifted her skirt and drew her underpants aside, scratching her thigh with his fingernail.

"Ouch!"

"I'm sorry," he said in a husky voice.

He forced his legs between hers and lifted her against the wall. As before, her woolen skirt snagged on the abrasive surface and when he lifted her, the skirt was tugged downward until it sat halfway down her hips. She tried to wiggle it back in place, but she was forced to give up and spread her arms back against the wall to relieve the pressure on her back. Her shoulder blades scraped against the rough cement surface. Her eyeglasses had come dislodged and sat askew on her nose. The swathe of moonlight was now a bright blur, shimmering. The Île aux Marins across the harbor appeared as two islands, two smudges on the close horizon.

Raymond leaned hard against her, slamming her back against the wall, knocking the breath from her.

"Ouch!"

"I'm sorry." His voice was husky, heavy with impulse.

"Be careful."

"Unngh."

Before Marie-Lisette could regain her breath, she felt another sharp pain. "Ow! Ow!"

"I'm sorry. Did I hurt you?"

"Unnh!"

"Unngh!"

Marie-Lisette grimaced. She winced her eyes shut. She felt like a fly pinned to a wall, writhing. Then, her arms splayed wide, an image of the crucified Christ flashed through her mind, a flush of shame. She tried to squirm her elbows inward. It threw Raymond off balance.

"What're you doing?"

"Can't ... our Savior ... No!"

"Hunh?"

"Unnh!"

Gradually, the pain subsided to be replaced by a hint of pleasure, a suggestion, a promise. She closed her eyes to focus on the sensations, to satisfy her curiosity.

But suddenly Raymond's face turned red and he grunted twice. He collapsed against her. Still pinned against the wall, she felt the sweat on his forehead against her cheek. A fishy smell rose from his spent body. A wave of revulsion overwhelmed her. Raymond released her and she slid down the wall, causing her snagged skirt to lift above her waist. She rearranged it with quick, angry motions and straightened her eyeglasses. There were smudges of sweat on the lenses.

Breathlessly, Raymond asked, "Was that your first time?"

She glared at him. "It was my *worst* time!"

But now as she remembered the satisfying shock of dismay in his face, she could also recall the brief sting of pleasure she'd experienced, just a tease, and she knew that same exquisite pleasure awaited her if only she could find a real man, a man with graces, a sophisticated man, a gentle man.

A man who didn't smell like fish.

A man like Jacques Bernis. For a brief moment, her made-up image of the pilot returned to her and her cat-like hand stretched languorously between her thighs.

But suddenly, the magic was shattered once more. This time it was the kitchen door being flung open and Gabriel's voice shouting, "I saw a zebra! I saw a zebra!"

Marie-Lisette wrinkled her forehead in bemusement, threw the duvet aside, and climbed out of bed with a sigh. She threw on a robe and went into the kitchen. The copper teakettle was starting to whistle. A column of steam gushed upwards and spread out along the ceiling. The two dogs, their massive heads thrown back and their dark eyes dancing, were barking a storm.

Her father said to her mother, "What is your little idiot talking about?" He always said "your" when referring to Gabriel because Gabriel had been fathered by her first husband, Antoine Douville.

Sylvie Morel, a small woman whose back had a permanent bend and whose shoulders seemed dragged downward with the weight of life, shrugged as she removed the kettle from the cast iron stove.

The dogs continued to bark.

"Shut up, you mutts!" shouted Marcel.

"Come and see," cried Gabriel.

"Goddamned idiot."

"It's true. Come see."

"Stop your idiot babbling."

Gabriel flashed an angry look at his stepfather. "Are you afraid to come see?"

Marcel's face turned red. He was a scrawny man whose eyes bulged unnaturally causing him to resemble the fish he caught for a living. "I ain't afraid." He turned to his wife. "Alright, I'll go see if your idiot son is imagining things or not. And if he's right for once, I'm gonna shoot this zebra. Think what the men will say."

"There are no zebras on Saint Pierre," said Marie-Lisette. "They live in Africa." She said it with a bemused laugh that she instantly regretted. She saw her half-brother give her what she thought was a conspiratorial look.

Marcel whirled to face Marie-Lisette. "Oh, you know everything, you with your books." He went into the storm vestibule, almost tripping over a small throw rug that was always being disarranged by the dogs. He muttered a curse at the dogs and pulled his shotgun from the wall. "Come on, idiot, show me this zebra." He turned to Marie-Lisette. "And you, if I see this zebra, I'll be back to take care of your superior ways; you thinking the rest of us are nothing but ignorant fishermen."

As they left the house, Gabriel leaned toward Marie-Lisette and whispered, "I'm not an idiot. He'll see."

At last Jérôme saw Gabriel and Marcel approaching *The Mountain*. Marcel carried a gun, the sun glinting off its barrel. Jérôme cursed; he hadn't counted on that. He watched the pair carefully, prepared to bolt if Marcel raised his gun to his skinny shoulder.

Gabriel and Marcel stopped. Jérôme saw Gabriel pointing in the direction of the wooden zebra. Marcel started to raise the gun to his shoulder but he apparently decided the distance was too great and lowered it. He scurried up the slope, stumbling several times. Gabriel trailed behind.

Moving quickly from behind his screen of scrub pine, Jérôme pulled the wooden zebra toward him. Crouching low, the zebra tucked under his arm, he hurried to his left until it was safe to descend the far side of the slope to his house.

After more than an hour, he began to worry that the plan had somehow gone wrong. When yet another fifteen minutes passed, he decided to go outside to see if there was any sign of Gabriel and Marcel. But when he opened his door, he found himself staring into the skinny, goggle-eyed face of Marcel.

"I just saw a zebra," sputtered Marcel.

"Hello, Marcel," said Jérôme with as casual a voice as he could manage.

"Didn't you hear what I said? I saw a zebra."

Jérôme looked past Marcel's shoulder. He made a show of surveying the road. "Where?"

"Not, there, damn it … there." Marcel pointed toward *The Mountain*.

"Up there?"

"Yes, you moron."

"A zebra?"

"Ain't that what I just told you?"

Jérôme whistled softly. He wished Gabriel would stop grinning. He paused a long while as if considering something. "You know, I heard there used to be zebras on Miquelon back long ago, but I never heard of one on Saint Pierre."

"There were zebras on Miquelon?"

Jérôme nodded gravely. "Long before our time. That's what I heard."

Marcel's mouth dropped open. He turned to gaze up *The Mountain*. Jérôme took the opportunity to frown at Gabriel, signaling him to stop grinning. To his relief, Gabriel got the message.

Marcel turned back to them. "Maybe it swam across from Miquelon."

Jérôme nodded thoughtfully. "Could be. I also heard they are good swimmers, just like our dogs."

"Jesus! Wait until the others hear about this."

"You know what else I heard?"

Marcel stared at him, eyes flashing with wonder. "What?"

"I heard they like to mate with cows."

"Cows?"

"Yuh, cows."

"No," Marcel whispered incredulously.

"Yuh, that's what I heard."

Marcel paused a moment, then said, "We better go over to warn Claude Cormier."

Jérôme nodded gravely. "Let's hope it's not too late."

Moments later, they were pounding on the door of the Cormier farmhouse. It was a tidy clapboard structure, neatly painted white, with a small porch. Alongside the porch was a patch of cabbage plants, each one protected from the wind by a tin can with the bottom cut out. The door swung open and Jérôme's heart skipped when he saw Adrienne standing in the doorway, a bemused expression on her face.

Marcel lifted the beret from his head, brushed back his thinning hair, and clutched the beret to his chest. "Madame Cormier, we've come to warn your husband about a zebra who may be messing with his cows."

"A zebra?" She glanced at Jérôme who merely shrugged his shoulders as if to say, "Life is full of strange things."

"Yes, Madame, I seen it with my own eyes. The idiot saw it, too. But that don't account for much."

"But a zebra?"

Marcel pointed to his round, gawking eyes with forked fingers. "With my own two eyes!"

Adrienne hesitated a moment, looking to Jérôme as though for guidance, but he remained stone-faced. Finally, she said, "I'll get my husband," and disappeared inside the house.

Moments later, Claude Cormier appeared, Adrienne at his shoulder. "A zebra?" he asked with no preamble as he adjusted his suspender. His voice rumbled.

Marcel, breathless, told him the whole story including what Jérôme had said about zebras mating with cows. "That's why we thought we oughta come and tell you."

Claude gazed at the man for a long moment, skepticism written in his face. "Marcel, you are so full of shit."

"But I saw it; I swear."

Claude look at the others, pulled a handkerchief from his back pocket, blew his nose, and carefully folded the handkerchief in quarters before returning it to his pocket. Lifting a coat from its peg, he said, "Let's go check out the barn."

Claude marched toward the barn, Marcel shuffled after him. They scattered chickens before them. Jérôme, Adrienne, and Gabriel trailed behind at a more casual pace. Jérôme took the opportunity to wink at Adrienne. It only seemed to increase her bewilderment.

When Claude slid the barn door open, its wheels squealing on the track, and stepped inside, he cried, "Mon Dieu!"

Marcel, at his shoulder, let out a gasp. The two men stepped up to the stall containing the cow and calf and peered over the top.

Jérôme peeked over their shoulders. He was amazed; the stripes looked even more real than he had hoped. They were subtle and faint and gave the appearance of being part of the natural hair of the calf, just as if they were emerging according to the calf's natural maturation process. I'm as good as a Parisian artist! he thought.

Adrienne walked up to the stall, gazed at the black-striped calf for a moment, then turned to look at Jérôme with a perplexed expression. Jérôme raised his eyebrows and held out his hands in a gesture that said, "What can I say?"

Adrienne narrowed her eyes at him.

"Look at the damned cow," said Claude, "she's trying to lick the stripes off her calf. She's trying to hide her shame that she'd mate with one who's not her natural mate."

Jérôme saw Adrienne shiver.

"I should get my gun and shoot the bitch," Claude continued.

Adrienne averted her eyes from Jérôme.

"There's no need to do that," said Jérôme. "Think how famous this will make you."

Claude gazed at Jérôme for a long moment, then nodded. Jérôme's heart skipped a beat when Claude reached out and brushed his fingers along one of the stripes. Will he feel the paint? But apparently, it felt just like the calf's natural hair, for Claude said, "But it had no stripes when it was born."

"I've heard that the stripes come only after several weeks," said Jérôme. "Kinda like teeth in babies, only sooner."

Claude and Marcel nodded knowingly at him. Claude said, "Wait until the men at the café hear about this."

"They ain't gonna believe it," said Marcel. "But I saw the zebra with my own two eyes."

Claude nodded. "And who can deny this? We'll bring them out here so they can see for themselves."

Adrienne glanced at Jérôme, a look of alarm on her face.

Fire in the Trenches

ARIE-LISETTE HAD JUST PUT *Southern Mail* in a safe place and brought out two new library books when her father burst into her room without a knock. She dropped the book she was reading and jumped out of bed, a look of fear on her face. Rearranging her clothes, she faced Marcel who was sweating. The cords in his neck stood out; his face was flushed. "I saw the goddamned zebra," he said.

Marie-Lisette wrinkled her brow, "Oh, don't be silly. It's just a joke."

"Just a joke?" The flush on his face deepened. "You don't know nothing, Marie-Lisette. All you do is read crap and you don't know nothing about real life." He picked up the two books that were sprawled on the bed and examined them. They were both by Amelia Earhart: *For The Fun Of It*, and *Last Flight*. "What are these about?"

"Flying."

"Flying, eh? Well, you have had *your* 'last flight'!" He stomped out of the room clutching the two books.

Marie-Lisette chased after him. "Leave those books alone; they belong to the library."

But Marcel ignored her. Instead, he opened the small door to the coal stove. Marie-Lisette saw the coals shimmer with heat and she sucked in her breath. A hissing sound came from the burning chamber. She grabbed at the books and tried to wrest them from her father's grasp, but he was too strong. He snatched them away from her and pushed her across the room. She stumbled into the kitchen table, knocking over a chair. It landed with a loud crack and Marie-Lisette slid to the floor.

Marcel heaved the books into the stove. He took a poker and prodded them deep into the hunkering red glow of the coals. The books caught with a sudden flash of flame.

Marie-Lisette rose to her feet and threw herself on him, beating him about the shoulders. Marcel grabbed her wrists, holding her arms extended in front of her, and squeezed. Marie-Lisette let out a cry of pain. She gritted her teeth and said, "Those were library books. You had no right."

"To hell with the library! It has no business keeping young women from their duties."

"What do you know about a woman's duties?"

"I know that it's long past time for you to forget your books and get yourself married … and get out of this house."

"I'd love to get out of this house. Who wants to live with a beast like you?"

"Watch what you say, girl."

"I mean it."

"Careful …."

"I want to leave this house."

"Fine. Then marry Raymond Pineau. If he was good enough to screw, he's good enough to marry."

She stared at him in shock. How did he know? Raymond must have told him … or somebody had seen them. "I don't want to marry Raymond Pineau," she said. Then, from a deep sense of anger, wanting to hurt her father, and throwing away all caution, she added, "He smells like fish."

Marcel glared at her, his face reddening. "Smells like fish, eh?" He yanked her violently toward him and forced her face against his chest. "Is there something wrong with that? Don't I smell like fish? Your own father? That's what an honest fisherman is *supposed* to smell like."

She struggled to escape, but it was useless.

"Go ahead, take a good whiff."

A wave of anger and shame came over her. She was eighteen, a grown woman, why did she allow herself to be treated this way? Was it to save her mother the agony of standing between her daughter and her husband? Her mother didn't deserve that. Or was she afraid of her father's violent streak? Feeling powerless, she let herself go limp.

Apparently satisfied that he had made his point, Marcel pushed her away from him. Marie-Lisette shot him a hate-filled glance and ran into her room, trying desperately to suppress the tears that were gathering in her eyes.

Marcel called after her, "I'm going to have a talk with Raymond Pineau. I'll coach him in how to handle you. That's all he needs, a little coaching. Then you two will be married, fish smell or not."

"You should have seen them, Antoine. They fell for it completely. What fools!" Jérôme lifted a coat off the peg adjoining the one he reserved for Antoine's trench coat and slipped it on. He rubbed his hands together to generate warmth. The house was unusually cold for July because of the damp fog that was rolling in from the battle zone between the ice-laden Baffin Current and the serpentine Gulf Stream that meandered toward the small archipelago before turning abruptly and making a dash for Europe. "I only wish you could have seen their faces when they saw the calf. It was …." Jérôme stopped to face the trench coat, searching for the right word. He put two fingers to his lips and kissed them. "It was delicious!" With the same two fingers, he touched the shoulder of the trench coat. His face fell for an instant before brightening again. "And your poor Gabriel, he played his role perfectly. You would have been proud. It was sweet revenge for the way Claude Cormier treats poor Adrienne. And as for your lovely Sylvie, and sweet Marie-Lisette, Marcel Morel won't be quite the big man he always likes to pretend he is."

There was a shy knock on the door. Jérôme, recognizing it with a flutter of his heart, hurried through the storm vestibule and opened the door. Adrienne Cormier asked, "May I come in, Monsieur Sabot?" A filament of fog drifted in over her shoulder.

"Yes, of course."

She slipped past him. He smelled her freshness. Shampoo? Perfume? It teased his nostrils—a frisson of arousal.

"Thank you," she said.

"Please call me Jérôme. After all, we're friends, aren't we?"

Adrienne smiled. "Yes, friends."

The way she said it caused a ripple of sadness in Jérôme's breast. It was as though the word had established a limit, a boundary that couldn't be passed, like the icebergs that sometimes ringed the archipelago in winter. "It's good to have you as a friend," he said cheerlessly.

Adrienne wrapped her arms under her breasts. Her knuckles were white. "It's so cold in here. You should light a fire when the fog comes in like this."

"I don't like fires."

"So you've told me."

"I only make them when absolutely necessary in the winter." He pulled a chair out from the table for her then, remembering it was the one with a loose slat, he slid it back and pulled out another one.

"You've said that to me before, but I guess I still don't understand it."

"It's just that I don't like fires."

"May I light one for you?"

Jérôme hesitated before saying, "Yes … yes, go ahead." He sat in the chair with the loose slat.

Adrienne moved to the cast iron stove, opened the door to the burning chamber, and poured coal from a tin bucket. She crumpled up some newspaper, stuffed it in among the coals, struck a match, and lit the paper. "My husband will be home soon. I mustn't stay long, so please pardon me for coming straight to the point. Are you responsible for that zebra trick?"

Jérôme said nothing. He only smiled. A hint of sulfur from the match Adrienne had struck wafted around his nose. His nostrils twitched.

A fleeting smile crossed Adrienne's face, followed quickly by a frown. She turned to prod the coal with a poker. "That was a rash thing to do. I don't believe you understand how dangerous my husband can be."

Jérôme gave a dismissive wave of his hand. "Pouf! He's a fool, if you don't mind me saying so."

"Yes, I know he's a fool, but he's still dangerous. He has a terrible temper."

"I've seen it."

"Especially when he thinks he's been made to look the fool." She propped the poker against a leg of the stove. "There, now you can offer me a cup of tea."

Jérôme saw the flames shoot up before Adrienne closed the stove door. He backed his chair further from the stove.

He is in a dugout several hundred yards behind the first trenches. He has just lit a cigarette and called "Hurry up!" to Antoine who is not far behind him, when he hears the high-pitched whine of an incoming shell. Instinctively, he throws himself to the earthen floor just as a deafening blast shatters his ears and the dugout erupts in flame. He is knocked unconscious momentarily and when he comes to, he doesn't know where he is. The world is strangely silent. There is only a dull ringing in his ears. He tries to get up, but finds he can't move. With rising panic, he sees first the decapitated body of the only other man who had been in the dugout with him, the man's clothes aflame and the skin of his hands already puckering with black blisters; then he sees the wall of flame all around him. He screams, but he can hear no sound coming from his throat. His face is unbearably hot and he throws his hands in front of it. Again, he tries to rise, but there is a searing pain in his right leg. He collapses again to the floor. Tears of frustration rise in his eyes.

He knows he's going to die. He tries to suck in a breath, but is rewarded only with a raw, scorching sensation in his throat. He's suffocating. A hand grabs his and starts to drag him brutally along the floor. The pain in his leg shrieks. Suddenly, he's through the fire and into the open air. Rain falls on his wracked body but it's long moments before he can feel the cooling effect. Antoine's mouth is moving absurdly, but Jérôme can't hear a word. He starts to cough. Every cough sends slivers of pain shooting up and down his right leg, but he can't stop. And, though he is outside the dugout, he can still see the flames all around him ... the hideous, consuming flames.

"Didn't you hear what I said?"

Jérôme gazed dumbly at Adrienne for a moment before answering. "Uh, yes ... Claude ….."

"He can be very dangerous. You know how he is when he gets a gun in his hands. He enjoys killing." She adjusted the stove's vents.

Jérôme felt strangely out of balance. Every time memories of the war struggled to the surface, they seemed to settle back into a different place, like a weight that he had to re-adjust before he could go on. He shook his head as though to clear it. "Did you see the doctor, today?"

Adrienne gave him an anxious glance. "You knew? I only told you I was going into town."

He shrugged. "It's a small island."

"Yes ... yes, I did," she said. Then, quickly, she added, "You mustn't let Claude be humiliated tomorrow."

"What for?"

"Because, I told you, he's likely to get violent."

"No, I mean why did you see the doctor?"

Adrienne gazed at him for a long moment. "It's very impertinent of you to ask. It was just … a womanly concern. Everything's alright."

"I'm glad for you."

"I'll be glad for you if you take my warning about my husband seriously." She went into the storm vestibule, took a broom and dustpan, returned to the kitchen, and began sweeping up the coal dust and the carcasses of dead wasps.

"The memories, they don't come back as often," he said. A worthwhile lie?

She seemed taken aback. "I'm … I'm glad."

"I mean we don't only have to talk about them, the memories … like before. When we're together, I mean … Adrienne."

"You shouldn't call me Adrienne."

"I mean we could talk about other things. I'm alright now." He waved at a fly buzzing around his ear.

"That zebra trick was a silly thing to do."

"Not that our talks haven't helped. They have. You're the only person I could talk with."

"Yes, I know."

"But that's all past, the memories, I mean."

"Why do you always have to play the clown? Whatever made you think about that zebra thing?"

Jérôme shrugged.

"It's a cover up—you know that, don't you?" When Jérôme still said nothing, Adrienne continued. "I'm sorry you have so much pain, but you must be careful it doesn't drive you to do crazy things that will cause trouble for yourself … and for others."

"But, Adrienne, we can talk about other things, you and me. The memories aren't such a problem anymore … other things …."

"You shouldn't call me Adrienne."

"I value your visits."

"Then be careful about Claude. I'd never be able to visit if he suspects you're trying to humiliate him."

Adrienne was no sooner back inside her house when she heard Claude's truck pull up, tires crunching the gravel. A jolt of fear ran through her at the realization that, had he been just a few moments earlier—he and Claudette, who was with him— they would have seen her emerge from Jérôme's house. There would have been questions and accusations from both of them and she would have been forced to answer their suspicions, defend herself. They would have been placed on alert and would start watching her. What little freedom she had would have melted away like snow in June, and she no longer would be able to see Jean-Luc.

Later, as they sat around the table at supper, steaming bowls of stew before them, Claudette said, "Me and Claude, we saw the Fournier family just now."

Adrienne had a sinking feeling. Here we go again, she thought. She knew exactly what Claudette would say next.

"Five kids, they have," said Claudette.

"Yes, I know."

"Three boys and two girls. Old Madame Fournier was with them."

"I'm sure she was very happy."

"Don't you think I would like to be happy, too?"

As if that were possible.

"I'd like to have grandchildren, too," continued Claudette. "Ain't you two trying hard enough?"

"Aw, Ma, leave it be, will you?" said Claude, pausing with a spoonful of stew before his lips. A trickle of liquid dribbled to the tablecloth. He leaned the hairy ham of a forearm on the table and pulled the handkerchief from his back pocket and mopped up the spot of stew and wiped his lips and stuffed the handkerchief back into his pocket.

Claudette watched him with narrowed eyes. "The problem is you two never think of me. How do you think I feel with no grandchildren to talk to my friends about?"

"Leave it alone, damn it," shouted Claude.

Under cover of the table, Adrienne slipped her hand across her belly. As she had so often in the last few weeks, she wondered when she would start showing and what would happen then.

"And Brigide Berteau, she has six grandchildren!"

"Christ!" muttered Claude. He sullenly dipped the spoon into the bowl and slurped another mouthful of stew.

Adrienne looked at him from the corner of her eye. She knew what she had to attempt, and the thought of it repelled her. But there was no other way to convince him that the baby was his. Even then, the timing would be all wrong, but perhaps he wouldn't notice. He might know a lot about the gestation period of calves, but when it came to people, he paid little attention. She doubted he was that much a fool, but it was worth a try. She had to get him to make love to her successfully, no matter how repulsive it might be. But how would she manage it? He had long ago given up the attempt, perhaps to avoid the humiliation of knowing he wasn't a complete man.

"What did the doctor say?' asked Claudette.

"About what?"

"About you being barren, of course. What'd you think I meant?"

"I didn't see him for that. I just had something wrong with my belly, a little discomfort. He said it was nothing to worry about. Just a bug of some kind."

Claude slurped his stew.

"Why don't you ask him about you being barren?"

"Christ, Ma, will you shut the hell up," shouted Claude. He slammed his spoon down on the table and pushed his chair back with a loud scrape. "I'm getting the hell out of here. I'll be at the café."

Adrienne watched him go. She knew that, with his sullen mood, there would be little chance of arousing him that night. Besides, he'd probably come home drunk. Perhaps the following night … if he wasn't totally humiliated by the zebra affair. She knew him well. He would never risk two humiliations in one day.

At the dimly lit Café Joinville, Jérôme sat at a corner table well away from the fireplace and sipped his pernod. Peter Pichot, Doctor Tréguy, and Gabriel Morel occupied the other chairs at the table. Cigarette butts overfilled the ashtrays and a scud of smoke licked at the ceiling.

Before the war, the Café Joinville had been the scene of frequent dances and dinners, but after the fall of Paris these affairs were thought to be too unseemly while the Motherland suffered under the Nazis. The large, adjoining room that had been used for dances was now overflowing with war bundles for people in France. But they piled up uselessly. There was no way of getting them to France unless *Le Celte* appeared.

"She'll never make it through," said Doctor Tréguy. "The Atlantic must be swarming with submarines."

"You give up hope too easily," said Pierre Pichot, a thin, nervous man whose bald pate shone with sweat. "She's been late before, but she's always come through."

"But there was no war before. It's different now."

"Well, my shelves are almost bare, so she'd better show up," replied Pichot. "People come in and I have nothing to sell them."

"Yes, I know," said Doctor Tréguy with a wistful sigh. "It's sad how many people come to me lately complaining of melancholy. The sight of *Le Celte* pulling into the harbor would be the best tonic anybody here could have."

From the next table, a man who was in his early nineties and who was wearing a threadbare French uniform from the Franco-Prussian War, growled across at them through yellowed, decayed teeth. "We'll beat the Bosch back to Germany in a week. Then *Le Celte* will make it through." A gray, unkempt handlebar mustache seemed to pull the man's wrinkled face even further downward.

"I wouldn't be so confident, Colonel Lafitte," said Doctor Tréguy with a laugh. "They ran over Paris like that!" He snapped his fingers forcefully. Although Auguste Lafitte's uniform was only that of a private, everyone deferred to his addled conceit that he had been a colonel.

"Colonel Lafitte, why do you wear your uniform all the time now," asked Gabriel. "You never used to."

Auguste Lafitte sat upright in his chair, thrust his cragged face toward Gabriel and said, "I will wear this uniform until the Bosch are driven out of France."

Jérôme leaned toward Pierre Pichot and whispered, "His clothes already smell like old piss. Imagine what it will be like if the incontinent bastard wears that thing for years."

Pichot smiled, wrinkled his nose.

Auguste Lafitte said, "The *Anciens Combattants* will send the government a telegram to tell them to keep fighting for France. I personally, will write it." As honorary head of the *Anciens Combattants*, the association of old soldiers on Saint Pierre and Miquelon, he had often said that his solemn duty was to state the position of the Saint Pierrais to the home government.

"And where will we send it? Which government? London? Vichy? General de Gaulle? Marshal Pétain?"

This ignited a brief but heated argument about the comparative merits of de Gaulle and Pétain, most of the men siding with de Gaulle. Auguste Lafitte attempted to end the discussion with one of his usual, peremptory pronouncements. "The *Anciens Combattants* support General de Gaulle. He is for Free France." But this only provoked a fresh outburst, several of the men protesting his presumption that he spoke for everybody. However, they were quickly shouted down by the vast majority of men who agreed with Lafitte.

At that moment, Claude Cormier and Marcel Morel walked in. After greeting several men, Claude walked straight over to Jérôme's table and asked, "Have you told them?"

"Told them what?"

Claude leaned close, whispered. "About the zebra."

Jérôme removed the cigarette from his mouth, blew out a stream of smoke, smiled, and shook his head. "I didn't want to rob you and Marcel of the experience."

Claude gave a smile of satisfaction. "Help me up," he said to the men at Jérôme's table, "I have something to announce."

Doctor Tréguy and Pierre Pichot helped him climb atop the table that creaked under his weight. Smoke from the many cigarettes wafted around his face. He stood teetering for a moment before proclaiming, in a loud voice, "I have something amazing to tell you all." He waited for the buzz of conversation to die down. Then, his massive chest thrust forward and his arms hanging by his sides, he announced, "My cow has given birth to a zebra."

A momentary stunned silence was followed by gales of laughter. "Have you been drinking before you got here?" someone called out from the far corner of the room.

"No, no, I tell you, it's true. Ask Marcel."

Marcel waved his hands then pointed to his eyes. "With these two eyes I have seen it myself."

But that provoked only more laughter, causing Marcel's face to turn red and his eyes go round with fury.

"Listen, you're all fools," cried Claude. "We're telling you the truth."

"Then it's you two who are the fools."

Now Claude's face turned as red as Marcel's. "If you won't believe us, ask Jérôme Sabot. He also saw this … this miracle."

Everyone turned toward Jérôme. "Well, what about it, Jérôme?" someone asked. "Have you, too, seen this?"

Jérôme smiled and spread out his arms in a gesture that said, "What can I say?" Then, in a loud voice, he said, "I can only say that I saw a calf with black stripes."

His announcement was greeted by silence and a room-full of bemused stares.

Finally, Auguste Lafitte said, "It could be a sign."

"A sign of what?" Doctor Tréguy asked.

Auguste pursed his lips, let out a puff of breath. He raised his shoulders in an exaggerated shrug and said, "I don't know. Perhaps that the Bosch will be beaten."

Gabriel giggled. Jérôme shot him a warning glance.

"I think you're looking for any sign that might deny the truth—that France has fallen to the Nazis."

"No, no," said Auguste. "I tell you it could be a sign of perversity to say that their occupation of Paris is also a perversity. It could be a sign that General de Gaulle should act. Perhaps we'll include this in the telegram."

"Tell General de Gaulle that on Saint Pierre a cow gave birth to a zebra?"

"Yes, why not?"

"They already think we're provincials."

"But if it truly happened …."

"*If* it truly happened. And even then, they'll still think we're crazy."

Doctor Tréguy rose from his chair. His eyes twinkled. "In that case, there is one thing we must do before we sign our names to such a telegram. We must inspect this claim scientifically. I propose that we all go out to Claude's farm in the morning and see for ourselves."

His proposal was greeted with immediate approval. It was as though the men were instantly relieved to find something to occupy their minds, to alleviate the boredom and suspense and heartache of waiting for *Le Celte*.

Claude and Marcel, beaming with the attention, bought a round of drinks for everyone.

It had been a cold, fog-bound day. Droplets of fog beaded every surface. Yet, despite the chill of her bedroom, Adrienne removed all her clothes and slipped under the blankets. If Claude kept to his normal schedule, he would be home soon and, if he wasn't too drunk, she would try to arouse him enough to make love.

The feel of the sheets against her nude body caused a sensual thrill to shiver through her. She thought of Jean-Luc Lavedan. She pictured the way he walked with that purposeful stride that excited her and she longed to be with him and not here, trapped in this cold bedroom. She glanced at the bureau where the empty jar of facial cream sat because she was unwilling to throw it away. Her heart started to beat faster with a sense of hopelessness … and with fear. Suddenly, the sheets no longer felt good on her body. Instead, they seemed to cling indecently to her.

Her husband's moods were too unpredictable. She knew she would be taking a great chance if her plan to arouse him didn't work and only ended in him feeling humiliated. But it was a risk she had to take. A flutter of guilt churned in her stomach, not only because she might be exposing her husband to humiliation, but because, in the process, she would be betraying Jean-Luc. It was an odd thought—that she should consider making love with her husband a betrayal of her lover—and it added to her anxiety and confusion.

She heard the front door open and close. She bit her lip. The gauze curtains filtered a miserly moonlight into the room. It blushed the empty facial cream jar with a dull glow.

Moments later, Claude appeared in the room, his unsnapped suspenders already bouncing against his hips. As he undressed to his underwear, he said, "At first the men didn't believe me about the zebra, but Marcel backed me up. And also Jérôme Sabot. They'll be out tomorrow to see for themselves."

"Are you sure you want that? What if it's some kind of trick?"

"It ain't no trick. Christ, you sound just like them fools." He pulled back the blankets and started to slide into bed.

Adrienne quivered with fear when she saw him gaze at her naked body. Her nipples, normally so easy to arouse, remained flat and soft. Were they slightly swollen? Would he notice?

"What the hell is this?" he said. There was an unfamiliar huskiness in his voice.

"Come to me, Claude." She hoped her revulsion wasn't betrayed by her voice.

He stared at her, bewildered for a moment, then said, "Oh, for Chrissakes, stop acting like a slut." He slid into bed and turned his back to her.

Adrienne's cheek muscles rippled with anger. She ground her teeth. A woman scorned. Even if it was the last thing she wanted. Not to be put off so quickly, she reached around his body and pressed her hand against his long johns. "Don't you remember our honeymoon? Halifax? The Lord Nelson Hotel?"

"Cost a fortune."

"But wasn't it worth it? The food?"

"Unnh."

"The huge bed?" She rubbed her hand against him.

He brushed her hand away, grumbled, "Jesus, Adrienne, leave me alone." He turned on his back to look at her, his dull eyes like raisins under his thick eyebrows.

Now that he was on his back and available, Adrienne slid deeper under the covers. Working quickly, she fumbled for the opening in his long johns. He shifted his body to pull away from her, but she followed it, lowering her hand to him. The rancid smell of his loins almost gagged her.

"What the hell are you doing?" Claude cried in a falsetto voice. But he made no effort to withdraw, so she continued to move her hand frantically. She was terrified. A shudder passed through her stomach. The beginning of a retch. Please, no!

Claude fell silent.

She could feel his body start to tense. She increased her efforts. He seemed to be enjoying the sensation and Adrienne was both shamed and encouraged. She closed her eyes tightly, the way one does when smelling rotten eggs. She tried to force herself to imagine this was Jean-Luc's flesh, as it so recently had been, but the effort was too great.

The tension in his body increased and all at once she recognized it for what it was—building anger rather than excitement. She had seen it so many times before in other situations. She started to panic, fearing an explosion at any moment. She worked faster. If she could only get him hard, she would straddle him quickly and then it would be done, then she wouldn't have to put herself through this misery ever again.

Not ever again!

Suddenly, Claude jerked himself away from her. He brought his open hand hard against her face, and shouted, "What are you trying to do, humiliate me, you goddamned whore?" He threw himself out of bed. "You slut!"

A wave of despair came over her. Her cheek stung. It felt hot with pain … and shame.

"You don't excite me," he said. "How am I supposed to get it up if you don't excite me?"

Adrienne glared at him, an almost overwhelming hatred and anger rising in her chest. She felt the heat of a blush on her cheeks.

Claude stormed out of the bedroom, slamming the door behind him. Adrienne heard Claudette ask, "What the hell's going on?" and Claude answer, "Nothing. I'm going out to look at my zebra."

Adrienne started to tremble. She pulled the covers up to her face and bit down hard on them, trying to will herself not to cry. It was now certain her infidelity would be discovered and she was sick at the prospect of what would happen then. For a long while, she lay in the bed staring at a bare spot in the ceiling, her mind spinning with thoughts about what to do next, thoughts that stubbornly refused to coalesce into anything resembling a plan.

At last, dejected, she climbed out of bed and put her robe on. She wanted to go into the kitchen, to the sink. She wanted to wash her hands. But she was afraid of encountering Claudette. She ran a finger on the inside of the jar of facial cream, hoping for just a little smear. But the walls of the jar had already dried with caked residue. A shudder ran through her body. A single tear left a cool track along her cheek.

Taking a deep breath, she slipped between the covers again. At least she would be safe this night because Claude would never return to the room feeling as humiliated as he did. She stared at the ceiling with its flaking paint and willed herself to still the turmoil in her mind.

Gradually, a thought began to take shape. She realized now, more than ever, that she couldn't stay in this house once the baby was born. She was determined not to expose the child to Claude's inevitable rage; it would be a constant reminder to him of his own impotence. Perhaps if she stopped being secretive about Jean-Luc, perhaps if she allowed herself to be seen in public with him. Surely, that would provoke the crisis and then, at least, she would be able to escape this household and stay with Jean-Luc. It would be done with and over with. She had been so pliant for so many years that the thought of such a bold action shivered her with excitement. She felt her resolve begin to stiffen.

But, then again, wouldn't that expose Jean-Luc to danger? An image of Claude sitting in a rocking chair in front of the house—blasting away with his shotgun, seagulls falling from the sky—came to her. How could she expose Jean-Luc to that sort of man?

Outside, a vast sprawl of stars shone on the tiny archipelago. The light glinted cold on the corroded bumpers of Claude's truck.

5
A Zebra Calf

SHORTLY AFTER DAWN the following morning a convoy of cars and trucks rolled up to the Cormier farm trailing billows of dust that shimmered in the slanting sunlight. The men climbed from their vehicles, gathered together, and approached as a group. Auguste Lafitte led them as though they were a squadron of soldiers.

Claude, along with Marcel who had come early, greeted the men and immediately led them to the barn with long purposeful strides through the striations of low morning light. Claude theatrically slid the barn door along its track as though drawing a stage curtain. To his obvious delight, several of the men gasped when they saw the striped calf. Auguste Lafitte made a quick sign of the cross across his forehead and said, "It truly is an omen. *Viva de Gaulle!*"

The cow stood over her calf, slobber from her nose dripping onto the calf's head. She gave a soft low.

Doctor Tréguy elbowed his way to the front and peered over the stall. He examined the calf closely, looking over the eyeglasses perched on the end of his nose. "May I go in?" he asked, turning to Claude.

"Of course. See for yourself."

Doctor Tréguy opened the stall door and dropped to his knees. He ran his fingers along one of the stripes. Leaning close, he lifted a section of the calf's hair to examine the underside of the bristles. He sniffed them. "It's paint ... or some kind of dye," he said.

"You're wrong," said Claude. "It can't be paint."

Doctor Tréguy only nodded gravely, an incipient smile on his face. "It's definitely paint or dye ... maybe ink. An excellent job, but you've been had all the same."

Claude's face turned red. He sputtered. "What do you know? You may be a good human doctor, but you don't know shit about animals."

"If you don't believe me, get some turpentine."

"I ain't got no turpentine."

"I do," said Jérôme. "Shall I go get it?"

Claude gazed at him a moment, then nodded hesitantly.

Jérôme dashed to his shed and returned with a can of turpentine and a rag. He handed them to Doctor Tréguy, who poured some of the turpentine onto the rag and began to wipe at one of the calf's stripes. The paint came off in a smear. He held the rag out to show Claude and Marcel.

The men who were gathered around started to laugh. Someone said, "What a wonderful trick! Who could have pulled it off?"

"Someone who's a great artist. Look how real it looks."

"Might have fooled me."

Jérôme beamed.

Well aware of Claude's temper, everyone was quick to deny responsibility. They looked around at each other for some sign of guilt—or, perhaps, pride. When several of the men looked at Jérôme, he extended his arms wide in an I-can't-possibly-guess gesture. But then he did the worst thing he could do. Despite his best intentions, he chuckled, and when he did, Gabriel picked up the chuckle like a contagion.

Claude gave him a gargoyle gaze.

Gabriel turned to face Doctor Tréguy. "I ain't an idiot. I'm good."

"Sure, Gabriel. I know."

"This proves it, don't it?" said Gabriel.

Claude and Marcel stared at Jérôme, their faces flushed.

"No, no, It wasn't me," Jérôme said to them. "It's just so … funny. Really, you have to admit …."

Claude and Marcel continued to glare at Jérôme.

"Truly, it wasn't me."

But as the men started to leave, several of them patted Jérôme heartily on the back. He felt a flush of pride, but he still wished they wouldn't congratulate him.

Claude whirled and strode angrily toward his house.

As the cars and trucks started to pull away, Jérôme headed for his own house. He had taken no more than a few steps when he heard Marcel say, "Come with me, you idiot."

"I ain't the idiot. You are."

Jérôme turned to see Marcel hauling Gabriel roughly by the arm across the gravel road.

When Marie-Lisette entered the tiny library with its musty smells and gloomy interior, she was agitated. Madame Leclair, the head librarian, greeted her at the door.

"Ah, Marie-Lisette, you've come for more books? You read faster than anyone else I know." She paused, frowned, and said, "But something is the matter. I see it in your face." She lifted her eyeglasses, which hung from a chord around her neck, to her eyes. The loops of the chord brushed against her large earrings. She had the complexion of unbleached linen.

Marie-Lisette said, "I'm afraid I have something terrible to tell you." She told Madame Leclair about the burning of the Amelia Earhart books.

Madame Leclair cried, "The nerve of the man! It's an outrage." Several white hairs had come loose from her French bun. She brushed them away.

"How can I repay the library for the books?" Marie-Lisette asked.

But Madame Leclair seemed not to hear. She said, "I'll have your father arrested for willfully destroying property."

"Oh, please, Madame Leclair, don't do that. It would only make matters worse at home. They're nearly intolerable as it is. I'll do anything to make it right for the library. Of course, I'll pay for the books … and any fine that might be attached."

"But why should you have to pay? Your father is the culprit."

"It's just that it would be easier that way."

"Do you always look for the easy way, Marie-Lisette?"

"Please, Madame …."

Madame Leclair gazed at her for a long time. Finally, she said, "I will not have you pay for the books. That would be unfair to you. But if you insist on making some kind of reparation—though, I repeat, you need not—then what do you say to taking a job with us cataloging books? We're rearranging the shelves. Madame Leneuf has just left us and we were about to look for someone new. You would be perfect."

"But I already have a job at the Hotel Lalanne."

"No matter. You can work for an hour or two in the mornings or evenings, whatever fits best with your job. It's not full time in any case."

"Then, yes, of course, I'll do it. You're very kind, Madame."

"Nonsense. I can think of no better person for the job and besides, what better way to punish Monsieur Morel? Here he does this horrible thing because he doesn't want you to spend your time reading, and what does he get for it? You end up surrounded by books!"

After returning to his house, Jérôme described the scene at Claude Cormier's farm that morning to Antoine's trench coat, then settled into his bed for a nap. He was in such a good mood that, for once, he wasn't visited by images of the war. He was dozing peacefully in that half-awake state that sometimes makes naps so pleasant when he was suddenly jolted by a sharp blast quickly followed by another. He jumped out of bed and rushed to the window. What he saw sent shivers through him.

Claude Cormier sat in front of his barn in a rocking chair, a shotgun propped at an angle on his hip. He fired two quick blasts and a seagull exploded in a smear of blood and feathers. Claude lowered the gun, slid two more shells into the breech, snapped it closed, and raised it again.

Soon, another seagull appeared overhead. It, too, was blasted out of the sky. Bloodied feathers drifted to the ground like large, bizarre snowflakes.

For the next hour Claude kept pumping his gun, ejecting buckshot into the sky, exploding seagulls. His barnyard was littered with a mess of blood and feathers.

Jérôme shuddered. Each blast of the shotgun struck a responsive chord in him. He felt an unholy kinship with Claude Cormier, except, in his case, the seagulls would have been German soldiers, French generals.

And for the first time, Jérôme wondered if he had gone too far with this man—and if he had come too close to revealing himself, revealing his own rage.

Adrienne cowered in her bedroom, flinching each time she heard Claude fire his shotgun. With every sharp blast she gripped the bedcovers until her knuckles turned white. She had seen Claude like this so many times before that she knew what would happen next. He would kill the birds until he had his fill of it and that would end it for a while. He would be like a drunk who had temporarily drowned his unhappiness. The initial force of his anger would have been vented, but it would sit inside him smoldering like a coal fire, or like magma deep inside a volcano, incandescent, ready to erupt any time in a flash of bitterness and hatred. It might take days, weeks, or months, but it would eventually spew forth in uncontrolled violence. She had seen it all before. Many times. And almost the worst part would be the waiting, worse even than the outburst when it came. Ahead of her was a long period of trying to avoid him, of being careful with every word she said, every gesture she made, of quailing every time she saw him. She dreaded going through it all again.

She shuddered again as he fired off two more quick blasts. She got out of bed, peeled the curtain back to peek out the window. He was loading more shells in the breech. A half empty box of cartridges sat at his feet. Spent cartridges littered the ground all about him along with a mess of blood and feathers and the barely recognizable carcasses of gulls. By all appearances he would be at it for some time to come.

She had to see Jean-Luc.

She couldn't stay imprisoned in her bedroom listening to Claude's rage. She put on an old cotton dress and stepped into the kitchen, hoping her mother-in-law wasn't around.

But the woman was standing at the sink. "Where are you going?" she asked Adrienne.

"I need to walk into town … get something." Adrienne didn't bother to hide her trembling hands.

"What?" Claudette gazed at Adrienne's hands.

"I don't know. Something."

Claudette stared at her suspiciously for a moment then shrugged as if to say it wasn't her business. But Adrienne wasn't fooled. She knew as soon as they were all together that night at supper, Claudette would press her unrelentingly for details of what she did in Saint Pierre, hoping, no doubt, to prove to Claude what an unworthy wife Adrienne was.

"I hate it when he gets like this," Claudette said. "He wasn't this way before his father left us. He was a sweet boy, so gentle."

Adrienne nodded, said nothing.

"It was before you knew him."

"I'm sure he was sweet."

"I brought him up right."

"Yes, of course you did."

"It was when his father left. That's what did it."

"Yes."

"There was nothing I could do."

"Of course."

"Does this have something to do with the fight you two had last night?" Claudette asked. "What did you say to him?"

"Nothing."

"You must have said or done something to set him off like this."

"It was probably the zebra joke."

"Maybe. He doesn't like to be shown up for the simple-minded man he is. But you had your fight before he knew the zebra was a joke. You must have said or done something."

"Jesus, I didn't say a thing."

Claudette made a hurried sign of the cross. "Don't use the name of Our Lord like that, you tramp."

"Sorry."

"Who brought you up, anyway?"

Adrienne glared at the woman for a long moment, then went out the door without saying a word. So what if Claudette runs straight out to tell Claude. What did she care? Besides, Claudette was just as frightened of Claude when he got into these moods as everyone else was. She'd probably wait a while before telling him.

Adrienne was no more than five minutes down the road to Saint Pierre when she heard a truck approaching from behind. It sounded like Claude's truck with its loose bumper. She turned to see it materialize slowly out of the ground fog as though forming itself out of the mist. It was bearing down on her and her heart gasped. She stepped to the side of the road, where some lilacs were blooming, but there was no shelter; she was fully exposed. She heard another blast of the shotgun and was confused for a moment. Claude must be still back at the farm venting himself. She peered at the oncoming truck. Finally, it drew close enough for her to see that it was Jérôme Sabot behind the wheel. Her breathing grew easier, but she still had an uneasy feeling. Jérôme would undoubtedly offer her a ride into town and people would see them together. It was the last thing she needed. She hoped he wouldn't stop, but she knew he would.

The truck slowed to a stop alongside her. Jérôme leaned over, rolled down the passenger-side window, and said, "Are you going into town, Adrienne? I'll give you a ride."

"That's kind of you Monsieur Sabot."

"Please, Adrienne, call me Jérôme."

"Please, Monsieur Sabot, we've been through that."

"But—"

"—It's best."

Jérôme spread his hands in a helpless gesture and said nothing.

Adrienne climbed into the truck and gave a determined shake of her head. "I mustn't call you by your Christian name and you mustn't address me like that either. You should call me Madame Cormier; it will be better for both of us."

"Has it come to that?"

Two more shotgun blasts buckled the air. They were followed by reverberating echoes.

Adrienne nodded, gave him an angry look. "Do you hear how he can be? You must not be familiar with me. You must call me Madame Cormier."

"But I—"

"—I insist."

Jérôme gave her a hurt expression, but said, "If that's the way it must be … Madame Cormier."

"That's the way it must be if we are to remain friends."

"Friends," he murmured with an edge of sadness.

They drove in silence for a long while, Jérôme guiding the truck slowly through the fog that shredded, then closed in again, after they passed. They came to a rise above the town where, on clear days, they would see the harbor and the sea beyond. From long habit, Adrienne scanned the harbor for a sign of *Le Celte*, but the fog lay like a curtain just beyond the docks, an impenetrable curtain. At last Adrienne saw the buildings of Saint Pierre begin to emerge like half-formed images on photographic paper. She wondered what she should say when Jérôme asked her where she would like to be dropped off. She couldn't tell him that she was going to the quay.

"How long will he go on like that?" Jérôme asked.

"You mean Claude? It could be a long time."

Jérôme shook his head. "I just couldn't stand it anymore. I figured I'd come in to have a drink at the café."

"Well, I warned you about him. Now you know. You should have known before. You've certainly known him long enough."

"All that because of a silly little zebra joke?"

Adrienne shrugged but said nothing. She'd decided where she would have Jérôme drop her off: The War Memorial. She remembered her uncle had been killed at Verdun. She would say she wanted to touch his name because it gave her comfort. She knew Jérôme would let her out and leave quickly because he hated to be anywhere near the memorial. It had something to do with his experiences in the war, but in all their conversations he would never tell her what, no matter how much she encouraged him. Perhaps it was cruel to make him go there, but what was she to do? She couldn't have him see her walking toward the quay.

But when she saw his reaction to the words "war memorial" she was saddened. There was so much pain in his countenance that she instantly regretted her choice and wished she could change it. However, she didn't know what else to say. As she had assumed, he dropped her off and quickly drove toward the Café Joinville.

A dense fog brooded among the trawlers from France that had been stranded in Saint Pierre when the war broke out. They were the ones that had not yet risked going back; nobody knew the fate of the ones that attempted to return. Adrienne could barely see the faint outline of the lighthouse at Pointe aux Canons, its light extinguished at the beginning of the war. It appeared lost in the cold mist, isolated from the town like a person trying to wade in from the sea but fixed in place, unable to move. Seagulls swirled and glided in and out of the fog with their raucous cries. She thought of Claude.

The fog deposited beads of moisture on her upper lip and she tasted them with her tongue.

Jean-Luc's trawler, *La Petite Fleur*, was about two-thirds of the way down the quay, rafted to another trawler dockside of her. Adrienne wished it was closer and tied directly to the quay so she wouldn't have to walk past all those marooned men and their mascot dogs, but she had no choice. The fog sat on the quay as easily as a sleeping cat. Her progress along the quay was marked by the barking dogs, one after the other, and, as always, it brought the men onto the decks to watch her walk by. She felt on display, almost as though she were walking nude. A rude, wet wind fingered her hair. Although the men said nothing, she could easily imagine what they were thinking. She took a deep, shuddering breath, and continued to walk towards *La Petite Fleur*.

Please let Jean-Luc be on deck! He usually was. Only once had she had to ask a man on the inboard trawler to summon him, and it had filled her with shame. Not that she feared they would talk and make her affair known to the Saint Pierrais, for there seemed to be a code of silence among them. Jean-Luc had told her as much. Many of them, lonely and far from home, were doubtless carrying on their own affairs.

To her great relief, Jean-Luc was on the bow of *La Petite Fleur* mopping the deck. He saw her immediately. Handing the mop to a shipmate, he bounded across the inshore trawler, and leaped to the quay. "Adrienne! What—?" Though he was short, the same height as she, his lean body, carried upright, made him look taller. A growth of whiskers softened the hard lines of his face, eased his Gallic nose. He had fans of wrinkles around his eyes, the look of a man who was perpetually sea-dazed.

"—We have to talk," Adrienne whispered.

Jean-Luc ran his hand across his chin. "I didn't know you were coming. I haven't shaved."

"No matter. Where can we talk?"

Jean-Luc pointed to a shack at the end of the quay. "There."

When they were behind the shack and hidden from view of the fleet, Jean-Luc gathered her in his arms. "You look worried."

"Shhh. Just hold me."

He held her closer and she nestled her head on his shoulder. His coat, damp with fog, was cool on her cheek. They stayed like that for a few long moments while Adrienne gathered her courage. A seagull alighted on a piling not ten feet from them. It looked at them with beady raisin-like eyes for a few moments, then flew off with a whisper of wings.

Jean-Luc said nothing, waiting for her to speak. That was one of the things she loved about him—he always seemed to know when to talk and when to be silent. Most men, certainly Claude, would pester her until she was forced to explain the unexplainable—every last detail of what she was feeling. But not Jean-Luc. Finally, she lifted her head, looked into his eyes, and said, "I'm going to have your baby." She felt an upwelling of guilt as she said it. It made her suck in her breath.

Jean-Luc's jaw dropped. She saw that he was stunned. But she also saw a new brightness in his eyes and that gave her comfort. Nervously, she smiled and said, "It's true." Deep inside her, she felt the guilt bubbling, but she was determined not to let it show.

"When?"

Adrienne attempted a light-hearted laugh. "You know when."

"No, no. I mean …."

She laughed again. "I know what you mean … January." She'd decided earlier that was the safest date to give. Later, when the baby came in early December, she would persuade him it was simply early. Men knew so little about these things.

Jean-Luc embraced her. "I'm so happy."

"Are you?"

He leaned back to gaze at her. "Of course." His expression turned serious. "This means you must leave your husband."

"I can't. Not just yet."

"But you—"

"—He's a very violent man. If I leave him now, he'll surely find out about you and he'll come after you."

A sudden, sharp horn blast made both of them jump.

"What's that?" cried Adrienne.

"One of the guys testing his fog horn," said Jean-Luc. "Listen, I'm not afraid of your husband."

"You should be."

"Why?"

"He's an excellent marksman and he would have no guilt about sneaking up on you."

"I've heard about him and his guns."

"I can't leave him, not just yet."

"But, when?"

"When are you leaving for France?"

Jean-Luc sighed. "That's hard to say. We can't leave without word getting back to France from the Vichy who run this place. All the men say that the boats would be impounded the minute we entered French waters."

Adrienne felt a knot of panic swell in her chest. She looked out to sea. The curtain of fog shrouded the horizon. "But that means you won't be able to leave until the war's over."

"Not necessarily. Haven't you heard the rumors?"

"What rumors?"

"Some of the men want to persuade General de Gaulle to liberate Saint Pierre and Miquelon. If that happens, then we'll be able to leave secretly. A Free French government wouldn't give us away."

"Do you think that will happen?"

Jean-Luc shrugged. "It's a crazy world right now. Nothing that happens would surprise me, but you have to understand this: If they go through with asking de Gaulle to take action, that would be considered treason by the Vichy. People could be shot."

"My god!"

"So, as I say, who knows if they'll go through with it, meaning who knows when I can leave?"

"I want to go with you when you leave."

He laughed. "Anything else is out of the question."

"But it can't be until after the baby is born. What if it came while we were at sea?"

Jean-Luc nodded gravely. "Then let's hope they find the courage to ask de Gaulle to liberate us … but not too soon."

"In the meantime, we must find ways to meet. It's too dangerous for you if I continue to come here."

"What can we do?" asked Jean-Luc.

"I don't know. I'll figure something out."

Bastille Day, 1941

JÉRÔME COULDN'T ESCAPE A FEELING of sadness because Adrienne made him drive up to the War Memorial. The sight of it was bound to stir up unhappy memories for the next week or so.

Indeed, it had disturbed him so much that he decided not to go to the Café Joinville after all; there would be too many veterans of the war there. Instead, he drove home.

When he arrived, he saw that Claude had finally stopped blowing seagulls out of the sky. The rocking chair was still there, along with dozens of spent cartridges and dead seagulls. The shotgun was propped against the chair, but there was no sign of Claude.

Once inside his house, he busied himself watering his many plants—anything to keep his mind occupied; anything to affirm the life of living things. That had always been their perverse purpose, after all. When he finished, he went out into the shed to inventory the cases of Miquelon whiskey, the cans of paint and grease, and the few tins of tobacco that were still left. With the fog filtering the sun, everything appeared washed in a gauzy gray light. He was expecting a smuggler from Newfoundland the next day and he wanted to be ready. Scribbling notes on a piece of paper with the stub of a pencil, he forced himself not to think of Adrienne. He worked deliberately, double-counting everything, but still it took him only a half hour. Soon he was back inside the house checking the plants again.

It was time for his customary nap, but he wasn't sure he should risk it. He could never predict when the memories would surface like some sea monster from the depths to savage his sleep. He made another round of his plants, wiping the leaves and adding a little more water against his better judgment. He had killed plants before by over-watering them, over-caring for them. Finally, he lay down on the bed and gingerly rested his head on the pillow. He stared at the ceiling for a while, half listening for Claude's shooting to start up again. The air still seemed to echo with the blasts. Gradually, his eyes closed.

A woman is standing naked before a fire. She's holding something at the end of a skewer over the flames. He asks what it is and she says it's a seagull. There has been a good crop of them this year, she says. He is confused. Suddenly the woman is in his bed and they are making love. Who is she? Her face is vague, foreign and familiar at the same time.

It is the face of Antoine. They are embracing each other in the trenches. The rain is pouring down; it has been for days. Shells burst on every side of them. Deafening blasts. Mud spraying through the air. A German soldier is charging at them with a shotgun. A shell detonates close by and the soldier disappears in a cloudburst of blood. Another shell, closer still, shudders the ground. He can feel it heave under him.

Jérôme's eyes snapped open. He saw blisters of paint on the ceiling. Vaguely, he remembered the dream, but its details had already faded. Then a real memory assaulted him.

The wall of the trench spasms and brings forth a corpse in a gush of mud. Jérôme clutches at Antoine. He screams.

Suddenly he heard a pounding. For a moment he was confused. Artillery shells? But he quickly recognized it as someone knocking frantically on his door. He heard Gabriel's voice. "Monsieur Sabot! Monsieur Sabot!"

Jérôme rushed to the door and opened it to see Gabriel with a terrified look in his eyes. His purple face was puffy and bruised. "What happened, Gabriel?"

"Monsieur Sabot, why were you screaming?"

"Your face, Gabriel, what happened?"

"I heard you scream."

Jérôme took hold of Gabriel's shoulders and shook him. "Never mind that. Just a nightmare. Now come in and tell me what happened." He guided Gabriel through the storm vestibule and to the sink. He primed the pump until cold water gushed out. He held a cloth under the water for a moment before ringing it out, leaning over Gabriel, and gingerly pressing the damp cloth against the largest of the bruises.

"He beat me," Gabriel muttered through clenched teeth.

"Your stepfather?"

Gabriel nodded.

"Does it hurt?"

"I'm not an idiot."

"No, you're not. Does it hurt?" Jérôme eased the pressure on the cloth.

"He's the idiot."

"Yes. Does it hurt, Gabriel?"

A dribble of water ran down Gabriel's face, wetting the collar of his shirt. "It hurts," he said.

Jérôme's shoulders sagged. Now he knew for certain that his zebra trick had gone too far and in that instant he resolved to take full responsibility for it. He decided he would go to Claude and Marcel and tell them that he was the one—the only one—to blame. Let whatever happens, happen.

As Marie-Lisette stacked books onto the shelves, pleasuring in their dusty scents, their heft, the comforting smell of binding glue, she asked, "How long do you think the war will last, Madame Leclair?"

Madame Leclair, handing books to her from a metal cart, replied, "Who knows? The last one lasted more than four years."

Marie-Lisette said, "When the war is over, I'd love to go to France to continue my studies." She arranged the books she'd just placed on the shelf so that each of them sat the exact same distance back from the edge of the shelf. A pleasant fusty smell wafted up from the shelves.

"That's a fine ambition. You should go to the Sorbonne."

"But I want to go to the University of Toulouse."

"Toulouse? But why?"

"It sounds so nice," replied Marie-Lisette. She thought of Jacques Bernis taking off in his France-America mail-plane from his home base of Toulouse. *On to Dakar ... Casablanca ... Buenos Aires ....*

"But the Sorbonne is where all the great ones are. Paul Valéry holds a chair there. You've said you wanted to become a writer. What better place is there?"

"The poet?"

"Of course."

"I don't know his work."

Madame Leclair gave her a feigned look of shock. "Don't know his work? My dear young woman, that must be corrected." She strode to another part of the room and returned moments later with a small volume. "Here, start with this. But mind you that your father doesn't see it."

Marie-Lisette took the book and fanned the pages with excitement. She could scarcely wait until she got home to begin reading it.

"But how will you afford to go to France?" Madame Leclair asked.

Marie-Lisette felt a sinking sensation. She had thought often about the problem and was certain her father wouldn't advance her one centime. "I'll continue to work at the Hotel Lalanne until I can save up enough. Perhaps I can book a cheap passage on *Le Celte*."

Madame Leclair gave a sardonic laugh. "If we ever see *Le Celte* again."

"She'll make it through some day," Marie-Lisette replied without conviction. "Then I'll learn if she even accepts passengers. I'll work as a deck hand if that's what I have to do."

Madame Leclair chuckled. "That'll be a fine sight, you working alongside those crude men. What makes you think they'd even take a woman aboard?"

Marie-Lisette shrugged. "If it weren't for the sea, I'd walk to France."

"Well, no matter," said Madame Leclair, "it all comes to nothing if *Le Celte* isn't able to visit us until the war's over."

"We'll see her soon," Marie-Lisette said with no more conviction than before.

"Well, I hope so." Madame Leclair leaned toward Marie-Lisette with a conspiratorial expression. "I've ordered some more of those delicious Collete novels. They're so … naughty!"

At that moment, Marcel Morel burst into the library. Raymond Pineau followed several steps behind.

"What are you doing here?" cried Marie-Lisette.

"How dare you Monsieur Morel?" Madame Leclair dropped the book she was holding onto the metal cart and stood to face Marcel.

"That's not the question," said Marcel to Marie-Lisette, ignoring Madame Leclair. "The question is why aren't you at home helping your mother with the chores?"

"I'm working."

"Working?"

"What's he doing here?" demanded Marie-Lisette, nodding toward Raymond Pineau.

Raymond blushed, shifted his feet.

"I've taken him on as my associate. Keep it in the family, you know."

"He's not family."

"He will be if I have anything to do with it. Now answer my question."

Madame Leclair stepped between them. "No, Monsieur Morel, I insist you answer *my* question. What gives you the right to burst in here like this with your imperious demands?" She leaned so far towards Marcel that her eyeglasses swung out from her chest and clicked against the metal cart.

"I don't care what kind of demands you call them. I insist that she leave this place."

"This place, as you call it, Monsieur, is a library. It is a place of reverence and you, Monsieur, are defiling it." Madame Leclair's face was splotched and the chords of her neck jutted. She was one of those women whose neck ages a decade before her face.

Several patrons of the library had gathered to witness the commotion. They looked at each other in apparent shock at the power of their gentle librarian's voice. "Oh shut up, you old bitch," said Marcel to gasps from the onlookers. "Marie-Lisette is coming home with me."

"She is doing no such thing. She will stay and finish the work that she has—work that she is doing to make up for your crime."

Marcel's expression faltered. His cheeks started to turn red. "And how will you keep her here?" he asked in a voice suddenly less demanding than a moment before.

"I'll report your crime to the authorities. You maliciously burned more than a dozen books that belonged to the library—two dozen, even."

"A dozen? Two dozen? You're crazy!"

"Do you deny it?"

"Of course, I deny it. I only burned two."

"Ah, so you admit it?" Madame Leclair turned to the five awe-struck spectators. "Did you hear him? He says he burned two library books. Will you be witnesses to his confession?"

Hesitantly, they nodded.

Marcel gave a weak laugh. "Who will believe you old biddies over me?"

"Anyone who has heard of the famous zebra."

"What does some damned zebra got to do with it?"

"Precisely this: they'll remember you for the fool you are and it won't be hard to persuade them that a man so foolish is likely to burn books as well."

Marcel glared at her. For a moment, Marie-Lisette thought he might attack Madame Leclair. But, instead, he said to Raymond Pineau, "Come on, let's get out of here." He whirled, and started out of the library.

Madame Leclair called after him, "And if I hear one word, just one, that you have treated Marie-Lisette badly because of this, it's straight to the authorities I'll go and have you arrested."

Jérôme saw from the moment Marcel Morel entered the Café Joinville with young Raymond Pineau, that the man was in an ugly mood. Jérôme had planned to make his confession about the zebra affair to Marcel and Claude that evening, but now, after seeing Marcel, he was having second thoughts. Besides, Claude Cormier had not been seen at the café for several days. There was no assurance he would show up that evening and it was Claude who was, by far, the more dangerous of the two. Perhaps if, instead of confessing, he tried to soothe Marcel's injured pride, then he would only have Claude to worry about. He ordered three pernods and carried them over to Marcel's table. "Marcel, Raymond, I've bought you each a drink."

Raymond smiled and said, "Thank you Monsieur Sabot. That's kind of you."

Marcel made only a growling sound. He brushed back his thinning hair, then fiddled with his beret which sat on the table in front of him.

Jérôme started by making idle chatter about how the cod fishing was going that season. He asked them what they thought of that year's capelin run, the tiny fish that usually arrive at the archipelago towards the end of June in the millions, turning the roiling waters green with their swarming frenzy. Then he asked the question that was on everyone's mind: when they thought *Le Celte* might appear.

He had to speak loudly because several dozen men were sitting around tables, smoking, and asking each other the same question. Through it all, young Raymond answered his questions while Marcel sat sullenly staring at his glass of pernod and twisting his beret. Jérôme ordered another round of drinks, then said, "You know, my dear friend, Marcel, you shouldn't feel badly about the zebra trick. Why, even I was fooled."

"Me too," said Raymond.

Jérôme smiled, nodded at the boy.

When Marcel didn't answer, Jérôme continued. "It took the trained, scientific eye of Doctor Tréguy to detect the deception."

"It was a good trick," said Raymond.

Jérôme nodded. "Very clever. Nobody could tell except for Doctor Tréguy."

At last, Marcel responded. "That's what I told Sylvie," he murmured.

"Yes. That's what I've been telling everyone."

They drank their pernods in silence for a while. The smoke became heavy in the room, curling about the light fixtures hanging from the ceiling, scudding along the walls. Jérôme saw that the alcohol was lightening Marcel's spirit; at last he might be getting somewhere with the stubborn man. Finally, Jérôme—himself feeling the effect of four pernods—said, "You must admit, though, the man who did it must be a great artist."

Marcel gave a harumph.

"No, really. It was quite a piece of work."

"I was fooled," said Raymond.

Marcel glowered at the boy.

Jérôme saw Doctor Tréguy walk into the café. He waved him over to the table. "I was just telling Marcel here that he shouldn't feel so bad about being fooled by the zebra trick."

Doctor Tréguy smiled. "It was clever all right."

"Were you fooled at first?" Marcel asked him.

"Why, of course." Doctor Tréguy looked as though he were trying not to laugh. "Who wouldn't have been? It was such a masterpiece." He winked at Jérôme.

After yet one more pernod which, of course, Jérôme bought, Marcel left in a far better mood than when he had arrived. Jérôme breathed a deep sigh of relief. He was confident he now had only Claude Cormier to deal with. But that thought left him with no great sense of security. An image of Claude in his rocking chair blasting seagulls out of the sky came to him and he shuddered. If Adrienne was right—that the man's anger would simmer and swell until it exploded in a new outburst of violence—Jérôme could only imagine the consequences.

One thing was sure: Claude would not be as easy to mollify as Marcel.

Bastille Day on Saint Pierre in that year of 1941 was not a happy time. Little more than a year before, Paris had fallen to the Nazis and Marshal Pétain had concluded what most thought was a dishonorable armistice with Germany. Now, he headed a collaborationist government in Vichy and all of France suffered under a dark cloud. There seemed little hope for her because the allies had yet to achieve a significant victory and America was refusing to enter the war. That summer, liberation seemed impossibly far away.

And still there was no sign of *Le Celte*.

The administrator of Saint Pierre and Miquelon, Count de Bournat, trapped between the overwhelming desire of the Saint Pierrais to support de Gaulle's Free French and the practical need to remain attached to the home government of Pétain, if only to continue the subsidy payments that were essential to the survival of the archipelago, chose the later. Thus, to the horror of the majority of Saint Pierrais, their islands were officially Vichy. As such, they saw themselves just as much occupied by the Nazis as their homeland. And they felt themselves just as much in need of liberation.

Under such conditions, no one felt that the normal celebrations of Bastille Day were appropriate, so the streets did not ring with cries of joy and singing and dancing as in the years before the war. The annual parade, for which Saint Pierre was famous, was cancelled and the day was declared a day of mourning.

Jérôme stood with Marie-Lisette in the square, watching people grimly mount the stairs and enter the church through the large wooden doors. They were going to hear Monsignor Bernard officiate at a solemn Mass for France and to hear his sermon.

Their unhappiness showed in their fallen faces.

A steady, light rain dimpled the pavement. The rainwater gurgled in the gutters. Jérôme waited for Adrienne to appear and enter the church and when, at last, he saw her, he, too entered. That way he could pretend they had come together to church.

As usual, the men mounted the stairways to the galleries while the women sat downstairs. Jérôme bounded up the stairs to find a place where he could have a good view of Adrienne. The air in the gallery was heavy with moist heat, almost suffocating. He took a seat next to one of the foreign fisherman who smiled a greeting and introduced himself as Jean-Luc Lavedan from Bordeaux. Jérôme nodded and whispered that at least Bordeaux was not yet occupied by the Nazis.

"But the Vichy are almost as bad," the man replied.

Gabriel entered and took a place on the other side of Jérôme with a broad smile. His bruises were almost healed. Jérôme patted his hand and told him he was looking much better.

Across the way, Jérôme saw Claude Cormier and Marcel Morel sitting together. Claude had a glassy look of anger in his eyes that made Jérôme shudder. Ever since the zebra incident, it had been the man's perpetual expression. Not far from Claude and Marcel, Doctor Tréguy and Pierre Pichot sat together quietly chatting in whispered voices. When they saw Jérôme, they both grinned broadly and nodded toward him. Not far from them, Auguste Lafitte sat stiffly in his Franco-Prussian-War uniform. Jérôme wasn't surprised to see that no one, as yet, was sitting beside the man on either side, for he knew from personal experience that the uniform, worn daily, was beginning to reek powerfully.

Downstairs, Marie-Lisette strode down the center aisle with her mother. When she saw Madame Leclair sitting in a pew on the left, she guided her mother to that pew and sat next to the librarian. As she sat down, she nudged Madame Leclair and showed her the little volume of Paul Valéry poems that she had secreted in her purse.

Her boldness in bringing a book of poetry into church thrilled her. It would have appalled the sisters of St. Joseph of Cluny who were gathered together at the front near the altar. She thought she might even sneak a peak at the book if the sermon became too boring. She had been reading the poetry nightly since the day Madame Leclair had given it to her and Valéry's words, his use of the language, excited her. Just that morning, with the blankets tucked over her, she had read his most famous poem *The Graveyard by the Sea*, a title she thought might well apply to Saint Pierre and Miquelon, garroted by an almost unbelievable six hundred shipwrecks. Words from the last stanza still resonated in her head: *"The wind is rising! … We must try to live!"*

Adrienne, sitting next to her mother-in-law several rows in front of Marie-Lisette, snatched a quick peak toward the gallery on her right. Jean-Luc was precisely where he had said he would be. He gave her a furtive smile. She didn't dare return the smile, for she saw that Jérôme Sabot was sitting next to him, something that vaguely disturbed her. She glanced to the other gallery, her husband's usual choice, to confirm his location. He was sitting near Marcel Morel and a fat man whom she recognized, but whose name she had forgotten. She wondered if Claude would be able to see her if she risked a glance now and then at Jean-Luc. She decided it would not be too risky, so she passed a hand slowly across her fecund belly and chanced another glance at Jean-Luc, wondering if he had seen her gesture. He smiled at her.

She quickly averted her gaze when she saw that Monsieur Sabot was smiling too.

Jérôme experienced a thrill when he saw Adrienne looking at him. He smiled at her, then looked out over the assembled people. Everyone was praying. Adrienne was praying. Marie-Lisette was praying. Doctor Tréguy, too. And Pierre Pichot. And so too, Gabriel.

They all prayed. They all prayed for a little gray freighter … and their homeland. Even Claude Cormier, leaning forward, the hams of his hairy forearms pressed into the gallery railing—even he seemed to be praying. It made quite a sight. Of course, Auguste Lafitte was also praying, perhaps demanding of God that He butcher all Nazis and restore the honor of France, if that could be called praying.

Then Jérôme thought of Antoine and he, too, prayed.

There was a stirring at the back of the church. The first phrases of the *Introit* filled the space, echoing from the walls and the ceiling. With the opening notes came a rolling rumble as everybody rose from their seats. People turned and craned their necks to see the grave procession move slowly toward the altar. Monsignor Bernard was engowned in the elaborate liturgical vestments reserved for such occasions—a white alb, cincture, a white chasuble, a maniple folded over his left arm, and a stole draped across his shoulders. He walked with solemn dignity, flanked by two altar boys carrying candles. As they walked, they shielded the guttering flames with cupped hands.

Shortly after the procession reached the front of the church, the Mass began and, later, after the reading of the Holy Gospel, Monsignor Bernard ascended the pulpit to begin his sermon. He spoke at length of the suffering of their beloved France and of the need for all citizens of Saint Pierre to fall down on their knees and pray for the life of the motherland. He spoke also of their lifeline to France, *Le Celte*, and offered prayers for her safe passage through the turbulent waters of war. His words brought tears to many.

Marie-Lisette was startled to feel Madame Leclair's hand slide over her own and grip it with fervor. She turned to see the librarian's watery eyes and the sight caused her own eyes to well with tears. She knew that Madame Leclair depended on the books from France just as much as she did, if not more. Each book brought a message that they were not completely isolated, that there was a rich world beyond the ragged reefs and shipwrecks of their tiny archipelago. And the books gave people like Marie-Lisette the hope that someday they might see that magnificent other world. It was a hope that, for the moment, lay dormant in their hearts, a victim of the war, and Marie-Lisette wondered if it could ever be revived again.

A few rows in front of Marie-Lisette, Adrienne held her hands over her belly and wondered if she and the child would ever see France. Would she ever be able to escape the misery of her life on Saint Pierre? Or would she be condemned to live in a perpetual state of fear, caught halfway between the husband she detested and the husband she dreamed of having one day? The hopelessness of her situation—brought home to her by Monsignor Bernard's remarks about France and by the continued absence of *Le Celte*— delivered fresh tears to her eyes.

Jérôme wept, too. But it was neither the words of the Monsignor, nor the missing *Le Celte*—which he alone among all the Saint Pierrais wished not to see—that elicited his tears. They had started long before, during the singing of the Kyrie. And when the tears had come, he had lowered his head and whispered, simply, "I'm sorry, Antoine. I'm truly sorry."

Far from the mourning church-goers, across the vast, secluding sea, the war wore on in its inexorable way. On this Bastille Day, a force of German Junkers bombed Suez causing considerable damage to harbor facilities and to unloading ships. The German army continued its advance on Leningrad, reaching the Luga River in the north.

And, as on every day, people died in droves in the concentration camps scattered across the continent, smoke from crematoria rising and mingling among the violated heavens.

In Paris, a small group of resistance fighters faced a firing squad near the German headquarters at the Hotel Meurice. Their deaths were meant as examples to anyone who dared resist the occupation by the *Wermacht*.

Meanwhile, deep in the heavens, Cassiopeia, low on the horizon, began its climb in the northern sky. It was followed by Perseus whose principal stars, Algenib and Algol, the Demon Star, were not yet visible. Slowly, month by month, the two constellations would rise in the sky and would be well overhead when the winter ice closed in once again around Saint Pierre and Miquelon. The earth had already started to tilt its axis away from the sun like a virgin shying from a kiss.

Part 2

September, 1941

A Visitor from the Sky

7

THE ALMOST CONSTANT FOG that from June to August enshrouded the archipelago stretched into September that year. It smothered the islands in its massive, moist flesh, leaving dew on every exposed surface, suffocating the people in their small isolation even as the necklace of six hundred shipwrecks strangled them.

In the waterways around Baffin Island, the ambient temperature had fallen. The color and texture of the sea's surface had changed as gray needles and plates crystallized to form a surface-thin sludge. The thin sheets of ice jostled each other and, in a matter of hours, formed a field of pancake ice.

More ice coalesced.

Snows came.

Wind created stresses and strains that produced hummocks and brine pockets and ridges on the growing ice pack. And then the ice pack started to slide south and east along the coasts of Baffin Island and Newfoundland. Soon it would curl around Cape Race and the Burin Peninsula, grinding and groaning, and it would form a ring around Saint Pierre and Miquelon and once more the isolation of the archipelago would be asserted. They would be sealed off from any chance of escape from loneliness before the spring thaw. Soon, the dories and wherries would be hauled onto the pebbled beaches and all thoughts of fishing would be forgotten until the following May. It might be, even, that the ocean would freeze over—it had as recently as 1929 when people could walk across from Saint Pierre to Île aux Marins.

And the incessant snows would arrive, and the *poudrin*—the terrible "dust storm" of sharp snow crystals—would appear driven by unrelenting winds into every tiny opening of house or clothes or skin. The wind, sharp with salt and ice, would scour the houses, peeling them of so much paint that they would have to be re-painted each spring.

And with the cold would come the danger of fires. Two years previous, three blocks of Saint Pierre, including the only movie theater, had been destroyed. So great was the danger, the government had required that all houses have ladders running up the side and onto the roof to aid the fire fighters.

As the curtain of isolation descended on the tiny archipelago, all hopes of seeing *Le Celte* that year faded. Because of the war, no other ships would call on Saint Pierre. Only the Vichy-controlled telegraph station, the smugglers' dories from Newfoundland, and the occasional airplane, would provide any contact with the outside world.

Perhaps because her mind was tuned to it, Marie-Lisette heard the drone of airplane motors before anyone else. She dropped her book on the bed and hurried outside to look into the sky. All she saw was an undifferentiated gray veil of fog. She listened closely. At first she thought it might have been only her imagination because she heard nothing except the lowing of one of Claude Cormier's cows. But then it came again, a low vibrating hum that gradually grew into a pulsing roar, a much louder version of the sound of her pumping blood that she sometimes heard against the pillow. The sound passed overhead, then turned toward the southeast. It started to fade again, but within moments it began to grow louder, this time from the southwest.

Circling.

All at once, Marie-Lisette realized it was lost, searching for the tiny airstrip in the dense floor of fog. Instantly, she knew what must be done. A phrase from *Southern Mail* came to her. "Casablanca now tested its ground landing lights. The red markers cut out a piece of night, a black rectangle." She saw Jacques Bernis in trouble. She ran back into the house. Only Gabriel was at home. "Gabriel," she cried, "there's a plane lost in the fog. We must light up the landing strip." She threw a coat over her shoulders and said, "Come on."

"Where?"

"To get Monsieur Sabot. We must get into town quickly and organize as many cars and trucks as we can." Before she finished, she was out the door and running as fast as she could toward Jérôme's house. Gabriel, throwing on a coat, followed her.

As she ran, Marie-Lisette kept glancing up at the sky. Nothing but fog. The air was cool and moist. It pressed on her. When they arrived at Jérôme's house, she pounded on the door. "Monsieur Sabot. Hurry!"

Within moments, Jérôme opened the door, a confused look on his face. "What is it, Marie-Lisette?"

Marie-Lisette explained about the airplane and her plan to organize people to take their cars and trucks out to the airstrip.

When she finished, Jérôme said, "The Café Joinville. Many of the men will be there."

As they ran to Jérôme's truck, they heard the plane make another pass. They stopped to listen, scanning the sky. The steady drone of the motors had now become a ragged pulsation.

"Oh God!" said Marie-Lisette, "They're having trouble with one of the motors."

"You can tell that just from the sound?"

"Yes, I think so." Or was she imagining it? She wondered.

The three of them squeezed into the truck and were soon barreling down the road toward Saint Pierre. Periodically, Marie-Lisette peered through the wet windshield up into the sky, yet could see nothing but a dark mass of fog. Despite the chilly air, she rolled down the window to see if she could still hear the plane but the clatter of the tires on the gravel road was too loud. She peered out the windshield again. Where was Saint Pierre? The whole town was swathed in fog. She had the sensation they could drive straight into the ocean without knowing it. But at last, images of the outlying buildings appeared wraithlike out of the mist, insubstantial.

When they finally pulled up in front of the Café Joinville, a number of people were standing in the street gazing up at the sky in various directions. Before the truck even came to a complete stop, Marie-Lisette leaped out. She listened for a moment, but couldn't hear the plane. That explained why people were looking in different directions; they had heard it once but no longer could; they had no idea where it was.

She shouted. "It's a lost plane. We must light up the airstrip."

Many of the men gazed dumbly at her.

"But the airstrip has no lights," someone said.

"We'll bring it lights. We'll line up cars and trucks on both sides and turn the headlights on."

Most of the people stared at her with bewildered expressions. Suddenly, Marie-Lisette heard the faint thrum of the twin engines. The plane was approaching again. "Listen!" she cried.

The people craned their necks to gaze up at the sky. Men started to shuffle out of the Café Joinville holding drinks, looking heavenward. The sound of the plane's motors became louder. Soon it was passing overhead. Marie-Lisette heard what she thought was a faint sputter from one of the motors. "They're running out of fuel. We must hurry."

When there was still no response from the men, Jérôme stepped forward. "What's the matter with all of you? You heard her. Get your asses to your cars and trucks and get out to the airstrip. Now!"

At last, two dozen men started to run for their cars and trucks. Jérôme called, "We'll meet you out there."

There was a roar of engines as more than a dozen cars and trucks came to life. Soon a conga line of vehicles was rolling along the Rue du 11 Novembre. Skirting the harbor, they turned onto the Route de la Pointe Blanche, heading for the airstrip. Marie-Lisette despaired of getting there in time. Repeatedly, she leaned out the open window of Jérôme's truck to scan the impenetrable sky. She was rewarded only with a cold, moist wind through her hair. The last time she had heard the plane, it sounded as though it were running on fumes. Perhaps it had already crashed somewhere on *The Mountain* or else in the sea to join the ring of shipwrecks strangling the archipelago. She glanced toward *The Mountain*. Surely, if it had crashed there, she would be able to see the bloom of fire even through the fog, but she saw nothing. Of course, their archipelago was like a tiny ship in the isolated vastness of the sea; there was a far greater chance the plane had crashed into the cold waters and they might never find it, never know who it was or why they were so desperately trying to land on Saint Pierre. The thought of it remaining a mystery forever appalled her. She would never know who the pilot was and whether or not he bore any resemblance to Jacques Bernis.

After what seemed an eternity, they finally pulled up to the airstrip. The cars and trucks that had preceded them were parked helter-skelter, with no organization to suggest their reason for being there. Marie-Lisette leaped from the truck and turned her ear to the sky. Nothing. But she refused to abandon hope. *Casablanca now tested its ground landing lights ....*

"We must get them to line up on both sides of the strip with their headlights on," she said to Jérôme.

All the men were standing outside their cars and trucks, milling about aimlessly, smoking.

"You take this side," she said to Jérôme. "I'll take the other." She ran across the airstrip and began to shout at the men, telling them to form a line with their cars and trucks and turn their headlights on.

No one moved. They seemed unwilling to follow the instructions of a young woman. Jérôme came running up behind her and yelled, "Get a move on! They might be running out of fuel."

Someone said, "But what if they're German?"

"Then we'll get Claude Cormier to shoot them when they come out of the goddamned plane!" He had seen Claude among the men and knew that he always carried his loaded shotgun in the truck.

Several men laughed. Claude glared at Jérôme for a moment, then turned to climb into his truck. All at once, the other men leaped into action. Again, there was a roar of engines starting up. Soon, they had formed a ragged line of cars and trucks on both sides of the airstrip. But some were pointing one way and some the other.

"They all have to be pointed away from the wind," said Marie-Lisette. "The pilot will want to land upwind." She and Jérôme ran along the two lines urging the wrongly-headed cars and trucks to turn around.

At last, the airstrip was bordered by two more or less straight lines of vehicles with their headlights pointing into the gloom. Marie-Lisette stood in the middle of the airstrip, listening. She still heard no sound. "Please let us not be too late," she murmured. "Please."

"It'll be alright, Marie-Lisette," said Gabriel who appeared at her side.

"I hope so."

"But I guess we better pray anyway, huh?"

Claudette said to Adrienne, "Where's your husband? He's almost never this late."

Adrienne placed checkered cloths over three bowls of stew to keep them warm and said, "Probably still drinking at the Café Joinville." She hoped, with a vague guilt, that he had been in some kind of accident—maybe shot himself accidentally. At least that would solve one of her problems.

The sound of airplane motors they had heard earlier returned, passing directly overhead. "What fools are trying to fly in this weather?" asked Claudette.

"It sounds like they could be in trouble," said Adrienne.

"Well, it would serve them right." Claudette glanced at the kitchen clock. "Ever since that stupid zebra affair, your husband's never spent much time at the café. He's afraid people are still laughing at him."

Adrienne said nothing. She busied herself laying out utensils and glasses. When she turned, she saw that Claudette was staring at her. "What is it?" she asked.

"Are you putting on weight?"

Adrienne felt a breathless sensation at the top of her throat as though her heart were lodged in her vocal cords. "No I … Well, yes, I guess a little. I should eat less."

Claudette tilted her head and gave her a narrow-eyed look of suspicion. Adrienne felt as though the woman was looking directly at her belly, trying to see through the dress … and the skin.

"It seems you're putting on weight."

"I guess. A little."

"Your face is fuller."

"Is it? I hadn't noticed."

"Now that I remember, weren't you retching a lot back a month or two ago?"

"I was sick. It's the weather."

After a long pause, Claudette asked, "Are you pregnant?"

"No, of course not."

Claudette said nothing. She continued to stare at Adrienne.

"Well, I would certainly know if I was pregnant," said Adrienne, feigning indignation.

Claudette said, "Yes, of course you would," but the note of suspicion was still there.

Adrienne busied herself cleaning the pot in which she had heated the left-over stew. She didn't dare look at her mother-in-law.

The sound of airplane engines came again and they both glanced instinctively at the ceiling.

The men climbed out of their cars and trucks to gaze up at the sky. And to listen. Minutes passed with no sound except the low rumble of their idling engines. Curls of mist floated in and out of sight at the outer limit of the bloom of headlights. Somewhere in the distance a dog barked and was answered by several others. The men stood about in small groups talking in low tones, then pausing to stare into the scrim of fog and to listen for any hint of an airplane's motors.

Jérôme came up to Marie-Lisette and Gabriel. "What do you think?"

"I don't know."

"Are we too late?"

Marie-Lisette didn't answer. She bit her lip. The headlights reflected in her eyeglasses.

"I've been praying," said Gabriel.

After several more minutes passed, Marie-Lisette said, "Let's tell them to turn their engines off so we can hear better."

Jérôme nodded. He and Marie-Lisette moved among the clusters of men to relay the message. Soon, the airstrip lay in near complete silence; the men even lowered their voices to whispers. The quiet was so complete that Marie-Lisette could hear the scritch of matches as the men lit cigarettes and she could hear the scrape of Auguste Lafitte's cane along the ground. He was pacing back and forth like an important man awaiting the arrival of an official delegation.

Marie-Lisette closed her eyes to concentrate all her alertness to her ears.

Far in the distance, under the soughing of the wind, she heard the faint sound of a motor dory crossing the harbor. She tilted her head.

"Do you hear something?" asked Jérôme.

At first, Marie-Lisette didn't answer. Then she said, "No … No, only a motor dory, I think."

"But everyone's in. No one's on the water right now," said Jérôme.

Marie-Lisette's eyes grew wide with hope. "Quiet everyone," she called.

Every conversation stopped abruptly. The men stood motionless, elbows bent in the arrested act of lifting cigarettes to lips.

She heard the sound again. It was growing louder. "You're right," she said to Jérôme. "That's no dory!" She heard the distinct sound of two motors, one thrumming in an even rhythm, the other sputtering raggedly. It was downwind of the airstrip, just where it ought to be. "It's them!"

Everyone peered into the gloom of fog. Marie-Lisette kept hoping to see the plane pop out of the mist, wheels down, low over the approach to the airstrip. But the sound of the plane grew louder and louder until it was directly overhead. Marie-Lisette tilted her head back and followed the sound but could see no sign of the plane. "They missed," she cried. "They can't see us."

The sound changed frequency and Marie-Lisette knew the plane was turning. She listened with growing hope as it made a wide turn until it was again downwind of them, the sound of its motors growing faint.

Marie-Lisette whispered, "Please, please." She traced the sign of the cross on her forehead. "Please, God."

"Please, God," repeated Gabriel.

"Let them see us, Dear God!" said Marie-Lisette.

Gabriel said, "Let them see us, Dear God!"

The sound started to grow louder. But this time, Marie-Lisette heard only one motor. "They only have one motor now," she said to Jérôme. "This is their last chance. Oh, God! Oh, God!"

"Oh God! Oh God!" said Gabriel.

Marie-Lisette opened her coat, un-tucked her shirt, removed her eyeglasses, wiped the lenses on the tail of her shirt, and placed them back on her nose. She peered into the fog with such concentration that she began to imagine phantom shapes coming in and out of view like the floating phantasms she sometimes saw on the insides of her eyelids. She was trying to make the plane appear through the power of her will. She blinked her eyes rapidly a few times and squinted. "I think I see them," she said in a tentative voice that conveyed little confidence.

"I see nothing," said Jérôme.

"I see nothing," said Gabriel. "Oh, God! Oh God!"

Marie-Lisette didn't answer. She shook her head as though to clear her vision and returned her gaze to the weak bloom of light that marked the limit of the headlights' reach. She adjusted her eyeglasses. To the extreme left of the wedge of light, the fog seemed slightly darker and she concentrated her gaze on that spot. Suddenly, a shape began to emerge, a wraithlike disturbance in the uniform gray veil. It grew. And it grew. Then, as if assembling itself into solidity out of insubstantial vapor, the plane appeared.

"There!" cried Marie-Lisette, pointing. She paused for a moment, then added, "Oh, no, they're not lined up properly!"

"Shit!"

"Oh, God! Oh, God!" cried Gabriel.

But just as suddenly, the left wing dipped and the plane banked to its left then straightened out again, heading for the center of the airstrip. Everyone watched breathlessly as the plane descended. Marie-Lisette could now clearly make out the wheels. The plane's wings wobbled once, first one, then the other dipping. Then it was level again, low to the ground. The sound of its one motor intensified until it was a roar. The blunt snub nose grew. The whirling propellers, grew, heading straight at them. Everyone scampered to the sides of the airstrip.

There was a loud squeal as the tires hit the ground. The plane bounced back into the air, then hit the airstrip again with a screech of rubber. The plane bounced along the airstrip, its one motor suddenly much quieter. It slowed. Finally, it rolled to a stop.

"That's a Lockheed Electra!" Marie-Lisette cried. "It's the plane Amelia Earhart used."

All at once, car and truck horns started to blare. It was a raucous, celebratory sound.

Marie-Lisette ran up to the plane. *As Bernis climbs out of the cockpit, his legs feel heavy ....* She peered up at the window by the pilot's seat, but couldn't make out the man's face. He slid the window open and leaned out. He was an old, bearded man wearing a World War I leather aviator's cap. A pair of old-fashioned goggles rested on his forehead. "Thanks," he said. "That was good thinking, whoever thought of it."

Marie-Lisette beamed—even if he wasn't at all like her vision of the young, handsome Jacques Bernis.

Then a figure emerged from around the other side of the plane and Jérôme let out a gasp. "*Mon Dieu*, it's Chrétien Bastarache!"

The man passed in front of the now-still propellers and smiled. "Jérôme! So this is Saint Pierre, after all. We were beginning to think we would land at the North Pole. Well, that's the Bastarache luck for you!" The man stomped the ground twice with his feet as if to express his joy at being on solid earth and held his arms out wide. "We were beginning to think we made a mistake not stopping in Halifax to refuel. I hope you folks have some fuel here, or you've just received new immigrants."

Jérôme ran up to embrace him. "We'll find fuel. How good to see you!"

Marie-Lisette gazed at the man. He was certainly no Jacques Bernis, but with his lean face, his bright eyes, and his extravagant manners, he seemed the kind of man she imagined Antoine de Saint-Exupéry might be.

Jérôme released his grip on the man, turned to Marie-Lisette, and said, "This is my old friend Chrétien Bastarache from Maine in the United States." He turned back to Chrétien. "This, my dear Chrétien, is your savior, Marie-Lisette Morel. She's the one who organized all of us to get out here with our cars and trucks."

Chrétien took Marie-Lisette's hand, bowed, and kissed it. "You will be forever in my debt, Mademoiselle Morel."

Marie-Lisette blushed. She attempted a curtsy, her eyes flashing with joy.

Chrétien gestured toward the pilot. "This here is Dave Lowe. He's the man who owns this plane and he charters it out to folks like me. I thought he was gonna have a heart attack when we couldn't find the runway."

Dave Lowe said, with a smile, "He ain't kiddin'. I have a weak heart, otherwise I'd be flyin' for the Army Air Corps."

Jérôme greeted the pilot then turned to Chrétien and asked, "What are you doing here, Chrétien? You're the last man I expected to see."

Chrétien held his arms out as if to say it was a ridiculous question. "You're suffering because of the war," he said. "I came to help."

When Claude finally returned to the house, more than two hours late, he could talk of nothing but the airplane that had appeared from out of nowhere on Saint Pierre. Adrienne was relieved because it meant that Claudette, once she finished berating Claude for keeping supper waiting, seemed to have forgotten Adrienne's apparent weight gain. All the same, Adrienne knew the persistence of the woman. She knew her mother-in-law would probe and prod, if not that night, then the next day, or the day after that. She would press on until she finally convinced Claude of her own suspicion that Adrienne was pregnant.

Adrienne wondered how she could prepare herself for the fallout that was sure to occur.

Exploding Whiskey

CHRÉTIEN BASTARACHE EMBRACED JÉRÔME AGAIN. "We're great friends, you and me, Jérôme, and you helped me back in the whiskey time. Now I've come to return the favor. I've come to see what you need, now that France is at war."

They were sitting, with Marie-Lisette and Gabriel, at the table in Jérôme's kitchen. Before each of them, a glass of Miquelon sat on the red checker cloth. At the center of the table sat a kerosene lantern, its flame guttering. It was two days after Chrétien had arrived and he had already talked with a number of people about what they needed.

Marie-Lisette lifted the whiskey to her lips and sipped cautiously. The liquid burned her throat, but she suppressed the cough that tried to escape.

Gabriel drank happily.

"I don't know what to say, Chrétien," said Jérôme.

"You must need something. With the war and everything, things must be hard to get."

"We need lots of things," said Marie-Lisette. "*Le Celte* never appeared and the things that she always brought us are either all used up or soon will be. Books …." Reflections from the lantern danced in her eyeglasses.

"*Le Celte*?"

"A little freighter that used to bring us things."

"Good things," said Gabriel.

"Books?"

"Yes … and many other things."

"Such as? What else do you need?" asked Chrétien. "Besides a fire, I mean. Do you always keep this place so cold?" he asked Jérôme.

"I don't often light a fire when I don't have to."

Chrétien gazed at him a moment then nodded as though he understood something about Jérôme that no one else did. "Well, do you mind if I light one? It was damned cold in that airplane."

Jérôme's expression faltered, but he said, "No, no. Go ahead."

Chrétien moved to the stove and started to pour coal into the burning chamber. Marie-Lisette said, "You said something about the whiskey time. Were you and Monsieur Sabot smugglers together?"

Chrétien laughed. "Smugglers? We don't like to use that word. We were ... businessmen. Jérôme delivered whiskey to me for a good price and I sold it in America at a better price. In America five or so years ago we had something called Prohibition."

"Yes, I know. I know all about the whiskey smuggling in Saint Pierre."

"You do?"

"Of course. Everyone did. It was our main business."

"Until our own damned government in France shut us down," Jérôme said. He made a sour expression and took a sip of whiskey.

"Oh, don't blame the French," said Chrétien as he adjusted the vents on the stove and the chimney. "It was the Americans and the Canadians who pressured them." He crumpled some newspaper, stuffed it among the coals, and lit it. Flames leaped in the burning chamber.

Jérôme averted his eyes from the fire and glanced at Antoine's trench coat.

Chrétien returned to the table, took a long sip of whiskey, and turned to Marie-Lisette. "Me and Jérôme had an arrangement. He and his men would sail their little schooner down to Maine and I would meet them out past the international limit. Then I would take the whiskey into this little town called Brooklin and from there I would sell it. We made a handsome profit, both of us."

"So you never actually went into America?" Marie-Lisette asked Jérôme.

"No," he replied. "It was safer that way."

"Well, that ain't exactly true," said Chrétien with a big laugh. "There was the one time you came to meet my relatives while your boys went on to Portland. Don't you remember the brush pile?"

Jérôme gave a weak grin. He nodded then looked away, glancing at Antoine's trench coat again.

"Tell us about it," said Marie-Lisette.

"Yes we want to hear," added Gabriel.

Chrétien was still laughing. "This one time, Jérôme decided to accept my invitation to come ashore and sample my sister's cooking. I knew she was making chiard—it's sort of a potato casserole with pork—and Jérôme always wanted to try it. Except, you see, we had a little problem and he ended up at the doctor's office with the rest of us."

"Oh, tell us," Marie-Lisette said with a delighted laugh.

Chrétien settled back into his chair and began to narrate the story to Marie-Lisette and Gabriel.

While he talked, vivid images of the scene ... and of the war ... passed through Jérôme's mind.

Chrétien, along with his brother-in-law, Pip Dupuy, had taken his lobster boat out to a red nun buoy near West Halibut Rock off the coast of Maine where Jérôme had arranged to meet up with them. It was during the height of the prosperous time known on Saint Pierre and Miquelon simply as "the whiskey" when many men had given up fishing for the more lucrative trade of helping to keep America lubricated.

When the schooner and the lobster boat finally found each other in the darkness and the fortuitous, covering fog, Jérôme had invited Chrétien and his brother-in-law to climb aboard the schooner and have a drink. One drink led to another and soon they had passed a couple of hours in happy conversation, Chrétien and Pip enjoying an opportunity to speak French for a change. As a result, by the time Jérôme, Chrétien, and Pip had stored the cases of whiskey under the false floor of the lobster boat, spread bait over it, and started to whisper their way homeward on an underwater exhaust, the fog had lifted and the first flush of dawn was appearing over Mount Desert Island.

Chrétien continued the story. "The American revenue men were all over the place in those days because Brooklin was a center of rum running, but they never suspected me because of the special work a friend had done with the boat's exhaust system." He told them how a local boat builder had rigged a mechanism that would allow Chrétien to change over from the extremely noisy external exhaust to an almost silent underwater exhaust whenever the need arose. Every time he left the anchorage, Chrétien would steer close by the revenue men waving cheerily and shouting something that, of course, they couldn't hear because of the racket of his normal exhaust. Then he would turn toward the sea and whatever rendezvous he had arranged. "The revenue guys, they would shake their heads then turn to watch other boats, figuring that nobody who was rum running would be idiot enough to have such a noisy boat," said Chrétien.

"I'm not an idiot," said Gabriel.

"Huh? No, I guess you're not."

"Hush, Gabriel," said Marie-Lisette. "Let him tell the story."

"Well, now, when the dawn came, I said to the others, 'We can't unload in daylight. We'll have to hide the whiskey somewhere.' " He told them how he had pulled out a crumbling chart and began perusing it. Jérôme had folded his arms across his chest to fend off the hour-before-dawn chill, and had asked, "Where are you going to hide so many cases of whiskey?"

"I don't know. You take the wheel and I'll look at the chart," Chrétien had replied.

After a few moments Chrétien chuckled and said, "I got it."

"I don't like it when you laugh like that," said Pip, a note of suspicion in his voice. Pip's face looked as though it had been etched by a lifetime of wind, like the rocks along the shores of Acadia, all crags and crevices.

"The Ashford fellow from Boston ain't at his summer place in Herrick Bay and he's got a small dock. We'll unload there."

"Makes sense," said Pip.

"Then we'll hide the whiskey in the big brush pile I saw in front of his house yesterday. It's right by the road, but you can't see any of his neighbors from there. Tonight, we'll take your truck, Pip, and get the whiskey."

Jérôme rolled his eyes but said nothing. It sounded to him like another one of Chrétien's famous stratagems that often backfired. Everyone who dealt with him knew about those crazy schemes. He turned the wheel back over to Chrétien. Pip pulled a crumbled pack of Chesterfields from the pocket of his slicker, tapped out a cigarette, and offered it to Jérôme. Pip cupped his hands to light it with his Zippo lighter then lit another for himself.

To Jérôme's surprise, the operation went without a hitch. He was certain no one had seen them stuff the cases of whiskey under the giant brush pile and was feeling greatly relieved when they finally pulled into Naskeag Harbor near Brooklin, waking everyone in hearing distance with the rattle, roar, and thunder of Chrétien's exhaust.

"Now let's go over to Gott's," said Chrétien. "I'll introduce you to some of the men."

The men sitting around the counter at Gott's, a combined grocery store and coffee counter, smiled when Chrétien entered and ordered a coffee with two sugars. As Chrétien had told Jérôme, everyone knew the signal. Since he normally took only one sugar, when he ordered two it meant he had a new consignment and interested buyers could come round to the disused shack at the edge of Pip's farm for their liquor. A man with a long straw-colored beard that came to a point at his belt took his coffee over to Chrétien and Pip. He smiled. "Long night?"

Chrétien nodded. He introduced Jérôme to the man. "This here's Ogden Gower. He's the genius who built my exhaust system." He turned to Ogden and said, "This heah is my friend from Saint Pierre. He's the man who keeps us in supply."

Ogden smiled and raised his coffee in a toast to Jérôme. "Eyuh, pleased to know yuh."

"Where's Buddy? I got a lobster for him," Chrétien asked Ogden.

"He's gone out to the Ashford place. Mr. Ashford telephoned from Boston. Said the town people was complainin' that his brush pile was too close to the road and he should burn it. He offered Buddy five dollars to do the job."

"What? He's doin' that now?"

"Eyuh. Something wrong?"

Chrétien didn't answer. Instead, he turned to Pip who was holding his head in his hands, rolling his eyes. "Come on. Maybe we can stop him."

Chrétien, Jérôme, and Pip bolted out of Gott's and jumped into Pip's truck. Pip threw it into gear and popped the clutch. The tires spun, spitting up dirt before gripping. Pip straightened the truck out and headed for Herrick Bay. After a few moments he muttered, "Merde!"

"What?" asked Chrétien.

Pip nodded toward the rear-view mirror. "The whole goddamn town's following us."

Chrétien looked over his shoulder. Jérôme turned to see where he was looking and saw a procession of three trucks and two cars.

When they arrived at the Ashford place, they found a young man cowering behind a big oak tree. The brush pile was ablaze. They skidded to a stop and ran up to him. It was Buddy. "Jesus Christ," he said. "The whole goldang pile started explodin' at me!"

"Merde!" said Chrétien.

"It's the goddamned devil," said Buddy.

There was an explosion. Shards of glass landed at their feet. Ogden Gower appeared, followed by a dozen other men. They all stood by the oak gazing at the fulminating brush pile.

Jérôme backed away a few steps.

As they advance across no-man's land on the third charge of the day, shells explode to the right and left. Jérôme hears fragments of metal whistle past his ear ... screams of wounded men ... dying men ....

"Gorry!"

Another detonation. More glass raining down.

"Merde!"

Suddenly there came a series of blasts. Whiskey bottles started to go off in rapid succession. Everyone backed away from the oak tree as glass showered all around them. One explosion after another, like the grand finale of a fireworks display.

Jérôme fell to the ground and covered his head. His whole body shook.

Shrapnel rains down on them as though the very sky is angry ....

"Gorry!" said Ogden Gower.

"Merde!"

Some of the men sniffed the air that was beginning to smell like a saloon. Recognizing the smell, their shoulders sagged, their mouths dropped. They turned sympathetic gazes on Chrétien. He replied with raised eyebrows and a look that said, "Sorry." But then his eyes started to twinkle, he squared his shoulders, looked at Pip, and said, "Look to the right side of the pile. There's a couple o' cases the fire ain't reached yet."

Pip gazed at him for a moment, the smile wrinkles around his eyes deepening. "We'd have to crawl. Too much glass flying 'round."

"It'll be just like the Meuse-Argonne."

Pip turned to the others. "Who's with us to save some o' the whiskey? Anything we save, everyone shares at no cost."

There was a buzzing among the men. Chrétien gave Pip a raised-eyebrow stare but then shrugged, let a bright smile lift his face, nodded. One of the men said, "Let's save the goddamn whiskey."

The others roared their approval.

In French, Chrétien explained to Jérôme what they were going to do and, before Jérôme could answer, Chrétien began crawling toward the pile. "Stay down. Make a line like a bucket brigade."

Pip dropped to his hands and knees and followed his brother-in-law.

Jérôme hesitated.

Chrétien, crawling fast, said, "Come on, Jérôme, you can't bring me all this good whiskey then watch it all go up. Either you help or we re-negotiate terms."

Reluctantly, Jérôme lowered himself to his hands and knees and started to crawl after the two men.

The ground feels hot, as though scorched from the white-hot metal piercing its skin. He slinks forward on his belly, bullets whistling over his head. He waits for the one that will pierce his helmet. Tears of human terror wet his cheeks .... "Oh, Dear God!" he mutters.

Jérôme heard other men drop to their knees behind him—in all, nine men, stretched out on their bellies, forming a line that snaked toward the right hand side of the pile. They were half way there when more bottles started to explode.

"Keep your head down," Pip cried to Chrétien.

A fragment of glass whistled past his ear. "Merde!"

The jagged shard landed just in front of Jérôme's face and he had to resist the urge to stand and run.

"We're almost there," cried Chrétien. But by the time Chrétien reached the pile, the fire was spreading rapidly. Jérôme could feel the heat of it. He started to pant as though he couldn't get enough oxygen.

He screams, but he can hear no sound from his throat. His face is unbearably hot and he throws his hands in front of it. He tries to suck in a breath, but is rewarded only with a raw, scorching sensation in his throat. He is suffocating ....

There was only time to save one or two of the cases. Chrétien groped under the lowest branches. "Got one." He levered it out and passed it back to Pip who passed it back to Jérôme and so on until the case was well on its way back to Buddy (who had refused to be anywhere near the pile).

Chrétien was just about to reach into the pile again when there was another salvo of bursting bottles. Glass shards flew everywhere. "Jesu, Marie, et Josef! Let's get the hell outa here!"

Jérôme screamed. He bolted to his feet and started to run as fast as he could away from the fire. Pip cried, "Stay down, Jérôme!" But Jérôme ignored him and continued to run. Everyone else in the column turned and started to scramble on hands and knees back toward the oak tree. More detonations. Pop! Pop! Pop! In rapid succession.

"Damned Germans are zeroing in," Chrétien cried with a laugh. Another pop. Chrétien reached behind him, felt his butt. "Merde! I've been hit."

"Me too," said Pip.

"Crawl faster."

Suddenly, all of the remaining bottles must have gone off together, for there was a tremendous explosion followed, an instant later, by a hail of glass shards.

"Ow!"

"Merde!"

"Goddamn!"

"Gorry!"

When at last the brush pile settled back to being just an ordinary burning brush pile, its explosive fuel spent, they discovered that five of them had been wounded, all in the butt. Jérôme was unhurt. He sat against the tree, trembling.

"Are you alright?" asked Chrétien, his brow furrowed.

Jérôme nodded, but his eyes must have betrayed him, for Chrétien said, "The war?"

Again, Jérôme nodded without saying anything.

"It's alright, Jérôme. Me and Pip, we understand. We was there, too." Then Chrétien laughed and said, "And the deal stays as it was. You don't owe me no money since it was my crazy idea to put the whiskey there."

As he finished telling the story to Marie-Lisette and Gabriel, Chrétien said, "All of us ended up at the doctor's office to have glass taken out of our butts—all, except Jérôme, here. Right, Jérôme?"

"What?" Jérôme had not been listening ever since the vision of the fire had come to his mind. Instead, he had been staring at Antoine's coat. Reflections from the kerosene lantern flickered on the wall and the stove.

"I said you were the only one not wounded by the whiskey bottles."

Jérôme nodded. "Yes, that's true."

"Did you smuggle more whiskey after that?" asked Marie-Lisette.

"Oh, yes. Many times. Right up to the end of Prohibition. Jérôme was a good partner … and a good friend." Chrétien turned to Jérôme. "And that's why I'm here, to pay back some of that friendship. So what do you need?"

After some gentle urging, Jérôme and Marie-Lisette listed a number of items that were in short supply because *Le Celte* hadn't been able to make it through, including good wine, cosmetics, perfumes, kid gloves and, as Marie-Lisette was careful to remind Chrétien, books. "I admit," she said, "I would like them. But mostly they would be for Madame LeClair at the library."

"Well, all the other stuff should be no problem, but I don't think I can get books in French."

"Oh, but Madame LeClair can read English. I can, too."

"Well, in that case, make me a list of the books you would like and I'll get them."

"I don't know any books in English. Anything will do."

"Oh, well I'll do the best I can," said Chrétien. He turned to Jérôme. "Anything else?"

"Yes," Jérôme said. "Some facial cream."

Chrétien gave him a bemused look. "Facial cream? For you?"

"No," Jérôme replied hesitantly. "I happen to know that Madame Cormier wants some." He glanced at Marie-Lisette and Gabriel. "She's run out."

Chrétien laughed. "Now it happens that I had an opportunity to ask this Madame Cormier what she needed and she didn't mention facial cream."

"What did she say?"

"All she asked for was a record for Doctor Tréguy." He pulled a slip of paper from his pocket. "Chopin's Second Piano Concerto by Arthur Rubinstein. It seems that everybody wants nothing for themselves, but something for everybody else."

At breakfast, Adrienne didn't have to wait long before her mother-in-law brought up her apparent weight gain. She guessed the woman had planned it all night.

"Claude, I was saying to Adrienne yesterday that she seems to be putting on weight," Claudette said, with what Adrienne thought was feigned casualness. "Don't you think so."

"Weight?" asked Claude, glancing at Adrienne. "No, I don't think so."

"Oh, but she is. Look at her."

Claude shrugged.

"Look at her face. It's fuller. And I think her dress is tight around the middle."

Claude poured milk into his bowl of porridge and looked at Adrienne again. He looked at her belly. "Well, maybe, but what's wrong with that? You ain't so skinny yourself. Women put on weight."

Claudette didn't answer at first. Instead, she rose from her chair to get more milk and bread. Then she said, again with an air of casualness that made Adrienne suspicious, "When do you think them foreign trawlers will be going back?"

Adrienne hoped her alarm didn't show in her face. She gazed at her bowl and took another spoonful of porridge, afraid to look up. She played with the chunk of bread sitting beside her plate and stared at the floor. An ant was making its way under the table. It stopped near her foot, paused, circled a bit, then retraced its path.

"I don't know," said Claude. "Besides, they ain't foreign. They're French."

"Some of them are Spanish. Anyway, you know what I mean. All them men who ain't from here causing trouble. Ain't that right, Adrienne?"

"Trouble?" murmured Adrienne, glancing quickly at Claudette then returning her gaze to her bowl.

"Sure. Drinking in the streets … and who knows what else. They've been a long time without their women."

"Aw, Ma, you're always imagining things," said Claude.

"You may think so, but I tell you, women ain't safe with them fishermen hanging around."

"What are you worried about? You hardly ever go into town anyway."

"It ain't me I'm worried about," she said, snapping a dishtowel at him.

"Who, then?" Claude said with an edge to his voice. It was clear he was becoming annoyed with the discussion.

"Oh … younger women, in general …."

The ant turned, apparently confused, then made for Adrienne's foot again. She pulled her foot back to clear its path. It continued, passing under the table towards Claude.

"You mean like Adrienne?"

"Sure. She's young."

Claude looked into Adrienne's eyes. He lowered his gaze, saw the ant, and stomped it.

Adrienne sucked in her breath. She managed a smile. "Don't be silly."

"All I'm saying," continued Claudette, "is that them men can be trouble. Maybe it's best if Adrienne stayed home."

Adrienne felt her stomach flop, a flush of anger rose to her face. She thought of Jean-Luc.

"Then who would do the shopping? You won't; that's for sure. And I sure the hell ain't."

"I'm only saying it could be trouble, that's all."

Claude dismissed her, shaking his head without answering. He lifted the last spoonful of porridge to his mouth. Milk dripped down his chin. He reached into his back pocket and pulled out his folded handkerchief, wiped the milk from his chin, and returned the handkerchief to the pocket.

Adrienne cleared her own plates, then took Claude's plates from the table. She busied herself brushing breadcrumbs from the table, silently hoping that Claude had put an end to the discussion.

"Don't listen to me, then," Claudette said. "It may happen some day that I'll say 'I told you so.'"

"Please be quiet!" snapped Claude.

For a long while, Claudette said nothing. Then, just as she was leaving the kitchen, she turned to Claude and said, "I don't care what you say, I'm telling you that your wife is putting on weight." She turned to Adrienne, narrowed her eyes, and said, "A woman knows these things."

Lafitte Hatches a Plot

IN THE EARLY MORNING, Jérôme and Chrétien drove into Saint Pierre to attend a meeting of the *Anciens Combattants*. Jérôme had explained that this was an association of veterans who had fought mainly in the Great War. "Except for Auguste Lafitte, who imagines himself a colonel and who fought in the Franco-Prussian War. We accept him as our leader because he would have it no other way. Besides, what do we care?"

"The Franco-Prussian War? That was a long time ago," said Chrétien with a laugh.

"Yuh, but he's still fighting it. He hates the Germans."

"These days, who doesn't?"

"But his hatred goes back a very long way."

"Even after we beat them in the last war?"

"But they're in France once more and Lafitte would like to expel them single-handedly if he could."

They approached the outskirts of Saint Pierre. The town was spread out below them and, for once, it was not swaddled in fog. It lay in a benediction of yellow light that seemed ladled from a melt of gold. One by one, windows flared with the rising sun, blinding Jérôme and Chrétien. All the buildings, normally white or gray depending on the quality of light, now took on a buttery tint. Out beyond the quay a band of golden flashes stretched across the rippling water all the way to the horizon—a sparkling tremolo of light. In the distance, Jérôme saw two lonely figures standing at the end of the quay gazing at this shining pathway.

He guessed they were watching for *Le Celte*.

The two men descended into the town and turned onto the Rue de 11 Novembre. Ahead was the War Memorial, its white marble glowing amber. Chrétien said he wanted to stop. "Maybe the names of some of my relatives are there."

"We'll be late for the meeting," said Jérôme.

"Oh, we can stop for just a minute."

Jérôme frowned, but said, "Alright, but only for a minute. I'll stay in the truck."

As Chrétien climbed out of the truck and mounted the curving steps of the memorial, Jérôme gazed off in the other direction. He knew where the name of Antoine Douville was; he didn't need to see it again. The war had been over long ago; why did they have to erect monuments to keep the memories alive?

After what seemed a long time to Jérôme, Chrétien finally returned to the truck "Not a Bastarache or a Dupuy among them," he said.

When they entered the big meeting room at the Hotel Lalanne, a lively debate was already raging. A canopy of cigarette smoke dimmed the ceiling lights like a fog. More coils of blue smoke drifted upwards from cigarettes held in hands that gesticulated in front of the men who were trying to make their points. The room was bedlam, men shouting and gesturing at one another. Incongruously, a solitary butterfly had somehow found its way into the room. It flitted around and through the clouds of smoke.

Auguste Lafitte was trying to shout something, waving his arms, but few men took notice of the slight man. He beckoned the two men closest to him to help him mount a rickety chair. As he stood on the chair—arrayed in the blue greatcoat, red trousers, and white gaiters of his grenadier's uniform—he swayed and struggled to hold his balance. The two men steadied him, one hand on the chair back and one pressed into the backside of his pee-stained red trousers. They wrinkled their noses.

Again Lafitte waved his hands—one of them holding a cigarette that sent swirls of smoke in front of his face—and shouted for order. But the din continued. The two men propping him up added their voices to his and at last the noise started to diminish.

Lafitte twitched his nostrils as the smoke from his cigarette irritated them. "I demand that everybody shut up," he cried in his thin voice.

The shouting continued.

"Shut up!" The butterfly floated past his face. He waved at it.

Gradually, and with some lingering grumbles, the men finally fell silent.

When he was satisfied he had their attention, Lafitte expanded his chest in an effort to fill the uniform into which, over the years, his aged body had shrunk, and proclaimed, "I repeat: I call for a full mobilization of Saint Pierre and Miquelon to fight the invading Hun."

This brought a renewed outburst of shouts and gesticulations. Someone called out, "What have we got to mobilize?"

"We have both an army and a navy, Monsieur Boullot," Lafitte said, pointing his cigarette-holding hand at the man.

"Navy? What navy?"

Lafitte scowled at Boullot. "We have three boats."

"Two of them are speedboats from the whiskey smuggling days. They have no guns."

"And we have the *Béarn*."

"The *Béarn*? She's a harbor boat. All she's good for is carrying the mail and supplies to Langlade and Miquelon."

"She has a cannon."

"A cannon that hasn't been fired for years because everybody's afraid it would rip the deck off the old tub."

Auguste Lafitte pressed his lips together in a scowl and extended a trembling finger toward the man. "I think that you, Monsieur Boullot, must be a collaborationist."

"Why you old fart," Boullot shouted. He whipped off his beret and advanced toward Lafitte.

Lafitte squared his shoulders, shot his chin forward, thrust his right arm, bent at the elbow, into the air and slapped his bicep with his other hand in the universal gesture that says, "Fuck you!"

Boullot, red faced, advanced closer but Lafitte's helpers rushed forward to restrain him. This left Lafitte teetering on the unsupported chair. Jérôme and Chrétien hurried to steady him. Lafitte, holding onto the shoulders of Jérôme and Chrétien, smiled at Boullot and said, "This I will tell you, Boullot, when I die it will be as a citizen of Free France and my last words to you will be 'Fuck you!' Those will be my last words and I will die a happy man."

Chrétien laughed, said, "Well spoken, Colonel."

Lafitte looked down at him. "Who the hell are you?"

Chrétien told him his name.

"But you're not an *Anciens Combattant*."

"I fought in the Great War with the Americans. The Meuse-Argonne."

"The Meuse-Argonne?" Lafitte paused to consider then, satisfied, said, "You are a welcome guest." Then, more loudly, pointing to Boullot, he added, "Do you see Monsieur Bastarache, what idiocy I have to put up with?" He leaned toward Boullot. "Remember, Boullot, my last words in this world will be 'Fuck you!' and they will be directed at you."

Boullot, the cords of his neck protruding, struggled to free himself from the men holding him.

Lafitte gave him a supercilious smile and stroked the loosely bent fingers of his right hand along his cheek in the gesture that said, "What a bore!"

Boullot sputtered, "You have no authority to call for a mobilization. That's up to the administrator."

Lafitte made a hitting motion with his right hand toward his shoulder in the gesture that said, "I don't give a damn." He made a scowling face at Boullot, bared his rotting teeth at the man.

"De Bournat will arrest you for … for usurpation," cried Boullot.

With the forefinger of his right hand, Lafitte tugged the skin under his right eye downward in the gesture that meant, "My eye." He turned his gaze to the entire room and shouted, "Who's with me and the Free French … and who's with Boullot, de Bournat, and the other dirty Vichy collaborationists and (here he stuck his two index fingers on each side of his head and wiggled them) … cuckolds? All who are for de Gaulle and the Free French, raise your hands."

There were shouts of glee. All but three or four men thrust their hands in the air. The only exceptions were Boullot, two other men standing close to him, and Claude Cormier who had just entered the room.

"Ah, so Monsieur Cormier, you are not with us?" asked Lafitte, eyebrows peaked. "Are you a collaborationist cuckold?"

Claude said nothing. Instead, he looked first at Auguste Lafitte, then at Jérôme who was still supporting the old man.

"The man has no tongue," said Lafitte. "Maybe he's still dumbstruck about his little zebra."

Claude breathed deeply in the manner of a man trying to control himself. "I think it makes more sense to stay with the Vichy since they control the government in France ... and our subsidies."

"What right do you even have to speak?' Jérôme asked. "You don't belong here. You never fought for your country." As soon as he said it, Jérôme regretted it.

Claude glared at him, a look filled with hatred.

"Monsieur Sabot is right," said Lafitte. "You don't have a vote here."

Claude was about to say something when another voice came from the back of the room. "Every citizen of Saint Pierre and Miquelon has a right to speak his mind during these terrible times."

The crowd in the back parted to reveal Count Gilbert de Bournat, the Administrator of Saint Pierre and Miquelon. He strode to the front of the room and turned to address the crowd, his beaked Gallic nose lending him an air of authority. "You say you want to side with General de Gaulle and the Free French instead of the Vichy government of Marshal Pétain. I must explain to you what that would mean." He went on to say that since the end of the prosperous days of *Le whiskey* they had become poor islands unable to sustain their former way of life. They depended, therefore, on subsidies from the home government for their survival and unless they could find other sources of support, say from the Canadians or the Americans, they would be unwise to cut themselves off from their only means of support.

It only made sense, he told them, that they remain loyal to the Vichy government, because the Free French hardly had so much money that they could divert some of it to their tiny archipelago. Furthermore, if they declared for de Gaulle, they might be inviting occupation by the Germans who would feel insecure with a Free French presence near the waters where they were conducting submarine warfare. And, he went on to say, occupation by the Germans would be a thousand times worse than subservience to the Vichy who, after all, continued to send subsidy payments. "The best bet for Saint Pierre would be to remain passive and wait for the liberation of France. If we ally ourselves with the British and the Americans, we will be in trouble since they don't have the armies or the will to oppose Hitler."

"But my dear count," said Lafitte from his shaky perch, "if, as you say, the British and the Americans cannot oppose Hitler, then who is going to bring about the liberation of France that you advise us to wait for? Tell me that."

"We must have faith that France will someday be liberated. There is no need for Saint Pierre to create difficulties for itself."

"But if we don't support the Free French, Saint Pierre will be used as a base for German submarines," said Doctor Tréguy.

"That's absurd," replied de Bournat. "Anyone who knows these islands would know that is impossible."

"Why is it impossible?"

Before the count could answer, someone said, "But the radio station could be used to broadcast weather bulletins to the Germans."

"Impossible," said de Bournat. "Saint Pierre Radio sends out its broadcasts by underwater cable. It is absolutely secure. Our neighbors, the Americans and Canadians, have no worries on that account. We must remain passive and neutral lest we invite the Germans to occupy us."

Boullot stepped forward. "He's right. If we invite the Germans to occupy us, we'll never again see *Le Celte*."

Lafitte, still wobbling on his chair, gave the "I don't give a damn!" gesture with his right hand and said, "What is money, what are all the little pleasures that *Le Celte* brings us, next to honor?"

"I agree with him," said Doctor Tréguy. His voice was so respected among the Saint Pierrais, that the room fell silent.

Lafitte took the opportunity to call for another vote. "We have heard the Vichy position and we know the position of the Free French who, like us, love France from the depths of their souls, from their very hearts. So who is for the Free French? Raise your hands."

As many hands as went up before, went up again.

Lafitte gave the "fuck you" gesture to de Bournat. "So, you see: They have voted for honor. *Le bras d'honneur* to you!" he said, using the supremely ironic name for the gesture of smacking your right bicep with your left palm, forming the arm of honor.

Everyone looked at Count de Bournat, waiting for his next move. Would he arrest Lafitte as an agitator? Would he arrest all those who voted for de Gaulle as traitors to the Pétain government?

But he did none of those things. Instead, shaking his head sadly, he strode from the room without a word. He was followed by Boullot and several other men, including Claude Cormier who shot Jérôme a hate-filled glance before leaving.

Tears formed in Lafitte's eyes and started to roll down his cheeks. He squared his shoulders, lifted his gaze to the ceiling, and started to sing in a cracked, thin voice. *"Alons enfants de la patrie, le jour de giorie et arrivè ...."*

Every man in the room, including Jérôme and Chrétien, joined him in full voice.

Gabriel's powerful baritone voice rose above all others, inspiring them to greater heights. They sang several verses of the *Marseillaise*, and when they finished, the men milled about the room congratulating each other.

Doctor Tréguy approached Auguste Lafitte who was being helped down from his perch by Jérôme and Chrétien. "Colonel Lafitte, I must say that you sing in the key of W flat. You should take lessons from Gabriel."

For the first time that night, Lafitte laughed; a rasping, eggshell of a laugh. His yellowed teeth gleamed dully with saliva. "I'm a warrior, not a singer. It may, as you say, leave my lips as W flat, but it leaves my heart like the voice of angels."

"Well said, my colonel," replied Doctor Tréguy with a chuckle. "But on a more serious note I must alert you to a problem. Considering what happened to Pierre Laval, I'd be careful if I were you. The Vichy are cracking down on dissidents."

"What do I care?" Lafitte grumbled. The butterfly fluttered near his nose. He snapped at it.

"You should care because the home government might very well order de Bournat to carry out his own crackdown," said Doctor Tréguy. "And take care with the butterfly; it should be long dead by this time of year. Perhaps it's a sign."

"A sign?"

"I assure you, it could well be."

"Who the hell is Pierre Laval," asked Chrétien.

"He's Pétain's top man. Some say he actually heads the Vichy government and Pétain's only a figurehead," Doctor Tréguy replied.

"What happened to this Laval?"

"Last month he and a newspaper editor, who is a German sympathizer, were shot by a young resistance fighter." Doctor Tréguy looked around, leaned closer to Chrétien, and said in a low voice, "Unfortunately this fellow wasn't a very good shot and they were only wounded." Then, turning toward Lafitte again, he said, "But it's given the Vichy an excuse to round up opponents."

"De Bournat would never arrest me or anyone else."

Doctor Tréguy nodded. "He's not a bad man. However, he's a loyal administrator who's caught in the middle. He might be forced to do something to prove his loyalty."

"We'll see," said Lafitte with a dismissive wave of his arm. "But there's not enough room in the prison for all of us."

Later, as they were leaving, Chrétien turned to Jérôme and said, "You know, where you are concerned, Count de Bournat isn't your main problem. That man … Cormier? I saw the way he looked at you. You have an enemy there. You better be careful."

When Adrienne arrived at the quay, she hesitated. She had to see Jean-Luc, but there were many men milling about and she imagined herself, with her swelling belly, as big as a house. Surely they would know she was pregnant and they would guess that Jean-Luc was the father. She looked down at the water. It seemed sluggish, wheezing against the walls of the quay as though anticipating the ice that would soon skirt its fringes. The trawlers rocked to lazy swells, remnants of storm waves far out to sea; their rubber tire bumpers sighing and groaning against each other. Their mooring lines creaked as they stretched. The conversations of the men were hushed, the sounds of a harbor between storms.

A few of the men glanced toward Adrienne.

A dog barked.

She studied her reflection. It was distorted, undulating to the slow heave of the waves. Her belly appeared huge, bloated. She covered it with her hands and snatched a glance along the quay. She paused, unsure. Then her courage failed her. She turned to retrace her steps across the square. She decided to stop at the Hotel Lalanne for a cup of coffee and time to think.

When Adrienne stepped inside the hotel, Marie-Lisette, who was working behind the registration desk, looked up. "Madame Cormier, you look worried. Is something wrong?"

"No, no, Marie-Lisette. Nothing. I thought I'd have a cup of coffee is all."

"Of course, Madame." Marie-Lisette disappeared into a small room behind the desk and emerged moments later carrying a cup balanced on a saucer. They rattled against each other as she walked.

Adrienne, now seated in an overstuffed chair, accepted the coffee with a weak smile.

"Are you sure nothing's wrong, Madame?"

"No, nothing."

"I see. Well, I'll be right over here if you need me." Marie-Lisette returned to her place behind the registration desk.

Adrienne sipped her coffee and listened to the sounds coming from the street: barking dogs; drivers tooting their horns; all muffled by the storm sashes that had been installed in the windows now that winter was just around the corner. She had convinced herself that her mother-in-law knew very well that she was pregnant. All of the woman's sly comments and insinuations said as much.

Furthermore, she was persuaded that Claudette knew the baby wasn't Claude's. Why else, the woman must be thinking, would Adrienne hide the fact that she was pregnant from her family, especially her husband? If Adrienne was right about her mother-in-law, and she knew the cunning woman's ways so well that she was sure of it, then it was only a matter of time before everything would explode. Either Claudette would press her unmercifully until she confessed, or she would start showing so much that it would no longer be possible to deny her pregnancy. In any case, Claude would learn she was going to have a baby and would know for a certainty that he was not the father. And when that happened, there was no way to predict what he would do, only that it would be violent. She had to think of something.

She held the cup and saucer in her lap to disguise her belly and gazed at Marie-Lisette who was reading a book behind the registration desk. Marie-Lisette's head was framed by a large begonia, its leaves stirring every time somebody walked past. How well did she know this young woman? Marie-Lisette was not like other people on Saint Pierre; Adrienne sensed in the young woman the same desire to escape the island that she, herself, felt so intensely. And she realized that for all the gossips on their little archipelago—and it seemed that every last person, men included, was a gossip—she had never heard a rumor, or a story, or any insulting kind of embellishment from Marie-Lisette about anyone else. As far as she could tell, Marie-Lisette was a model of discretion.

But could she trust her? She needed somebody on her side, somebody who might be willing to carry messages to Jean-Luc and, perhaps, somebody who could advise her when everything blew up. And besides, what was the risk? Soon, everyone on Saint Pierre would know the truth anyway. What was there to lose?

Marie-Lisette appeared at her side. "Another coffee, Madame?"

"No thank you, Marie-Lisette." Adrienne took a deep breath, glanced to right and left, and said, "May I talk with you … woman to woman?"

A crease of concern appeared on Marie-Lisette's forehead. "Why, of course, Madame."

"I need your help. Can I trust you?"

"Absolutely."

Adrienne looked around again. "Is there a place we can talk?"

"What Count de Bournat said about the Americans and British not being able to stop Hitler," Jérôme asked Chrétien, "what do you think?"

They were sitting at Jérôme's kitchen table. Coils of smoke rose from their cigarettes and fanned out along the ceiling. The ashtray between them overflowed with crumpled butts and an un-labeled, half empty whiskey bottle sat between two glasses, themselves half empty. Jérôme's beret rested limply on the table. The two men sat in a fug of smoke. The air in the room was stale and fusty, for Jérôme had already secured the windows and storm sashes against the coming winter.

"Well, us Americans ain't gonna do nothin' 'bout Hitler if we don't get into the war," replied Chrétien.

"Do you think Roosevelt will get you into the war?"

Chrétien shrugged. "Don't know. We saw his presidential yacht a little while ago; it stopped into Buck's Harbor where we live so he could get some ice cream. But, Mister Roosevelt, he didn't come ashore and say, 'Chrétien, I'm gonna tell you what I'm gonna do.' So who knows?"

"What do the American people think?"

"There's many, like my nephew Gil, who say we oughta be over there fightin' right now. But there's many others who say it ain't none of our business. And there are others who are afraid of what might happen. My grandnephew Jordi, for example, is afraid of losin' his father. So, you see, there are both sides even within my own family."

"But unless the Americans enter, I'm afraid France is lost for good."

"Maybe what happened to the *Greer* will help."

"What's the *Greer*?" Jérôme poured more whiskey into each of their glasses. A narrow slant of sunlight, edging through the almost closed curtains, luminesced the bottle. Faint, dancing reflections played on Jérôme's face, caught his eyes. He squinted.

"One of our destroyers. She was in a convoy a few weeks ago when a German sub attacked her. Roosevelt made a big deal about it with the American people, so I guess he's *tryin'* to get us into the war."

"Well, I only hope—"

Suddenly, there were two deafening blasts and the kitchen window exploded into fragments. Jérôme and Chrétien dove for the floor, shards of glass flying about their heads. A rush of cold wind invaded the room through the shattered window. Jérôme felt something rip into him. There was a sharp pain around his eyes. He rolled under the table and reached up to feel his head.

His hand came away with blood.

Le Mort-Homme

W HEN THEY WERE ALONE in the business office of Hotel Lalanne, Adrienne hesitated for a long moment, then blurted, "I'm going to have a baby."

Marie-Lisette stared at the woman for a moment, stunned, then said, flatly, "And your husband isn't the father."

A look of alarm came across Adrienne's face. "How did you know?" She brushed back a loose strand of hair.

"Why else would it be a problem?"

"Yes … yes, I suppose."

"This is serious, isn't it?" Everybody knew about Claude Cormier's temper. Marie-Lisette could scarcely imagine what might happen if he found out.

"Very serious." A strand of hair fell over Adrienne's forehead again. She brushed it back.

Marie-Lisette pulled a bobby pin from her own hair and offered it to Adrienne. "How can I help?" Marie-Lisette had to admit to herself that she was flattered Madame Cormier had come to her for help rather than to someone else. And, despite her alarm, she also recognized within herself a wicked pleasure at the prospect of being involved in an intrigue.

"Can you take a message for me?" Adrienne anchored the stubborn strand of hair with the bobby pin then let her fingers play with a button on her dress. Marie-Lisette saw that they were shaking.

A courier between lovers! This was, for Marie-Lisette, as good as it gets. It was straight from a novel by Colette. "Of course. Where?"

Adrienne paused. Her expression seemed to beg for empathy and Marie-Lisette instantly felt guilty about her salacious excitement. "The quay."

"The quay?"

"I'm ... I'm afraid to go there again. All the men look at me."

"They're like that."

"I'm sure that I'm starting to show." Adrienne passed a hand over her belly and indicated the tiny strain wrinkles at the middle button of her dress.

"Not enough so one would notice."

"Perhaps, but soon, there'll be no hiding it."

"A foreign fisherman?"

Adrienne nodded.

"Who?" Marie-Lisette wondered if she was being too bold by asking.

"His name is Jean-Luc Lavedan. His trawler is *La Petite Fleur*."

"I know of him."

"He's a good man."

"And he ... he's the father?"

Adrienne nodded quickly but averted her eyes. "Yes."

There was something in the way she said it that aroused Marie-Lisette's suspicion. She felt that Madame Cormier wasn't telling her everything. She gazed into Adrienne's eyes. "Yes ... of course I'll take your message."

"I need to see him, to talk with him." Her fingers continued to play with the straining button.

"I understand. When are you due?"

"In about two months."

Marie-Lisette frowned. "But you don't look that far along."

"I'm lucky. Some women don't show almost up to the time they deliver. But my mother-in-law is suspicious. She keeps saying that I've gained weight. I'm sure she knows and I'm afraid she'll tell my husband."

"But so what? He'll just think the child is his. Both men are French. Who will know the difference?"

Adrienne blushed. She shook her head, averted her eyes. "He'll know it's impossible for him to be the father."

"But how?"

Adrienne's blush deepened. "Because it ... it's literally impossible."

"But ...." Marie-Lisette started to say before she stopped and gazed wide-eyed at Madame Cormier. "You mean you and ... Monsieur Cormier ... haven't ... haven't ...." Now it was Marie-Lisette who was blushing.

Adrienne gazed at the floor, undid and redid the button. "No, we haven't had relations."

"No relations?"

"It's … it's impossible." She didn't care if Marie-Lisette knew about Claude.

Marie-Lisette put a hand to her mouth. "Oh my!"

"So you see my problem."

"Yes, yes. I most certainly do."

"Will you help me?"

"You can count on me, Madame Cormier … in all ways."

Adrienne took a piece of paper from her purse and handed it to Marie-Lisette. "This is the message. And considering what you are doing for me, perhaps you should call me Adrienne."

Marie-Lisette took the message, noticing that it was not sealed. She was moved by the woman's trust in her. "And what about a reply? Should I wait?"

Adrienne nodded. "Otherwise, I won't know where we can meet … or when."

"I can arrange that," Marie-Lisette heard herself say. Suddenly, her heart was racing.

"You? How?"

Marie-Lisette took a deep breath. "With the war and no tourists, the hotel has many vacancies. I can arrange a room for you. No one has to know." Again, she blushed.

"But we … Jean-Luc and I have no money. He's been unable to fish and I—"

"—As I said, no one need know. Money is not a problem. As far as the hotel is concerned, the room will still be vacant."

"You would do that for us?"

Marie-Lisette gave a hesitant nod. She wondered how she would keep it secret from the hotel's owners.

Adrienne threw her arms around Marie-Lisette. "You're an angel," she murmured through tears of gratitude. Then she pulled back and asked, "Can it be as soon as tomorrow?"

"Leave it to me," replied Marie-Lisette, her courage returning.

As Adrienne neared home, filled with a sense of relief and anticipation for the next day, two shotgun blasts buckled the air. She flinched, almost expecting to feel the hot pain of buckshot tear into her body. Instinctively, she covered her bloated, distended belly with both arms. But when she felt no pain, she cautiously approached the turn up ahead. Her house, and Monsieur Sabot's, came into full view. She saw Claude standing before Jérôme Sabot's house, his shotgun pointed at the ground.

"Oh my God," she cried. "Jérôme!" She broke into a run.

When he saw the blood on his hand, when he smelled it's salt heat, a vision of the war returned to Jérôme.

He is trudging toward a line of battle near the hill called Le Mort-Homme overlooking Verdun ... The unrelenting gunfire has become a thrumming in his temples; he can feel them vibrate like the skin of a drum ... Bullets hiss by his ears but it's useless to duck ... He trudges on ... Each time he lifts his foot, it comes up out of the swampy soil with a sickening sucking sound; each time he has to check to be sure his boot is still on his foot ... All around him, soldiers are walking, if that's what you can call the plod of dead men, in their socks or puttees or even barefoot ... no time to stop and retrieve boots sucked from them by the mud. It's as though the earth itself is stripping them, preparing them for embalming, preparing to enfold them ... He passes a pond with a vile greenish slick covering its surface ... A soldier near him, insane with thirst, falls to his knees and drinks from the pond ... In the middle, a corpse floats on its back, its face black, its belly bloated, distended ... Other men tell the thirsty man to stop, but their voices are too weak, too weary, and they move on ... Jérôme looks up ahead, trying to spot Antoine, but his friend is too far in front ... Suddenly, he hears a scream to his left and turns in time for the man who has just taken a bullet in the face to fall into his arms ... Blood is pumping from the wound ... It gushes over Jérôme's hands ....

Jérôme was jerked back to the moment by Chrétien's cry. "Jérôme, move! Get up against the wall."

Jérôme snatched a quick glance at Antoine's coat then half-crawled, half-rolled, to the wall under the shattered window where Chrétien already crouched.

"What the hell was that?" asked Chrétien.

"Sounded like a shotgun."

"Two barrels?"

"That's what I heard."

"Me too. He hasn't had time to reload," said Chrétien as he raised himself up to peer out the shattered window. "I hope."

Jérôme, following Chrétien's lead, raised his head above the windowsill. He saw Claude Cormier standing not ten yards from them, staring at the window. The man held his shotgun pointed at the ground and seemed to be making no effort to reload.

"Let's get him before he reloads," Jérôme whispered.

Chrétien nodded and crawled through the storm vestibule toward the outer door. Jérôme crawled after him.

"Ready?" whispered Chrétien.

Jérôme nodded. "I go first. He's my problem." Jérôme rose to his feet and burst through the door into the yard, his heart pounding. Chrétien came stumbling after him.

Claude barely flinched. He stood staring dumbly at them as if not comprehending what was happening. He made no effort to reach for more shells in the pouch that hung at his hip.

"What the hell?" Jérôme yelled.

Claude shook his head, side to side, slowly. "I was shooting at a bird ... I missed."

"You *never* miss. You're the best damned shot on all of Saint Pierre and Miquelon."

"I was distracted."

"What kind of bird?" demanded Chrétien, his voice betraying his disbelief.

"It was a seagu ... no a razorbill."

Jérôme glared at the man. "Are you trying to tell us you can't even say what kind of bird it was ... you, the master slaughterer of birds?"

Claude didn't answer.

"You were shooting at us," said Jérôme. "At me."

Claude shook his head slowly. "I ... I wasn't ...." His voice trailed off.

At that moment, Adrienne Cormier ran up to them. "What happened? My God, Jérôme, you're hurt." She rushed to him, pulled a handkerchief from her pocket, and held it to his forehead. The handkerchief started to turn red.

"I thought it was my eyes," Jérôme said.

"It's your forehead." She dabbed the handkerchief over the wound.

Jérôme winced.

Adrienne took the handkerchief away. "I hurt you. I'm sorry." She leaned close to examine the wound. "There's a piece of glass stuck in your forehead."

"You called him Jérôme?"

They turned to see Claude slowly backing away from them. "You called him Jérôme?" he repeated.

"It's not—"

"—Mama says you're pregnant. Is he the son-of-a-bitch?"

Jérôme felt his heart begin to race faster. "Claude, you're crazy."

Claude backed up a few more steps and reached into his pouch for shells. He snapped the shotgun in half and, with the practiced quickness of a man who had done it thousands of times, inserted the shells and snapped the gun closed. "I'll kill you both."

Jérôme was frozen, unsure what to do.

Chrétien lunged at the man.

Claude raised the shotgun with trembling hands.

Jérôme sucked in his breath. He closed his eyes.

A German machine gunner is less than twenty yards in front of him. He can see the bloodshot eyes ...

A single shotgun blast shattered the air.

A flock of sea pigeons rose from the roof of the Cormier barn some fifty yards away. The rustle of their wings was the only sound other than the reverberating echo of the gun's blast.

Jérôme opened his eyes to see Chrétien struggling with Claude. Chrétien had both hands wrapped around the gun barrel and was trying to wrest the gun from Claude's grip. Jérôme rushed to them and threw his arms around Claude from behind, causing the man to lose his grip on the shotgun. They wrestled Claude to the ground.

Jérôme looked up. "Adri ... Madame Cormier, call the police."

Adrienne stared at them, her face twisted in horror.

"Madame Cormier, you must!" shouted Jérôme.

"It's for his own good," added Chrétien. Then he said to Jérôme, "Sit on him."

Jérôme sat on the backs of Claude's thighs while Chrétien sat on the man's back. Claude squirmed under them, face in the dust.

When the police arrived ten minutes later, Jérôme and Chrétien were still sitting atop Claude. By the time they let him up, it took four men to force Claude into the car. After they finally had him subdued, the police drove off toward Saint Pierre. Telling Adrienne to stay, Jérôme and Chrétien piled into Jérôme's truck and followed the police car into town.

At the police station, Inspector Bernard said, "So you say Monsieur Cormier was going to shoot you?"

"Yes," said Jérôme. "He said as much."

"He had already emptied two barrels through Monsieur Sabot's kitchen window," said Chrétien.

"I was shooting at a bird," insisted Claude. "A razorbill."

Inspector Bernard arched his eyebrows. "You were shooting at a bird and you missed?" He shook his head and made a series of tsk-tsk sounds.

"You see," said Chrétien. "He's lying."

"Monsieur Cormier, you'll have to do better than that," the inspector said.

"I tell you, I was shooting at a bird."

"And you expect me to believe that? A marksman like you?"

Claude glared at Jérôme. It was a hate-filled stare. "And do you expect me to believe that you didn't sleep with my wife?"

A flush rose to Jérôme's cheeks. "That's absurd! You do your wife a terrible injustice."

Inspector Bernard stared goggle-eyed at Jérôme. "So I see. This is a crime of passion."

"Absolutely not," cried Jérôme. "At least not on my part. I mean ... on his part ... who can say?"

"She called him by his Christian name," Claude said to the inspector.

"And that's a reason to shoot at him?" The inspector shook his head sadly from side to side. "Monsieur, Monsieur, we may be under the Vichy but it's still a crime to shoot at people. Perhaps a few months locked up will give you a chance to regain your senses."

After the police took Claude away, Jérôme and Chrétien signed the papers that the inspector handed them, then left.

As they drove back to Jérôme's place, Chrétien asked, "This thing with Madame Cormier; is it true?"

Jérôme stared at Chrétien. "Of course it's not true. How can you say such a thing?"

"Well, to tell you the truth, I didn't believe it. It's too absurd, the thought of you with a woman that young."

"There, you see," said Jérôme through tight lips. "I told you it was impossible."

"But he doesn't think it's impossible. He believes it; probably because his mother told him so."

"Well his imagination is none of my concern."

"Oh, but it is, my friend, it is. He'll have two months to imagine all sorts of things. And to remember the zebra affair ... and the way you had him booted out of the meeting of the *Anciens Combattants*. Two months is a long time to think about such things."

Jérôme didn't answer. He was thinking of Adrienne, how helpless she must be feeling after all this.

"But, unfortunately, two months is a short time, too," said Chrétien. "What happens when he gets out?"

After a few inquiries, Marie-Lisette found Jean-Luc Lavedan at the end of the quay. He was smoking and chatting with another of the trawler fishermen. Instantly, she recognized why Madame Cormier loved this man. With his thin, Gallic nose and his rugged good looks, he could easily have been Jacques Bernis—if only it was an airplane that he piloted rather than a fishing trawler.

He certainly was no Raymond Pineau; he probably didn't even smell like fish though fishing was his profession. Momentarily, she experienced a strange regret, an emptiness, though she could not identify its source. It caused her to be speechless for a moment, even a little disoriented. Over Jean-Luc's shoulder she watched a pair of seagulls descend in a swooping spiral to alight on the stern of one of the trawlers. She read the name: *La Petite Fleur*.

Jean-Luc, seemingly amused at the sight of this speechless young woman, raised his eyebrows inquisitively.

At last Marie-Lisette introduced herself.

"Of course. I've seen you at the hotel," said Jean-Luc.

"Yes … I … I work there."

"I know."

"Yes." She paused, glanced at the other man.

Jean-Luc turned to the man and said, "Would you leave us alone, Henri?"

The man smiled then sauntered down the quay towards another group of men.

Marie-Lisette said, "I have a message for you from Madame … from Adrienne." She handed him the slip of paper.

He took it and read it quickly with excitement in his eyes. "She says we must meet."

"I know."

"When? Where?"

"I've arranged for you to have a room tomorrow at Hotel Lalanne. No one must know of it."

"But why?"

"Well, because … because …." She didn't know what to say.

"No, I mean why do you do this?"

She hesitated, then said, "Because I, too, long to go to France. I understand her soul." Marie-Lisette paused, gazing at the seagulls. Jean-Luc's eyes were too intense. Finally, she added, "And I know about her husband."

Jean-Luc threw his arms around her and hugged her. "I thank you," he said with a smile.

His strong embrace left her breathless and, as she'd suspected, he didn't smell like fish. Reluctantly, she withdrew from his embrace, mumbled, "Tomorrow, then, early afternoon," turned, and hurried down the quay.

As Marie-Lisette returned to the hotel, she tried to identify the odd sense of sorrow she'd felt when she first met Jean-Luc Lavedan. It wasn't anguish for Madame Cormier; of that, she was certain. In fact the instant she saw the man, she was filled with joy for her new friend. But the joy was mixed with melancholy, and she recognized it now as a heartache for herself. Jean-Luc was, for Adrienne, a means of escape from the boredom and isolation of Saint Pierre—an escape that she, herself, could not hope to achieve, at least as long as the war was on. And even when the war ended, how could she possibly afford to follow her dream to a French university? Just as she had seen the possibility of hope for Adrienne, she had seen her own hope diminished.

As she crossed the street in front of the Hotel Lalanne, she saw a police car drive past. She caught a quick glimpse of a sullen Claude Cormier sitting in the back seat. Immediately behind the car came Jérôme Sabot in his truck with Chrétien Bastarache in the passenger seat. She wanted to stop them and ask what was happening, but they were past her before she could call out. She watched the truck, with its salt-corroded bumper, disappear, then went into the hotel to prepare a room for Adrienne and Jean-Luc. After that, she planned to start the new Colette novel that Madame Leclair had given her.

What else could she do?

Deadeyes in the Sand
11

THE FOLLOWING DAY, Jérôme took Chrétien and Marie-Lisette across to Miquelon in his motor dory. They were headed for the Dune where Jérôme often combed the beach for cargo washed ashore by shipwrecks.

The body of water separating Saint Pierre from Miquelon—which was officially called "The Bay" but which most people called "The Mouth of Hell" for its turbulent waters—was on this day relatively placid. No more than a two-foot chop was running and the motor dory bounced from wave to wave at full speed, flinging sheets of sun-saturated water to the sides. Jérôme, Chrétien, and Marie-Lisette sat gripping the gunwales and ducking the wind-blown spray. As they rounded the promontory guarding the Cove of Soldiers, Jérôme asked Chrétien, "Do you know how many wrecks surround these islands?"

"Lots?"

"More than six hundred. God seems determined to make them pay a high price for disturbing our isolation."

"But I thought you all resented the isolation."

Jérôme shrugged. "If it cuts us off from some of the good things, it also helps protect us from the outside world."

"But Monsieur Sabot," said Marie-Lisette, "I think it cuts us off more than it protects us." The pang of regret she'd felt the day before had returned. Indeed, it had never left her.

"You haven't been to France," replied Jérôme with a note of bitterness.

"But I would love to go to France." Marie-Lisette heard the fervor in her voice and her sorrow deepened.

"Why, Marie-Lisette," asked Chrétien with a smile. "Why do you want to go to France?"

"To study. I want to go to university."

"That sounds like a good plan."

Marie-Lisette shook her head. "Not a plan; a dream. I could work at the hotel all my life and never save enough to afford it."

"But what about your family?"

Marie-Lisette gave a wry laugh. "My father doesn't believe in education. He wants me to stay on Saint Pierre all my life and marry a local boy— Raymond Pineau." Her entire body shuddered visibly.

"But you don't like this Raymond Pineau?"

Marie-Lisette made a face. "He smells like fish."

Chrétien laughed. "I guess that means 'No'."

Jérôme interrupted them by calling out, "Hang on. We're about to run up." Moments latter, the dory nosed onto the beach with a grinding of sand under its keel and shuddered to a stop.

They had arrived at the southern end of the north-south isthmus that separated Langlade from Miquelon like an elongated cleavage furrow between dividing cells . They hopped out of the boat into knee-deep water and shimmied the boat further up onto the beach. Its bottom ground deeper into the sand. By now, a fog had rolled in, blotting out the sun, shrinking their world to a half mile in any direction before it ended in an undifferentiated mist. As they stepped ashore, there was a great fluttering of wings. The place was a cacophony of birds and ducks. They heard the haunting wail and laughter of the loon, the infant-like cries of the oldsquaw, the barking yelps and cackles of snow geese, the honks of Canadian geese, the shrill cries of the gulls. Several cormorants bobbed in the waves some distance off the western shore of the flat dune not far from the rotting hulk of a ship.

"Sometimes I think God gives us fog so we can't see the sky and the ocean and know how isolated we are," said Marie-Lisette.

"Now you sound like my brother-in-law, Pip," said Chrétien. "He's a minor philosopher of sorts."

"Philosophy is what I'd like to study ... and literature."

"Perhaps you will, Marie-Lisette. Someday."

Marie-Lisette felt a heaviness in her chest. "I'll never get to France." She hated the morose tone in her voice, but that was how she felt.

Chrétien gazed at her a long time, then said, "Well, perhaps things might change for you somehow. Don't ever give up hoping."

They strode casually along the Dune toward Miquelon, the sand hard and packed under their feet. As they walked, Jérôme explained to Chrétien that the shipwrecks—some of which were still visible along the western boundary of the Dune where the cormorants bobbed—brought them windfalls: barrels of rum, gasoline, cans of paint, grease, cases of preserves, and many other goods.

"Much of which seems to end up in your shed," said Chrétien with a sly smile.

Jérôme shrugged. "If that's the way God has decided to deliver us goods from the outside world, then so be it. Who am I to refuse his gifts? He's a kind of middle man."

"And are you certain you don't provide the Lord with assistance?"

"How do you mean?"

"I've heard that sometimes ships are lured onto the rocks by false lights. There was a story about a man who attached lanterns to the horns of his cow. Things like that." Chrétien turned an amused, conspiratorial gaze on Jérôme.

Jérôme shook his head vigorously. "I have no qualms about taking what is offered, but I would never put lives in danger that way."

"Well, I remember years ago, during Prohibition, you said God meant for Americans to be drinking and you were only there to help."

"True."

"So you don't seem opposed to being God's agent."

"Of course. But, as to false lights, you can get that out of your head," said Jérôme. "I don't even own a cow."

After they had been walking about ten minutes, they came upon a partially buried wreck that had been washed up on the sand, probably during one of those storms that so often submerged the isthmus. What timbers remained of the wreck were completely buried by the sand, but a row of four iron bands—chainplates—protruded from the sand like grave markers. At the end of each was a deadeye, a flat disk with three holes through which standing rigging once ran. The holes—two above, one below—appeared to Marie-Lisette as the eyes and noses of dead men. Four corpses lost for all eternity on a tiny archipelago in a vast ocean, under a complete isolation of sky.

Against Marie-Lisette's will, tears formed in her eyes.

Chrétien asked, "What is it Marie-Lisette?" Creases formed a triangle on his forehead.

She was unable to answer. She shook her head from side to side.

Chrétien pulled her close and let her rest her head on his shoulder. He stroked her hair. "You're so sad. Why?"

Her chest heaved, her shoulders shuddered as she tried to catch her breath to answer him. Sputtering through sobs, she said at last, "Everything here … is … is … so dead!"

"But it's a dangerous isthmus, this Dune."

Marie-Lisette shook her head vigorously. "No. The whole … all of this place … the whole of Saint Pierre. The sea around us." She looked up at Jérôme, who was standing before her, for confirmation. But he had only a confused expression, as though he didn't know what to do. It was a hard look, and it made her only sadder. She pressed her head into Chrétien's shoulder, skewing her eyeglasses, feeling the heat of her tears as they slid down her cheeks.

Chrétien continued to stroke her hair. "Have a good cry for yourself," he said. "It's the best way."

"I feel so stupid. Why do I have to be so different from everybody else here? Madame Leclair seems happy on Saint Pierre."

"You ain't Madame Leclair, you're somebody else. Besides, how do you know Madame Leclair isn't just putting on a face?"

"I'm so lonely. I want to meet people like the ones I read about."

"What people?"

"The people in France who think big thoughts … and talk about them … and who go to concerts … and museums … and who fly in airplanes … and who … who …." A fresh surge of tears made her unable to finish.

"We'll help you find a way," said Chrétien. "We must definitely help you find a way."

"I feel like a child."

"You're no child. You're a bright young woman with ambitions. You shouldn't be ashamed of that."

She buried her face deeper into his shoulder. After a while, the tears subsided and Marie-Lisette started to feel that strange glow that so often comes after a good cry. A new warmth rose in her. She raised her eyes to Chrétien, adjusted her eyeglasses. "My father never let me cry like this."

"I'm sorry."

"He never held me like this."

Chrétien squeezed her shoulder.

"Thank you," she said through a sniffle.

Chrétien tightened his grip on her shoulder.

She told them about Jacques Bernis flying his France-America mail-plane over the deserts of North Africa and the cities of South America, places like Toulouse, Alicante, Port-Etienne, Dakar, Casablanca, Buenos Aires, Santiago. "These are the places I want to go," she said.

"Perhaps after the war."

"Those places don't exist," Jérôme suddenly said.

Marie-Lisette stared at him. Chrétien frowned. "What do you mean, 'don't exist'?"

Jérôme shook his head sadly. "Look out there. Do you see them? Can you touch them? The only thing that's real is this place and this sea. Marie-Lisette, you complained about Raymond Pineau smelling like fish. We *all* smell like fish. The sea is around us and inside of us; there's no escaping it. This is the truth we can't hide from."

Marie-Lisette and Chrétien had no answer so they gathered themselves in silence and made for the dory and set out for Saint Pierre. Marie-Lisette was drained of emotion by her tears. Despite what Jérôme had said, it was as though the monster of her isolation, that reared itself from time to time, had been put at bay—at least for a short while. They crossed the "Mouth of Hell" quickly with a following current and soon shuddered to a stop on Saint Pierre. After they secured Jérôme's motor dory on the pebbled beach, Marie-Lisette invited the two men to the Hotel Lalanne for cups of coffee. It was where Chrétien was staying anyway. "I'd suggest the Café Joinville for drinks, but women aren't allowed there," she said with a hint of resentment.

"Coffee will be fine," said Chrétien.

Over their coffees, Chrétien said he would be leaving soon for the States. "But I promise to return as soon as I can with at least some of the things you need. It's the least I can do for my friends."

"After all you plan to do for us," said Jérôme, "I hate to ask for more …."

"But there's something else. What is it?"

"As you've seen for yourself today, unless we can plant vines in rock and extract sunlight from fog, this is not wine-growing country. Our stocks of good wine are depleted and with *Le Celte* unable to make it through from France …."

"That's an easy one," Chrétien said with a laugh. "You shall have some good wine. Is California alright?"

Jérôme shrugged. "Who are we to complain?"

Indeed, thought Marie-Lisette, who are they to complain when, in France, their countrymen were experiencing the war firsthand. All the same, she would rather taste French wine again … but in France. Once more, the knot of despair at such a futile dream pulsed like an old wound. She knew it was only a matter of time before it became inflamed again.

It had felt so good making love to Jean-Luc that Adrienne wanted never to leave the room on the third floor of the Hotel Lalanne. Marie-Lisette had given them a corner room on the top floor, well removed from the usual traffic of the hotel. It was a small room with only a bed, a bureau with a ceramic water basin, a single straight-backed chair, and a faded print of a sailing schooner over the bedboard. The wallpaper, peeling in places, was a rose-colored pattern and lace curtains hung at the tiny dormer window. Their clothes sat commingled on the solitary chair. A late-season fly buzzed around the room, bumping repeatedly against the window.

Adrienne curled against Jean-Luc's body as he lay on his back smoking a cigarette. She watched the columns of blue smoke rise and spread out and took comfort in them. There was a way that Jean-Luc smoked, a way that he held the cigarette between the thumb and middle finger of his inverted right hand, a way that he exhaled that was, at least to her, unlike anybody else. She could feel she was, for the moment, at peace with the man she loved. But it wouldn't last. It never did and it never would until they escaped together back to France where they could be with each other permanently.

They had to talk.

"My husband's in jail," she said tentatively.

Jean-Luc turned to gaze at her, alarm written on his face. "Did he do something to you?"

"No, no ... well he tried, but I'm alright."

"What did he do?"

"The baby's alright, too."

"Thank God! What did he do?"

She explained what happened at Jérôme's house, being careful to refer to Jérôme as Monsieur Sabot. The fly made a circuit of the room then returned to the window. It resumed bouncing against the radiant illusion of an opening.

"Your husband's a crazy man. It's good he's locked up."

"But it's only for two months."

"That gives us two months to be together every day and night."

"But that's impossible."

"Why? Why is it impossible?"

"Don't you see? Everybody will know about us then."

"So, let them."

"My mother-in-law will know and she'll tell him. You can count on that."

"Perhaps it's best. Then everything will be in the open."

Adrienne shook her head. "He'll stew in jail thinking about it and the anger will grow and grow in him like steam in a kettle. When his two months are up ... well, who knows what will happen then?"

Jean-Luc placed his hand over Adrienne's bare belly. He kissed her breast. "I'll protect you and the baby, don't worry," he murmured against her flesh.

"The best way to do that would be to take us to France before I'm due."

"But we already talked about that. We can't return to France as long as the Vichy control Saint Pierre."

"Someplace else, then. Martinique."

Jean-Luc exhaled a stream of smoke and shook his head. "Also controlled by the Vichy. In fact, part of the Vichy fleet is there."

"America?"

"They're trying to get along with the Vichy. Besides, we have no passports. The same applies to Canada."

"What about de Gaulle? Didn't you say there were rumors he would liberate Saint Pierre?"

Jean-Luc nodded. "Yes. But as to when …."

"But what can we do?"

Jean-Luc put his arms around her. "We must wait. I can't risk taking you and the baby across without a convoy. The Germans are blasting everything out of the water."

"Oh, God …."

"We have to hope Saint Pierre is liberated and we can leave with the rest of the trawlers, under escort, to some neutral place such as Portugal. If conditions are right, we might even be able to make it into France … or at least England."

"But when?"

"I wish I could say." He held her close to him for a moment, then lay his head gently on her belly. "You two are so important to me."

Adrienne ran her fingers through his hair. "Do you know when the baby is due?"

"January?"

Adrienne shook her head. "Now the doctor says late November."

"Late November?"

"That's the same time my husband is released from jail."

Once more, the buzzing fly threw itself against the window.

Because Dave Lowe and Chrétien Bastarache had joined Jérôme in smuggling whiskey blanc to Newfoundland and Prince Edward Island, using the Electra to make more and faster deliveries, they always stayed at the Hotel Lalanne when they were not on a run. Thus, Marie-Lisette saw them often, frequently serving them coffee. And every chance she got, she made it clear in many subtle and not-so-subtle ways that she was interested in learning all she could about the Lockheed Electra 10A.

One morning, as she placed coffee cups on the table, she asked Dave, "Do you have a manual that tells you how to fly the plane?"

"Sure do," he replied.

"Do you think I could borrow it for a little while?"

"I'd be happy to let you borrow it, only it's not exactly a manual on how to fly the plane such that a beginner could read it, then go off flyin' without lots of lessons. It mainly tells an experienced pilot how this particular aircraft differs from other aircraft so you don't go and try to do somethin' that it ain't designed for."

"Oh, I see. I guess Amelia Earhart must have had lessons, then."

"Must have."

"Maybe she needed even more lessons," said Chrétien. "Didn't she crash a plane in Hawaii?"

Dave nodded. "Ground looped an Electra. In fact, the same plane that dropped me and Chrétien in on you folks and that now is sittin' out at the airstrip," he said to Marie-Lisette.

"Ground looped?" she asked.

"Instead of goin' straight down the runway, the plane started to drift to the right, she over-corrected and spun the plane almost an entire three-sixty. Anyway, that's what I read."

"How did she over-correct?"

"Well, I wasn't there so I can't say for sure, but the Electra is a tail dragger and—"

"—Tail dragger?"

"Means it has a wheel at the back of the fuselage instead of at the front."

"Why is that important?"

Dave smiled. "I think it's swell you have so many questions. It means the plane has a tendency to wander on takeoff or landing."

"Wander?"

"Has a mind of its own. If you ain't real skilled, the plane may refuse to go straight. Sorta like tryin' to drive a car real fast in reverse gear. Not particularly hard, but you gotta know how to do it and have practiced it."

"So you think the plane wandered on Amelia Earhart?"

"Yup. And the way to correct that is with the rudder. You kinda dance lightly on the pedals, little right, little left. Except in Earhart's case, she probably stomped on them, then hit them the other way too hard. Maybe she panicked."

"Does your manual tell you about all that? Not Amelia Earhart, of course, but about the tendencies of the aircraft." She felt a frisson of pleasure at her use of the professional-sounding word "aircraft."

He shook his head. "A little bit, maybe. But that ain't nearly enough."

"Why not?"

" 'Cause no book can push back on your hands like a yoke can, or press back on your ankles, or sink you into your seat, or rattle your teeth. You gotta fly for that. It's the only way you learn."

"I see," said Marie-Lisette. She fell silent, idly rearranging the sugar bowl and the salt and pepper shakers on the table.

"You still wanna borrow my manual?" asked Dave.

Marie-Lisette shrugged. "I guess."

Dave shot Chrétien a silent question. Chrétien nodded. Dave returned his gaze to Marie-Lisette and said, "But what you really want is some flyin' lessons."

Marie-Lisette looked into his eyes, afraid to say anything.

"What time to you start work tomorrow."

"Ten."

"Perfect! Can you be ready at seven o'clock for your first lesson?"

Marie-Lisette's eyes grew round. All she could say was, "Yes."

Marie-Lisette's knees shook as she slipped into the right hand seat of the Lockheed Electra.

She had spent hours the previous night reading Dave's copy of *A Pilot's Operating Handbook for the Electra 10A* under her bed covers. Now, she would get to experience in reality some of the sensations she had only been able to imagine.

"So let's see what we can do about teachin' you to fly this chariot," said Dave.

"Tell me what to do," said Marie-Lisette. "I promise I'll be a good student."

He held several sheets of paper out to her. "First, help me go through the checklist for takeoff. "Read me the items and make sure I respond correctly."

"Where do I start?" she asked.

"With the pre-start checklist."

"Okay," she replied. Then, trying to make her voice sound professional, she said, "Parking brakes set."

"Brakes set, check," Dave replied.

"Throttles idle."

"Idle, check."

They went quickly through several other checklists: startup, taxi, before take-off, then came to the take-off checklist. After completing it, Dave said, "Okay, here's how we're gonna work together at first. Put one hand on the yoke and one on the throttle, here. Don't do anything; just feel what I do with them during takeoff."

Her hands trembling with excitement, Marie-Lisette carefully placed them where he said.

"Good. Now put your feet on the rudder pedals and place your heels on the floor. Think of using your ankles to control the rudder. If you stomp on it with the weight of your legs, you'll way overdo it and only bad things will happen."

Marie-Lisette felt the throttles slide forward and she turned to watch Dave's hands.

"Notice how I keep my hands on the throttles?" Dave said. "That's 'cause I want to be ready in case we need to abort. Same thing applies on landing if we need to make a go around. Ready?"

Marie-Lisette nodded.

The engines roared. She looked up quickly to see the runway sliding past. She returned her gaze to Dave's hands. The plane gathered speed, lumbering down the runway. She felt the vibrations through her seat. The plane bounced several times on the rough runway. She saw the nose of the plane slide right. *Just like Amelia Earhart!* Her heart beat faster. Dave applied subtle pressure on the rudder and the nose swung back left until they were pointed straight down the runway. Then, suddenly, Marie-Lisette felt the plane lift from the runway and her eyebrows lifted in unison. A thrill passed through her. She shivered with joy as the plane climbed. She looked out the window and saw Saint Pierre slipping away under them. Moments later, the five-mile-long isthmus between Langlade and Grande Miquelon, slid beneath them. Still, they gained altitude. *Toulouse ... Dakar ... Casablanca ... Buenos Aires;* it was just as she imagined. They turned to the east and she saw crepuscular rays shooting through a broken layer of stratocumulus clouds. They splashed a circle of radiance on the blue ocean beneath them.

"Crepuscular rays always make me think of angels," she said.

"What rays?" asked Dave, bemused.

"Crepuscular."

"Criminy, you sure must read a lot! You even know words like that in English?"

"I look up every word I don't know."

Dave gestured toward the horizon. "That there what you're callin' crepuscular rays?"

"Yes."

"Hmm. I always called 'em 'fingers of God'."

As they flew out over the Atlantic south of the Burin Peninsular of Newfoundland, Dave let Marie-Lisette try a few small turns. "Be very gentle," he said. "It don't take much."

They spent more than two hours flying around with Dave frequently handing over the controls to Marie-Lisette while he, nevertheless, kept his own hands on his yoke. He let her bring the nose up and down with gentle climbs and descents.

"You like funny words," Dave said. "What we're doin' now is called fugoids. It's like bein' on a small roller coaster."

Marie-Lisette smiled at the sound of the word and repeated it silently to herself several times.

A half hour later, she studied Dave's actions and concentrated on the sensations communicated to her by the plane as Dave brought them in for a landing.

"Remember what I told you about this here plane bein' a tail dragger?" he asked.

"Yes."

"This is where you can go squirmin' all over the goddamned runway like a drunk if you ain't careful." But Dave managed to keep the plane tracked down the center of the runway. They glided to a gentle stop and Marie-Lisette took a deep, satisfied breath.

In the weeks that followed, Dave took Marie-Lisette flying at every opportunity. The only times she could not go up with him was when he and Chrétien were doing a run. Jérôme and Chrétien refused to involve her in their smuggling in case they should ever get caught.

There soon came a time when she began practicing takeoffs and landings. After more than two months of lessons, Dave said, "Criminy, you almost have enough hours for a certificate! You're sure gettin' good enough." His comment thrilled her and allowed her to think that someday she could be a bona fide pilot.

When Jérôme and Chrétien appeared at the Café Joinville Doctor Tréguy pulled them aside. "I called you here because there's a meeting in my office in ten minutes," he whispered.

"A meeting?" asked Jérôme. "What about?"

The doctor glanced from left to right. "Not here. I'll tell you then. Let's go."

They strode the two blocks to the doctor's office and when they arrived they found Colonel Lafitte sitting behind Doctor Tréguy's desk. "Have you told them?" Lafitte asked.

"No," replied Doctor Tréguy. "I thought you should do the honors."

"Told us what? What's this about?"

Instead of answering, Colonel Lafitte held out a sheaf of papers to Jérôme. Jérôme saw that they were blank except for an official-looking seal at the bottom of each sheet. "Do you know what that is?" Colonel Lafitte asked.

"A seal of some kind."

"It's de Bournat's official seal."

"How did you get it?"

Doctor Tréguy laughed. "Security isn't that tight here. What's there to protect?"

"But what do you plan to do with these papers? How does it involve me and Chrétien?"

"We are going to deliver a message to General de Gaulle," replied Colonel Lafitte. "Or, I should say, de Bournat is going to deliver the message, only he won't know it."

"And the message?" Jérôme asked, already knowing the answer.

"The good general will be informed that the Saint Pierrais are prepared to overthrow the Vichy regime and establish a government of Free French.

Count de Bournat will say that he will not resist a liberation and will change allegiance should the general decide to take action."

Chrétien let out a soft whistle. "That sounds like treason to me. At least your Vichy masters will see it that way."

"We see it as patriotism," said Colonel Lafitte.

Doctor Tréguy looked at each of them in turn, letting the implications of what Chrétien had said sink in. Then he said, "We not only have the seal. I also have copies of the good count's signature which, I'm proud to say, I've mastered."

Jérôme said, "This is very dangerous business."

"War is dangerous, Monsieur Sabot," said Colonel Lafitte. "And what do I care? I'm more than ninety years old. What can they do to me?"

"And as for me," said Doctor Tréguy, "Everyone knows I'm for Free French, always have been. Plus, I'm tired of not being able to do anything for all the people who come to me complaining of melancholy."

"But how do you plan to get this message to de Gaulle?" asked Chrétien. "You can't send it from here; everything's controlled by the Vichy."

"Ah, Monsieur Bastarache, but that's where you come in," said Lafitte.

Chrétien nodded. "I was afraid you were goin' to say that."

"You're leaving shortly. Would you be willing to travel to Washington and deliver the message to a representative of General de Gaulle?"

"How do you even know de Gaulle has a representative in Washington? Don't forget, the Americans are trying to make a go of it with the Vichy."

"Perhaps. But it's my bet that they're also smart enough to be in contact with de Gaulle, just in case."

"That may be, but it would be unofficial. What do you expect me to do—walk up to the State Department and say to Mister Hull, 'Can I please speak to the secret Free French representative'?"

"But surely, there must be a way to find him."

"There's a better way."

"What do you propose?"

"If you're going in for treason, why not go all the way? Take the message straight to de Gaulle himself."

"In London? You could do that?"

"If I pay my pilot enough, he's always up for a little adventure," Chrétien replied. "But that's assuming the airplane has the range." He turned to Doctor Tréguy. "Do you have an atlas?"

Doctor Tréguy went to his bookcase, withdrew a large book, and laid it on the desk. Chrétien flipped the pages until he found a map of the North Atlantic. As he studied it, the others remained silent. Finally, he said, "The plane has a range of eight hundred miles, not nearly enough to go directly from here to London. Besides, I think any plane approaching London would be shot down. However ..." He motioned for the others to look at the map with him. "If we can approach from the west, land in a remote area of Scotland, and go by road from there ...."

"They wouldn't think you were German."

"Exactly."

"But what about the range of your airplane?"

With his forefinger, Chrétien traced a line from Saint Pierre-Miquelon to Labrador, from there to Greenland, from Greenland to Iceland, and from Iceland to the Outer Hebrides. "We'll puddle jump. The longest leg—Greenland to Iceland—is a little over seven hundred miles. We'd just make it."

"But are you sure there are airstrips in all those places?"

"There are airstrips everywhere."

Colonel Lafitte rose from his chair, approached Chrétien, and placed a trembling hand on each of the man's shoulders. "You would do this for us?"

"When I arrived, I said I was here to help."

"You're a saint. We will supply you with a letter for General de Gaulle."

"Also," said Doctor Tréguy, "you'll have official letters authorizing your mission from de Bournat. We thought you should leave a letter with every official who questions you."

"What are these letters?"

The doctor laughed. "We don't actually know; we found some examples in the administrator's office and they looked official enough. Obviously, it will be impossible to get passports so you'll need something to get past the authorities, most of whom will be minor functionaries. We're hoping something so official-looking with a grand title like 'letter of authorization' for an emissary of the administrator of Saint Pierre-Miquelon will do the job."

"Why should we leave a letter with each person who questions us? Wouldn't it be better to keep them for later use?"

"We'll make plenty of copies," said Doctor Tréguy. "With all those letters out there as evidence of his treason, de Bournat will likely not think twice about joining us when the time comes."

"But there's another problem," Chrétien said.

"What's that?"

"Who will be the person to actually deliver the message into General de Gaulle's hands? It can't be me or Dave; we're Americans. Given the state of relations, de Gaulle would never believe us. It needs to be a citizen of Saint Pierre."

"I'll go," said Doctor Tréguy.

"It's admirable of you to offer," said Chrétien, "but it won't work. First, you're the only doctor here; you're needed. Second, forgive me, but you weigh too much. We need somebody light if we're not going to run into trouble on that Greenland to Iceland leg. Just a little too much head wind and we'd be swimming with the German submarines." He turned to Jérôme. "And before you say anything, you're too heavy, too. As it is, we're going to have to strip equipment from the plane and add containers of spare fuel to give us a safety margin. We can't be guaranteed there'll be fuel at the places where we stop and we can't re-fuel in mid air."

"Then who can go?"

Chrétien glanced at each of the men in turn, then said, "Someone who is smart; someone who commands respect; someone with courage; someone who is in love with the idea of flight and who can function as co-pilot. And, of course, someone who is light."

"Who?" asked Doctor Tréguy. "As if I didn't know."

"Yes, of course you know. It has to be Marie-Lisette Morel."

Jérôme stared at Chrétien. "What are you saying? It would be a dangerous journey. There's the weather; there's a war; you can't know what to expect. Besides, we already agreed it would be treason. You can't ask her to do that."

"You're right: it would be dangerous, and she must be told exactly how dangerous. But she's a grown woman and she must be allowed to make her own decisions. There's a war on. People must take extraordinary risks in war."

12 Grand Circle Flight

WHEN THEY TOLD Marie-Lisette of the consequences they would all face if the Vichy authorities discovered their treasonous plan, plus the physical dangers of flying to Europe in the northern latitudes, a danger enhanced by the presence of war, Marie-Lisette didn't hesitate for a moment. Thus it was that a little before sunrise two days later a group of six people stood between Doctor Tréguy's idling Citroën Deux Cheveaux and the Lockheed Electra, whose aluminum fuselage reflected the fingernail sliver of sunlight that was rising above the horizon.

"Don't take any unnecessary risks," said Doctor Tréguy.

"Too late for cautions, Doc," said Chrétien. "As soon as this plane gets airborne, we're committed."

"Well, just be careful."

"And make sure to salute General de Gaulle when you get to London," said Auguste Lafitte. "We military types like that."

"Doctor Tréguy is right," Jérôme said to Marie-Lisette. "Don't try to be a hero."

"We'll be fine," she replied.

Chrétien said, "Enough discussion. Time to go." He, Marie-Lisette and Dave Lowe climbed aboard the Electra and, moments later, the plane hurtled down the airstrip and its nose lifted and the wheels left the ground. Marie-Lisette concentrated on every sensation the plane was communicating to her through the yoke. Straining as if to shake itself of annoying rivets, the plane lumbered into the sky and Marie-Lisette felt Dave turn the yoke to the left and they made a long, looping turn until it they were heading south.

If anybody was watching from below, they would have reason to believe the story that Doctor Tréguy had conceived to explain Marie-Lisette's absence: that because of her fascination with flying and her recent lessons, Chrétien Bastarache had offered to fly her to Maine and back. It was a reward for her efforts to marshal the cars and trucks to light the airstrip when he had difficulty landing in the fog.

Marie-Lisette turned to smile at Dave. But instead of smiling, she frowned. "Was that a difficult takeoff?" she asked.

"Of course not," Dave replied. "Why do you ask?"

"You're sweating."

"It's the heat in this damned cockpit."

Marie-Lisette gazed at him a long moment. She was confused because her fingers were numb with cold. Then she shrugged it off with the thought that different people had different temperature tolerances.

As soon as they were well clear of the archipelago, Dave made a one-hundred-and-eighty degree turn and settled on a course slightly west of north, heading for Goose Bay, Labrador. At first it seemed strange to Marie-Lisette that they would start out flying in that direction when London was to the east, but when she studied the charts she saw that it was the route that offered the most fuel stops and was also most closely on the great circle route to Britain. Also, their first stop in Britain, the Isle of Benbecula, was more than ten degrees of latitude further north than Saint Pierre.

As they gained altitude, Marie-Lisette saw the rim of the sun swell on the horizon, a sight Jacques Bernis must have witnessed countless times. When they leveled off, the engines settled into a modulating harmonic drone that seemed to mirror the surge of blood through Marie-Lisette's veins. Soon, they were over the fractured southern coast of Newfoundland and shortly afterwards they were again over water. Marie-Lisette knew this was the eastern embayment of the Gulf of Saint Lawrence and that, further to her right where it squeezed between Newfoundland and Labrador, was the Strait of Belle Isle.

She'd memorized their destinations: Goose Bay; Narsarsuaq; Reykjavik; Faroe Islands; Benbecula; Glasgow; London. It wasn't Toulouse, Alicante, Port-Etienne, Dakar, Casablanca, but for her, their destinations held equal excitement. She was still flushed with it an hour later as they prepared for landing. They descended quickly over the eroded green and brown glacial hills of Labrador into Goose Bay where, as part of the lend-lease arrangement with Great Britain, the United States was building an air base.

"I know a man who's working on it," Chrétien said, leaning into the cockpit from the main fuselage. "It's being built by a Canadian corporation for the air force."

"*Being* built?" asked Dave.

"Yuh. We better hope they've made good progress."

When they found the airstrip at the foot of Lake Melville, they descended to a few hundred feet to do a fly-by, surveying the area before landing. They flew over what seemed a long, narrow scar on the land that had pieces of construction equipment squatting along its edges. They were low enough to see workers gazing up at them.

"The strip's been cleared, but it has no surface," said Dave. "We better hope that's not mud."

They made a long, looping circle before lining up for the tiny airstrip.

"Okay," said Dave, "time to read the landing checklist."

Marie-Lisette reached for the papers and started to read the items. "Landing gear down."

She felt a heavy jolt when Dave lowered the landing gear. "Check, down. Three green."

"Speed eighty," she said.

"Speed eighty, check."

Moments later, they were bouncing along the ground. To their relief, although rough, the surface seemed to be solid. "Probably frozen," said Dave.

The Electra came to a stop and they climbed down from the plane to be greeted by several men. One of them, a slight man with a mustache who appeared to be in charge, asked, "What the hell do you folks think you're doing? This airstrip ain't finished."

"Yuh, we could tell that," replied Chrétien.

"I asked you a question: What the hell are you doing?"

Marie-Lisette was startled to hear Chrétien say, assertively, "Can't tell you that."

"What the hell do you mean, you can't tell me?"

Chrétien proffered one of the letters of authorization. "Here, maybe this will help."

The man took the letter and read it quickly. "I don't understand what this is," he said.

"It says we are emissaries on a secret mission for the administrator of Saint Pierre-Miquelon. It guarantees us safe passage."

The man paused before asking, "Where are you headed?"

"East."

"Toward the war?"

Chrétien shrugged. "Do you have fuel?"

"We got fuel for our equipment, probably not for that thing. What's it take?"

"Ninety-five, ninety-eight octane."

"Not a chance," the man replied sullenly.

"Then we'll just dump in some of our reserves and be on our way." Chrétien turned his back on the man and said to Dave, "Let's top off and leave these folks to their work."

In all, they used four 50-liter Jerry cans to top off the fuel before taking off in front of the curious gazes of the assembled work crew. As they taxied, Marie-Lisette saw the supervisor staring at them, the letter of authorization fluttering in his hand from the propeller backwash.

The flight to Narsarsuaq was uneventful and soon Marie-Lisette, looking down through the side window, saw that the sea was mottled with broken ice, an unhappy reminder of what was in store for her archipelago in a short time when the Baffin Current delivered its load of drift ice. As she held the yoke, she heard a change in the tone of the engines and felt the plane descending. She made a rapid sweep of the instruments with her eyes then raised her gaze to look out the windshield. Before them was the huge land mass of Greenland totally covered with snow except for a ragged green-brown fringe where the land plunged into the sea.

They soon found the airstrip tucked in a valley that was surrounded by glacial fingers descending from the high plateau of the central ice cap. The airstrip, although clearly outlined, appeared white—not the black surface Marie-Lisette had expected.

"Probably rolled snow," said Dave. "It'll be fine."

As at Goose Bay, they made a low pass over the airstrip before circling around and landing. Like before, Marie-Lisette concentrated on the feel of the yoke as Dave maneuvered onto the landing strip. Before they took off on the trip Dave said that he would do all the take-offs and landings because they would be dealing with unfamiliar airstrips. Marie-Lisette was disappointed, but she understood his reasoning.

Once again, they found themselves surrounded by construction equipment and workers.

"Seems everybody is building airstrips these days for the war," said Chrétien.

"Or else, they're building 'em for us," Dave replied with a chuckle. "Maybe every place we go they'll have just laid out a runway for us."

"Yuh, except these guys ain't civilian workers like at Goose Bay. Those are American Air Force guys. This may be a little more difficult."

No one came out to meet them and they had to walk several hundred yards to a small shack before which stood a clutch of men in uniforms. By the time they arrived, Dave was breathing heavily.

"Are you okay?" asked Marie-Lisette.

He dismissed her concern with a wave of his hand. "No problem. Just a little out of shape."

Chrétien approached a tall man who wore the twin bars of a captain. "You're wondering who the hell we are," he said. "Perhaps this will explain." He handed the captain the authorization letter.

The man read the letter quickly and accepted it without question. He offered them a place to stay for the night. "You'll want to be rested before getting on with your mission," he said. "The food ain't great, but we have some beer."

"That's real kind of you, Captain …."

"LeBlanc," the man said with a smile. "My father emigrated to the states from Newfoundland. I know Saint Pierre well."

They took off at 3:00 a.m. the following morning for the long, five-hour flight to Iceland. The moon, a day past full, glinted on the wings as they gained altitude. "I can't believe this great weather," said Dave.

"It's the Bastarache luck," Chrétien replied.

They flew north, skirting the western shore of Greenland, before finally turning east toward Iceland. Marie-Lisette gazed out at the panoply of stars that shone more brilliantly than she'd ever seen them. Dave brought the plane down to a few hundred feet over the water because he was worried about ice that was beginning to form on the wings. Marie-Lisette, huddled in her heavy overcoat, wrapped her arms around herself. Her teeth chattered. Out the left hand window, she saw nothing but an endless vista of snow and ice, and through the opposite window, the immensity of the sea. She thought of her little archipelago and hoped that when they arrived in Scotland she would at last see some soft green earth below them. Warm earth.

The engines droned.

Marie-Lisette dozed.

In her half sleep she imagined persuading Doctor Tréguy, Jérôme Sabot, and others on Saint Pierre to organize a committee for the purpose of buying a plane which she could then fly to provide better mail service for Saint Pierre.

Suddenly, her body lurched forward violently and she was startled awake.

From behind her she heard Chrétien shout, "What the hell is goin' on?" He stumbled downhill into the cockpit.

Marie-Lisette saw Dave slumped against the yoke which was angled forward. She realized they were in a steep dive. She grabbed the yoke and pulled back. But it wouldn't budge. "We have to get him off the yoke!" she cried. She leaned to her left and, grabbed Dave's shirt sleeve, and tugged hard. Reaching across the cockpit, without leverage, she found he was too heavy for her to move. "I can't pull back on the yoke!" she cried over her shoulder to Chrétien.

Chrétien wrapped his arms around Dave's chest and heaved back against the pull of gravity of their plunge toward the ocean. His face flushed with the effort. He failed. He gathered his breath and launched himself backward. At last, he managed to haul Dave back upright in the pilot's seat.

Marie-Lisette pulled back on the yoke. The airframe was shaking violently. Marie-Lisette's arms shook in sympathy. "Don't pull back too hard," she coached herself. "Easy! Easy! Don't overcorrect! Watch out for flutter!" A harmonic buzz passed through the airframe. "No flutter!" Marie-Lisette shouted as she eased the pressure on the yoke.

"I think Dave's dead," said Chrétien.

Marie-Lisette scanned the instruments. "No, both engines are running."

"You didn't hear me," Chrétien said. "Dave is dead. Can you fly this thing?"

She didn't answer immediately. Instead, she concentrated on what the plane was telling her. Slowly the nose came up. The frightening buzz had disappeared. The cockpit window was no longer filled with the sea; slowly, a horizon appeared. Finally, she was able to level the plane off and hold a level flight.

"Marie-Lisette," Chrétien asked in a loud voice. "I asked you if you can fly this thing."

"I think so. Yes, yes I think so," she replied. "But I'd prefer to watch Dave land a few more times before I do it."

"Didn't you hear me before? Dave is dead. I think it's a heart attack."

Marie-Lisette gasped and looked over to Dave whose face was ashen.

Jérôme lay on his small bed staring at the flaking ceiling and sniffing the sea air that insinuated itself through the cracks of his house. He tried to think why he'd been so disturbed when Marie-Lisette broke down and cried on the Dune. Part of it was that he had been so helpless, staring at her, unable to console her the way Chrétien had. But the sight of the chainplates with their staring deadeyes had also shaken him to his soul. He rolled his head on the pillow and looked towards Antoine's trench coat. "We saw men like that in France, you and me, Antoine. So many men. Propped up on the barbed wire." A tear slithered down his cheek and soaked into the pillow. "It's the sea, Antoine, it's this damned sea that surrounds us. It creates fog; it feeds the clouds that bring snow and ice. It's in our souls, this sea; it's what separates us. But can we ever escape it? No. Not even deep in France, especially in France."

But it was when Marie-Lisette said how lonely she was that he felt as though someone had punched him in the chest. For the first time in a long time he had been confronted squarely with his own loneliness on this sea-surrounded island. It had been festering inside him ever since Adrienne, with her offer of friendship, had stirred it up. And now that Claude Cormier was, at least for the moment, out of the way, the very possibility of being with Adrienne, of ending his loneliness, of living once again, made it all the more biting.

He loved Adrienne.

For the first time, he had to admit it to himself. And he made it public by admitting it also to Antoine's trench coat. "I love that woman," he said. "I love her more than I've loved anyone … except you, my dear friend. She is the only person I've been able to talk with since the war. It's amazing, but I've even been able to tell her about some of the things you and I saw and did—all the killing, all the dead men, all the trenches. And it helped. Perhaps, sometime I'll be able to tell her about that day … that day you …." A sob wracked his body. "I'm so sorry, Antoine."

He remembered what Claude Cormier had said: that Adrienne was pregnant. Can it be true she is going to have a baby? If Claude was the father of a child, would he make it even more impossible for someone to take Adrienne from him? Would that put an end to Jérôme's dream?

He continued to sob.

For Antoine.

For all they had seen.

For his own loneliness.

And when he finished sobbing, he vowed he would do whatever it took to make Adrienne his.

"You're gonna have to land this airplane, Marie-Lisette," Chrétien said when he returned to the cockpit after dragging Dave's body back into the main cabin. "We have no other choice."

"But what about navigation? Dave was doing all of that."

"I can navigate a boat and I know how an RDF works. I'll have to use what I know."

She gave him a skeptical look.

"There's nothing more we can do," he said, replying to her unspoken question. "Now pass me his clipboard."

Marie-Lisette, who had shifted to the left seat on Chrétien's suggestion, handed him the clipboard. He studied it for a few moments then said, "It looks like we're approaching Reykjavik now. I'm gonna get on the RDF. You better start thinking about how you're gonna land this thing."

Marie-Lisette wanted to grasp the yoke like it was a handhold preventing a fall from a cliff. She concentrated on relaxing her grip, knowing instinctively that she and the plane would perform better as a single being if she was as gentle with it as she was with an obedient horse. Her gaze shifted several times between the artificial horizon in the center of the instrument panel and the real horizon before she satisfied herself that she could trust the instrument. Lower, and to the left, the turn indicator also reported a level flight. Just above it was the airspeed indicator which she checked repeatedly though it held steady at one-hundred-and-eighty-fifty knots. She also scanned the engine instruments frequently—temperature, manifold pressure, fuel levels, tachometer—until she was satisfied that the steady throb she heard truly did indicate that the twin Pratt & Whitney R-985s were performing smoothly. She was so busy, she failed to notice that Chrétien had climbed into the seat beside her.

"Can you bring us down close to the water?" he asked.

Marie-Lisette snapped her head to the right. "What?"

"Bring us down close to the water; can you do it?"

"I suppose. But why?"

"You're not gonna like the answer."

"What do you mean?"

"If we drop out of the sky with a dead body aboard, there's bound to be an investigation. There's too much of a risk they'd turn us around."

"What are you saying?" she asked.

Instead of answering, he just stared into her eyes.

Creases formed on her forehead. "You don't mean ...."

"It has to be done. Otherwise we risk the entire mission."

"But ...."

"Look, you're an air Jane; that, right there, is gonna raise some questions."

"What's an air Jane; I don't know that expression."

"It's American for a girl aviator. Not only that, you're age is gonna lift some eyebrows. It's just you and me; they're gonna think we're cookin' with stardust."

"What?"

"In love. They may arrest me for robbin' the cradle."

"I'll say you're my uncle. But do we really have to—"

"—Marie-Lisette, everybody on Saint Pierre is depending on us."

For a long while, Marie-Lisette said nothing. Finally, she eased the yoke gently forward and the nose dipped and they began a slow descent toward the ocean.

Chrétien rose from the co-pilot's seat. "I'll give a shout before I open the door. I don't know what it will feel like on the yoke. You might have to make some corrections." He returned to the main cabin.

Marie-Lisette felt the tears slide down her cheeks as she monitored the instruments for their descent. Several minutes later she shouted back, "How low?"

"Couple hundred feet."

She glanced at the altimeter to the right of the artificial horizon. It read four hundred feet. She eased the yoke forward and continued to watch the altimeter. When it reached three hundred feet, she was afraid to go any lower. She bottomed out the descent and shouted over her shoulder, "Three hundred; that's as low as I want to go."

There was a brief pause, then Chrétien shouted back, "That will be good." Seconds later, he shouted, "Opening the door!"

Marie-Lisette felt a sudden drag that wanted to bank the plane to the left. She corrected for it. Behind her, she heard the roar of wind through the open door. After what seemed an eternity, the sound stopped and the pressure on the yoke eased. Chrétien returned to the cockpit and slipped into the co-pilot's seat.

Marie-Lisette slowly climbed back up to a thousand feet, remembering that Dave had said they should fly low to avoid ice buildup on the wings. During the climb, and for at least ten minutes after they leveled off, neither of them spoke. Finally, Chrétien said, "You're angry with me."

"No, not really."

"Yes you are. You're all hot and bothered."

"You're much older than me," said Marie-Lisette. "I have to assume you're right."

"If you're saying that my age gives me a different perspective, you're correct. But it's not what you think it is. I was pretty certain about things when I was younger; say, when I was about your age. Now, I'm not as certain. But when I make a choice, as I did today, I realize that although I can't be certain it's the right thing to do, I also realize it's the best I can do if I'm honest with myself. Does that make sense to you?"

"I suppose," Marie-Lisette replied.

They flew on for another hour in silence. At last, Chrétien said, "If my calculations are right, we should be picking up radio signals from Reykjavik any time now. Are you ready to land this thing?"

"I'll need you to read the landing checklist to me."

He looked at her for a moment, then went aft in the plane. Moments later, he returned with a roll of cellulose tape. He taped the checklist to Marie-Lisette's yoke. "You'll have to read it to yourself. I'm gonna stay on the RDF."

A half hour later, Chrétien muttered, "Criminy!"

"What?"

"Look to your right."

Marie-Lisette looked. "It's land!"

"Not just any land; that's Iceland! Look straight ahead."

Marie-Lisette squinted into the haze. The sun was still low in the east over the land.

"See it?" Chrétien asked. "Them buildin's? That, there, is Reykjavik."

"Yes, I see it!" cried Marie-Lisette. "Your navigation was perfect!"

"You shred it, wheat!"

Marie-Lisette frowned. She'd never heard that expression before. But there was no time to wonder about it. Her hands began to tremble a little. She had become accustomed to flying the plane, but now she was about to do something she had never done before: land on a foreign airstrip. The only experience of landing she had was at Saint Pierre.

She began to read the approach checklist.

"Landing lights … landing lights on, check … flaps … flaps set one … speed one hundred and five … one hundred and five, check."

"I didn't think it would be this clear," said Chrétien. "We don't need the RDF; I can read the list to you."

Marie-Lisette shook her head. "No. It may be zero visibility next time. We should practice."

Chrétien smiled.

Marie-Lisette continued. "Landing gear … landing gear down …." She felt the thunk as the landing gear locked in place. "Three green. Flaps … elevator trim tab …." She lined up on the runway. She backed off on the throttle. She opened her eyes and her mouth wide as the plane sank. She sucked in her breath. The plane continued to sink. It seemed suspended in air, suspended in time. Then it hit the tarmac hard, bounced, hovered for an instant, hit again and this time stayed on the ground as if it had taken over the controls to save itself. Marie-Lisette retracted the flaps, hit the brakes, and the plane slowly rolled to a stop.

The airfield was teeming with British and American warplanes. "It looks like we're about to enter the war," Chrétien said. "Last year, the Brits invaded Iceland, and this year the Americans took over. Nobody wants the Germans to be here. Too close to the Atlantic shipping lanes."

Marie-Lisette said, "I have a terrible feeling our so-called authorization papers are about to be tested for real."

"Yuh, I think you're right," Chrétien replied. "Good thing we …. Well, you know."

"I suppose," she replied.

Upon disembarking the plane, they were met by an American colonel who demanded to know who they were and what they were doing. When the letter of authorization didn't seem to appease him, Chrétien invited him to board the plane and look around. "You won't find anything except spare fuel. No weapons; nothin' at all." He gestured to Marie-Lisette. "Do we look like spies or enemy combatants to you?" When the man still seemed skeptical, Chrétien added, "Look, all we want to do is re-fuel and be off. We'll be gone in an hour and you won't know we've ever been here. If you stop us, on the other hand, it could cause a real international mess. Things between us Americans, the Vichy, and the Free French are real delicate. Are you willing to risk upsetting things?" He paused, then added, "Would some good whiskey help?"

At last, Chrétien seemed to have captured the man's interest. "Whiskey?"

"Search the plane. Satisfy yourself there ain't nothin' that shouldn't be there. And if you happen to find a case of whisky, we won't resist if you confiscate it."

Ten minutes later, the man emerged from the plane carrying a wooden case. He smiled at Chrétien and said, "Listen, if you're going to the continent you better tell me exactly where you're going. I can radio ahead and get you clearance. You don't want those RAF guys shooting you out of the sky."

"We're going to the Faroe Islands, then Benbecula in the Outer Hebrides, then on to Glasgow. From there, we'll go by land to London."

The colonel nodded. "I'll radio ahead to the Brits in the Faroe Islands, Benbecula and Glasgow. But when you get to each place, you'd better have them repeat the message down the line, especially to Glasgow. The Krauts were bombing there just a few months ago and you don't want the air defenses to think you're German."

"You're most kind, Colonel."

"Are you returning by the same route?"

Chrétien smiled. "Given the war, I don't know if they have whiskey, but if I can I'll bring you some."

An hour later, Marie-Lisette made her first takeoff without Dave and was thrilled when they climbed smoothly into the sky. She leveled off at three hundred feet. "Your course is east-northeast, seventy degrees magnetic, for now" said Chrétien, looking up from his clipboard. "I think that will adjust for the wind direction, near as I can tell. When we get closer the RDF will guide us in."

Several hours later, they made a quick stop for refueling at the Faroe Islands then took off for Benbecula and finally for Glasgow. Marie-Lisette was proving to be a quick learner and her landings and takeoffs were getting progressively better.

They arrived safely in the Glasgow vicinity late that afternoon. Using the radio direction finder, Chrétien called for a few minor course corrections and they soon saw the runway. After Marie-Lisette executed another smooth landing, an officer ushered them into an office at the airport where they were questioned extensively about their intentions. Once again, Doctor Tréguy's forged authorization papers did the trick and Chrétien and Marie-Lisette were cleared to go on to London.

After thanking the bespectacled airport official, Chrétien asked, "Any suggestions on how we get to London? Train?"

The man shook his head. "It's bloody tough to travel by train these days. And motor car is out because of the rationing on fuel. Your best bet is a motorcycle with a sidecar."

"Do you have any idea where I can get one?"

"How long will you be, Mate?"

"No more than one or two days."

"It so happens, then, I have just such a motorcycle. It's a nineteen-thirty BSA that's seen its day, but it'll get you there. What would you be willing to exchange for its use? Do you have any American cigarettes?"

"In the plane," Chrétien replied. "How about I give you two packs?"

"Four."

"Three."

"Done," the man said gleefully.

As they were preparing to leave, the man pressed several leaflets upon them. "Mind you, read these; they're important. And you will observe the headlight is tilted down and has a cover. Regulations. Mind you don't use any other lights. Follow the white center line they painted to help motorists at night. Lucky for you, there's plenty of moonlight."

Chrétien glanced at the leaflets from the Civil Defence: "Your Gas Mask: How to keep it, How to use it", "Masking Your Windows", and "Your Food in War-Time." Thus armed with the cautionary advice of the Lord Privy's Office of the British Government, they climbed aboard the motorcycle and set off for London, Chrétien astride the driver's seat and Marie-Lisette in the sidecar.

They rode through the night with only a few rest stops. When they stopped in Coventry, Marie-Lisette said, "London's a big place. How do we find where General de Gaulle is staying?"

Chrétien replied, distractedly. "We ask around." He walked toward a pile of rubble. Beyond the pile was the shell of what used to be Coventry Cathedral. The roof was completely gone. The east wall, with the apse stood starkly against a brightening sky. "This is Coventry Cathedral," he said to Marie-Lisette. "I was here back in thirty-one. Cripes, they sure wrecked the place, the bastards!"

"Do you think it's like this in London?"

Chrétien nodded. "Probably worse from what I've heard."

It was mid morning when they pulled to a stop alongside Green Park opposite Buckingham Palace. The low sun flooded the walls of the palace with golden light. Marie-Lisette was awestruck. She had never seen anything so magnificent. It was especially impressive after they had passed through streets littered with debris from buildings destroyed by the blitz.

"Should we go in and ask the king where he's keeping the good general?" asked Chrétien.

Marie-Lisette laughed. "What about asking a taxi driver instead? I've never seen so many of them."

"Excellent idea."

"There are more taxi drivers here than there are people in Saint Pierre."

The first man they asked, said, "The bloody French bloke? Can't say he's kept me informed of his whereabouts."

Several other taxi drivers near Buckingham Palace either didn't know or refused to answer, one saying, "We're bloody well careful about loose lips here."

Finally, near Marble Arch, after asking yet a dozen more drivers, they found one who said, "Just yesterday I took some mucky-muck Frenchies to a place near Regent's Park. I'm guessing that's where the man is. One Dorset Square it was."

After getting directions from him, they found Balcombe Street and turned right onto Dorset Square. There was a guard standing at the doorway to 1 Dorset Square. Chrétien approached the man and said, "Good morning, Sir. We're here to see General de Gaulle."

The man raised his eyebrows, went inside, and emerged a moment later with another man. The second man said, "You say you want to see the general? About what?"

"We have a letter. It's for his eyes only."

"I'm his personal secretary. You may give it to me."

"Sorry, Sir. But our instructions from the Vichy administrator of Saint Pierre and Miquelon say to give the letter personally to the general."

"The Vichy administrator of Saint Pierre and Miquelon?"

"Yuh. The very fellow himself."

The man studied them for a moment then said, "Wait here."

They waited five minutes before the man reappeared and said, "Follow me." He ushered them through a corridor and into a spacious room with high ceilings and large windows. Bordering the windows were rich curtains. A desk stood in front of the windows and, off to the side, a flag stand. The flag was the traditional tricolor of blue, white, and red except that in the center of the white stripe was a red Cross of Lorraine. It was the flag of the Free French. Moments after they entered the room, the leader of the Free French appeared through another door. He stopped before them, standing rigidly upright to his full, impressive height. His hands were clasped behind his back and he gazed expectantly at them, his Gallic nose like the prow of a ship. "You are American?" he asked Chrétien.

"Yes, sir, but my family is from Acadia. And Marie-Lisette here is Saint Pierrais.

"Yes, the general said to Chrétien, "you have a French-Canadian accent."

He turned and studied Marie-Lisette for a moment before saying, "You have a communiqué for me."

Marie-Lisette took two steps toward the general and attempted a curtsy. The beginning of a smile formed on de Gaulle's lips. He extended his hand. Marie-Lisette held the letter out to him and he, in turn, gave it to his secretary. "Read it."

The secretary tore the envelope open, unfolded the single sheet, and read, "'To General Charles de Gaulle from Count Gilbert de Bournat, administrator of Saint Pierre and Miquelon, greetings. Top secret. I wish to inform the general that, should he deem it wise to liberate Saint Pierre and Miquelon, he will not encounter any resistance. We are a small, peaceful people and wish nothing more than to be allowed to live our lives without oppression and we recognize that you represent the true France. *Viva la France!*'" The secretary folded the letter and stuffed it back into the envelope. "That is all, *Mon General.*"

"That is all? Such a brief offer of surrender?" de Gaulle asked. He turned to Chrétien and Marie-Lisette. "Does Count de Bournat understand that he would be executed for treason if his Vichy overlords learned of this?"

Marie-Lisette swallowed hard.

Chrétien said, "Perhaps that's why he made it top secret."

The incipient smile appeared again, "Yes, just so." He turned, hands behind his back, and gazed out the window for a moment before abruptly turning and saying, "Thank you for your efforts. I wish you a safe return journey."

Chrétien and Marie-Lisette stared at him.

"Jacques, please show them out."

Bemused and crestfallen, they followed the secretary out into Dorset Square. Marie-Lisette was just about to climb into the sidecar when she paused, then bolted back toward the building.

De Gaulle's secretary chased after her. "Mademoiselle! You can't go in there."

Marie-Lisette ignored him and pushed past the startled guard. She ran along the corridor and burst through the general's door. De Gaulle, bent over papers at his desk, looked up.

"Mon General," Marie-Lisette said, "you must permit me to say more."

The secretary appeared, breathing hard. "Mademoiselle, you must leave." He grabbed her left arm.

Marie-Lisette pulled her arm free and approached de Gaulle who gazed at her with an amused expression. "The people on Saint Pierre long for liberation," Marie-Lisette said. "Colonel Lafitte—but he's not a colonel; he's really only a private from the war with the Prussians— Colonel Lafitte is more than ninety years old and he won't give up until the Germans are defeated and France and Saint Pierre are free."

"Mademoiselle!" the secretary said insistently as he approached her again.

She stepped away from him. "Even today, *even today*, if you called for him he would come to you ready to fight. And Jérôme Sabot: he fought in the Great War against the Germans and something terrible happened to him …. And there's Doctor Tréguy who is unhappy because he has nothing to offer all his patients who come to him because of their melancholy that Le Celte cannot make it through with all the wonderful things that remind us of France."

"Mademoiselle, I must insist!"

De Gaulle held a restraining hand up to his secretary.

"And Madame Leclair needs more books for the library, and Madame Cormier needs facial cream, and Monsieur Pichot needs goods for his shop so he can sell people what they need, and Madame Imatz says she is running out of pernod at the cafe and that would be a disaster for the men, and Jean-Luc Lavedan needs to be able to take his fishing boat to France so he and Madame …." Marie-Lisette brought a hand to her mouth. "Oh, I'm sorry, but that's a secret."

"I see," said de Gaulle.

Marie-Lisette, exhausted, gave de Gaulle a pleading stare, then offered an awkward curtsy and turned to leave. As she reached the door, de Gaulle asked, "And you, Mademoiselle? What do you want?"

Marie-Lisette stared at him. She shook her head as if to say she could think of nothing.

"I thought as much," the general said.

Marie-Lisette turned back toward the door, paused, turned back again, and said, "After the war, I would like to go to the University of Toulouse."

"Toulouse? Why not the Sorbonne?"

"Because Toulouse is where Jacques Bernis was based."

De Gaulle gave her a bemused look as she bowed again, and left. She found Chrétien waiting for her at the curb and they mounted the motorcycle and headed back to Glasgow in silence.

Marie-Lisette and Chrétien could scarcely believe their luck. All along the return journey through Scotland, the Faroe Islands, Iceland, Greenland, Labrador and Newfoundland, the weather was perfect with light upper level winds and unlimited visibility the whole way.

"That's the Bastarache luck for you," Chrétien said as they lifted off from Goose Bay, Newfoundland for the final five-hundred-mile leg to Saint Pierre.

The weather remained perfect for the first two hours and forty-five minutes of the expected three hours of the flight. Then as they began their descent over Fortune Bay, Newfoundland and corrected their course, since they had drifted several miles eastward of the rhumb line course, Marie-Lisette said, "I don't see Langlade. We should see Langlade from here."

Chrétien lifted his eyes from his clipboard and peered out the right hand window of the cockpit. Instead of the hazy green hills of Miquelon-Langlade, he saw nothing but a canopy of white, a dome of fog. He turned to look out the opposite window. "It's clear to the east. I can even make out some of the buildings in Fortune."

"But look ahead," replied Marie-Lisette. "Shouldn't we be able to see Saint Pierre by now?"

Chrétien glanced down at his clipboard. "I have us about twenty miles out. We should definitely see it."

"Well, I don't."

Ahead of them was nothing but an undifferentiated whiteness.

"*Merde!* This place has not been kind to me."

"You made it down last time." It came out with less assertiveness than Marie-Lisette had wanted.

"Only because of you, but now you're up here with me."

"So we'll do the same thing you and Dave did."

"What's that?" Chrétien asked.

"We'll fly low so they hear us." Marie-Lisette spoke bravely, but she couldn't deny the terror she felt. She had never before flown blind. She desperately wanted to stay where they were at four hundred feet, where the sky was cobalt blue and the sun glinted off their wings. But of course they didn't have the fuel for that; they had to descend into the murkiness … and hope.

Marie-Lisette gazed at the instrument panel. Was she brave enough to trust the various instruments? She had read about the phenomenon of pilots, in zero visibility, flying upside down without knowing it. What if she became disoriented and did that?

What if she intended to decrease altitude and instead climbed briefly and stalled? And if she did somehow invert the plane, would the fuel slip to the top of the tank and starve the engines? Would the oil flow to the top of the engines and cause them to seize? They were questions she would love to have asked Dave.

She blinked her eyes several times and focused on the altimeter: four-hundred-seventy feet; the artificial horizon: level (but level to what?); airspeed: one-eighty-five; compass: one-eighty-five. *Wait! How can they be the same? She thought: I'm reading it wrong!* She double checked. The airspeed indicator did, indeed, read one-hundred-eighty five. She looked at the compass: one-eighty-five. "What should our heading be?" she asked.

"Just slightly west of dead south, replied Chrétien.

"One eighty?"

"More like one-eighty-five."

Coincidence!

She nudged the throttle back a little until the airspeed read one-seventy-five.

"We have to go in," said Chrétien. "We have no choice."

"I know." She turned to look at him. "Mister Bastarache, please, I'd feel a lot better if you read the checklist to me."

He smiled. "Of course." He reached across her to remove the checklist from the yoke. "Descent speed: one-forty."

"One-forty. Check." She eased back on the throttles and the plane began to sink. She checked the barometric setting in the Kollsman window of the altimeter. It was set at twenty-nine point nine. As she had the whole trip, she worried that she wasn't totally sure how to set this to the proper pressure; a fact she'd kept from Chrétien. But it affects the accuracy of the altimeter reading which, until now, she hadn't needed to rely upon because she'd always had excellent visibility. Now, she watched the hands of the altimeter move counter-clockwise around the face of the altimeter.

"Marie-Lisette, you aren't listening," said Chrétien. "I said: Landing lights, on."

"Oh. Yes." She flipped the switch. "Landing lights on, check."

"Maybe they'll be able to see us."

"Yes. But we're not really landing now?"

"Of course not. My navigation can get us over Saint Pierre, but that's as accurate as I can get. If we tried to land in this, we might end up in the lobby of the Hotel Lalanne."

"What can we do?"

"Fly over in a crisscross pattern and hope there's somebody like you down there," Chrétien replied. "I'll call the turns."

"Okay."

"What's the highest point?"

"The northern end of Langlade. It's about two-hundred-and-fifty meters."

"Okay. Climb to fifteen hundred feet and we'll begin crisscrossing. That's low enough for them to hear us," said Chrétien. "And bring the speed down as much as you feel comfortable without stalling."

Marie-Lisette climbed to fifteen hundred feet then backed off the airspeed and leveled the nose, her eyes glued to the altimeter and airspeed indicators. She dropped their speed to ninety knots. "That's as slow as I want to go," she said.

"Swell. We'll hold this course for about ten minutes, then we'll make a sweeping turn to the west."

Ten minutes later, Chrétien said, "Okay, we've probably passed over both Saint Pierre and Grande Miquelon. Let's turn to the north for one minute, then back to the east."

Marie-Lisette banked the plane slowly to the right and waited for Chrétien to call out the next turn. A minute passed.

"Now, let's turn back to the east," said Chrétien. "That should bring us back over Saint Pierre."

They repeated this pattern: east, north, west, north, east, north, west, north several more times until Chrétien was certain they had covered all of Saint Pierre and were heading toward Fortune Bay again. He shook his head. "We'll have to try again. Let's turn back south."

Marie-Lisette, her heart beating faster, turned to the left and kept the plane banked until the compass swung to dead south. All the while she looked at the fuel gauges. They were beginning to run low, something they'd worried about since Goose Bay where, because of the war, the amount of fuel they could take on board was limited.

Fifteen minutes later, when Chrétien calculated they were crossing the southern coast of Saint Pierre, they started the tight crisscross pattern again. They had gone through several turns with growing despair when Marie-Lisette cried, "Look!" She pointed ahead and to the right where a bloom of light had suddenly appeared.

Chrétien smiled. "That's what it looked like from up here the time you organized all them cars and trucks. Let's head on over there and lose some altitude."

"Yes, Sir!" Marie-Lisette made a long, looping turn, reduced speed, and began a smooth descent toward the light. She kept her gaze fixed on it, afraid it would disappear if she lost sight of it. As they got closer, the light revealed itself as a line, exactly like the one Marie-Lisette had created with the cars and trucks. Confident now, she reduced speed even more and started the plane heading away from the lights for a short distance before executing a one-hundred-and-eighty degree turn and lining up on the row of lights. She prayed that whoever organized the makeshift lighting system knew enough to arrange the cars and trucks so they were pointing upwind.

"Landing gear, down," said Chrétien.

"Landing gear down, check, three green," replied Marie-Lisette.

As they neared the ground, the line of lights became two lines with an inviting lane between them. Marie-Lisette focused her entire attention on the center of the runway; she desperately wanted to make this a perfect landing. At last, she felt the shock of the wheels hitting the ground and she gradually brought the plane to a stop before a crowd of people who, though she could not hear them, appeared to be gesturing happily.

When, finally, Marie-Lisette and Chrétien stepped down from the plane they were greeted with enthusiastic shouts and applause. Doctor Tréguy, Jérôme and Gabriel were the first to greet them. "Dave must be tired of landing between a line of cars and trucks," said Doctor Tréguy.

"Oh, that wasn't Dave that landed the plane," replied Chrétien. "It was Marie-Lisette."

"What?"

"Pretty swell, huh?"

"But what happened to Dave?"

"Dave?" Chrétien said. "Oh, I bought this here plane from him. I intend to start a business flyin' mail and goods between Maine and Saint Pierre." He looked at Marie-Lisette and winked. "Marie-Lisette is gonna be one of my pilots after Dave taught her all he knew."

Cassiopeia was high in the northern sky. Perseus, also. And almost directly overhead, Cygnus, the Northern Cross, spread its arms over the world.

Around Baffin Island, ice flows collided, icebergs ruptured—sounds of the earth stretching and forming, preparing. The whole mass of ice and snow started to slide southward toward Newfoundland and the archipelago of Saint Pierre and Miquelon.

Above the small town, and around the trawlers bobbing in captivity at the quay, seabirds were a-swoop with arctic air in their wings.

Part 3

November - December, 1941

13
Northern Lights

URKY DRAMAS PLAYED out on the backs of Marie-Lisette's eyelids. Faces flashed before her, limned in black-green, moving through the vitreous fluid of her eyeballs—across, up, down, in, out—and then as soon as they appeared they disappeared again in an instant. Each face—there were dozens of them—was somehow familiar, but she couldn't identify a single one. She saw fascinating details—a bouffant, a mustache, oval eyes, bushy eyebrows, a straight nose—but they were as difficult to grasp as, say, the precise sensation of longing. Yet they all seemed so real. People she had met in previous lives? It was a pleasant thought, for she was convinced her previous lives hadn't played themselves out on Saint Pierre, but in France, perhaps other places as well. And each face had a story attached to it. Of that, she was certain. If only she could hear them, if only she could decipher their stories, then she would know more about herself.

Raymond Pineau appeared briefly and she felt a tightening in her chest, a certain rudeness. It made her wince and, in the wincing, the play of faces vanished. She sighed and rolled over to switch the bed lamp on and pick up the book she had been reading: *Claudine In Paris* by Collete.

My mouth open ... head thrown back ... him leaning over me ... tortured with desire ... trembled ... opened my arms ....

She read with growing excitement and a yearning for consummation, if only imagined. But Reynaud had said, "No!"

How could he? How could he tell Claudine he would take her only as his wife or not at all?

Marie-Lisette's hand slid, seemingly of its own will, under the covers. And it consoled her like a cat sensing an owner's distress. She closed her eyes again. A flush of excitement mottled her chest and the cords of her neck protruded with her effort to imagine a lover. She tried to control her breathing lest her parents in the next room hear her. Or Gabriel. She imagined a man with her. At first the man resembled Chrétien Bastarache, but she quickly dismissed that image with a silent, shame-filled, giggle; he was far too old for her, wasn't he? All at once, she realized she had no idea how old he was. And besides, she had known of other young women who married men much older than they.

It had been two months since Chrétien left after their secret journey to London, promising to return soon. Had he changed his mind? Would he keep his promise? Marie-Lisette had begun to despair.

Now, Chrétien left her imagination to be replaced by Jean-Luc Lavedan. It was easy to imagine his hands on her body. Undoubtedly, they would be sure hands, hands that knew how to touch a woman, hands that didn't smell like fish. She pressed her lips together as an image of Raymond re-entered her mind. She concentrated, trying to summon back Jean-Luc. But the man who now assumed center stage in her imagination was not Jean-Luc but some odd melding of him and Chrétien Bastarache.

He was, she decided, Jacques Bernis, the man to whom she felt much closer after her long flight over the Atlantic.

Her breathing became more labored as her little finger teased. "I love you, Marie-Lisette," she heard Jacques whisper. She gave a gasp of pleasure as waves of sensation coursed through her body and her skin burned. The mottled spots on her chest deepened.

"Jacques, take me away," she murmured.

And soon, they were driving through the French countryside—Marie-Lisette-Geneviève and her lover, Jacques Bernis—driving through the night with rain drumming on the roof of the car, stopping at a hotel in Sens that turned out to be full and her saying, "It doesn't matter, darling, one must work for one's happiness," and he replying, "Marie-Lisette, my little one, my Geneviève, think about the future, think of Spain," and her gazing at him, and him asking, "Do you think you'll like Spain?" and her thinking, perhaps saying, "But it's France where I want to be ... it's France."

She shifted under the covers and, with a sigh, felt a tiny wet spot on the sheet.

Adrienne woke to a strange wetness. Her eyes opened wide, staring uncomprehendingly at the peeling paint of the ceiling. Tentatively, she felt under the blankets. The sheets were soaked and she knew instantly that her water had broken. *Oh God, not now!* She glanced at the window. As she suspected, it was the middle of the night. With Claude still in jail and her mother-in-law unable to drive, there was no way to get to the hospital. Unless ....

"Mama," she called tentatively, panic edging her voice.

There was no response.

"Mama!" She tried to rise, but was pulled back by an odd heaviness. The sweet, earthy smell of her amniotic fluid filled her nostrils.

"Mama!"

After several minutes, Claudette Cormier appeared at the door rubbing her eyes. "What in heaven is all the shouting about?"

"It's happening."

Claudette stared at her for a long moment, a heartless, hostile look. Finally, she said, "I'll call Doctor Tréguy."

"No, there's no time. Please run over and wake Monsieur Sabot."

"What can he do? He ain't no midwife."

"He'll drive me to the hospital. Hurry!"

"If you didn't have my boy arrested, he'd be able to drive you."

"Mama, there's no time for that."

"I ain't bringing Monsieur Sabot into this. Not after he played Claude for a fool the way he did."

"Please!"

"Why are you so interested in involving Monsieur Sabot anyway? Is he the father?"

Adrienne stared at her mother-in-law in amazement. "No, he's not the father!" she finally said, barely above a whisper.

"Then don't you think it's time to tell me who the father is? I know damn well it ain't my Claude; he told me so."

"Mama, I'm having a baby!"

"Whose?"

Adrienne grimaced with the pain of a contraction. "The baby's coming soon. Please help me!"

"Why should I? You're nothing but an unfaithful whore. You're no better than my husband who ran off with a young bitch."

"I'm sorry that your husband left you, but that was many years ago. It has nothing to do with me."

"Left me alone with Claude."

"Mama, think of this baby." Adrienne's voice was pitched high with panic. "It's coming."

"No more than four years old, he was."

Adrienne let her head fall back on the pillow. Beads of sweat gathered on her forehead. She sobbed. In a pleading voice, she whispered, "Please don't take your bitterness out on the baby. It's innocent. It did nothing to harm you."

Claudette didn't answer for a moment. Instead, she stared at Adrienne with a cold, dispassionate expression.

"For God's sake, Mama!"

Still, Claudette said nothing.

"Call me anything you want. Call me a whore. Call me an adulteress. Call me the devil himself. Anything." Adrienne's voice became garbled with her sobbing. "But please God, help the baby!"

"Finally, Claudette said, "I ain't about to help you—" Adrienne stared in shock at her mother-in-law, tears coursing down her cheeks. "—But I ain't got nothing against the baby. It can't help who it has for a mother."

"Thank God," whispered Adrienne.

"I'll call Doctor Tréguy."

When Claudette left the room, Adrienne fell back on the pillow. A second wave of pain crashed over her body. She muttered a prayer between clenched teeth, wishing Jean-Luc could be there. When the pain abated, she tried to regain control of her breathing. Perhaps if she could remain perfectly still, the baby wouldn't come as quickly. How long would it take Doctor Tréguy to get here? She guessed twenty minutes, maybe thirty. She rolled her head carefully to look at the clock beside her bed. *3:25.* He should be here by quarter to four. A rivulet of sweat caught in her eyebrow, then slid along the corner of her eye. She wanted to wipe it away, but she was afraid to move. She wanted to bring her hand to her mouth, to chew on the stubs of her fingernails, but she willed herself not to move.

Her breaths were quick and shallow. She kept playing the conversation with her mother-in-law over and over. How spiteful the woman is! How horrible it must have been for poor Claude growing up with such a mother. But then another wave of pain came and her entire being was again focused on the baby ... and herself.

He and Antoine hunker in the trench, afraid to move. The water is ankle deep from days of rain. It soaks into their uniforms, through their boots, but still they do not move. Even when a half-dozen rats scamper over their bodies, they remain still. The detonations all around them are unceasing, raining earth and hot metal down on them. The hot shrapnel sizzles in the cold mud. Repeatedly, the air is buckled; it hits their ears like a whip. But they don't want the bombardment to stop because they know as soon as it does, the generals will order a counter-attack. The trench water shivers, rippled by the unending tremors of the earth, and Jérôme sees his reflection squirming in the ripples. They wince to the terrifying shriek of a shell coming close. An instant later, the earth heaves, a paroxysm of agony shudders through it.

The walls of the trench spasm and discharge a corpse, squeezing it out slick with amniotic mud and maggots, and it rolls face up into the water at their feet, dead eyes staring at the sky.

They clutch each other and scream.

Jérôme heard the last notes of his scream as he sat bolt upright in the bed. His face was beaded with sweat. The pillow was drenched. He looked at Antoine's coat and shuddered. He couldn't stay in bed; it was too dangerous. He would be plagued once more with the horrible memories. He must get up. He scrambled across the room and fumbled with his clothes, his hands trembling.

At that moment, a diffuse light shot across the ceiling and down one wall. At the same time, he heard a car passing in front of his house. At this hour? He rushed to the window. The car continued past and stopped at the Cormier house. Jérôme watched as the driver emerged, satchel in hand. Cold moonlight illuminated the man's face. It was Doctor Tréguy.

Adrienne? The baby?

Hurriedly, he slipped into a pair of boots and a coat then stepped out into the rude moonlight. Cassiopeia was high in the northern sky, its stars burning faintly like the butt ends of cigarettes seen across a half mile of no-man's-land. Further overhead, the outstretched arms of the Northern Cross like a blessing upon the earth. Or forgiveness. In the east, the moon shone four days past full.

His boots crunched on the snow—a thin, harsh sound as though the air was too cold to give it resonance. He made his way, crouched, across the field toward the Cormier house. A pool of light softened the snow at the base of the window that opened onto Adrienne's bedroom. It was toward that window that he now skulked.

The spasms of pain became more frequent. Tears of frustration filled Adrienne's eyes as she clenched the bed sheet and screwed up her face, trying to hold back the contractions. But they kept coming; the baby was willing itself to be born and there was nothing Adrienne could do to delay it. She rolled her head to look at the clock. 3:45. *Where was Doctor Tréguy?* What would she do if the baby came before the doctor arrived? As soon as the last wave of pain had subsided, she was overcome by a sense of panic.

Then another spasm gripped her. A searing pain burned between her legs, migrated to her belly, and rippled across her lower back.

"Mama!" she cried. "It's coming!" She squeezed her eyes shut and muttered a prayer into the darkness behind her eyelids. "Oh, God, please help me," she murmured.

The door burst open. Her mother-in-law said, "Doctor Tréguy is here." *Thank God!*

She felt a hand on her forehead and looked up to see Doctor Tréguy smiling at her. "It's alright Adrienne. Everything will be fine."

"Doctor, it's coming."

"That's what babies do. Now I want you to raise your knees and keep your feet flat on the bed."

She raised her knees.

"I can see the head already," said Doctor Tréguy. "The baby's well positioned. Nothing to worry about."

Adrienne risked a smile. Then another wave of pain cascaded through her. She cried out.

Tears came to Jérôme's eyes when he heard Adrienne's cry of pain. He wanted to go to the front door, to go in, to help. But he knew he wouldn't be welcome. Adrienne would be embarrassed, perhaps even angry. And her mother-in-law—the old hag!—would run straight to her son who, though still in jail, was due to be released any time.

He hunkered under the window, afraid to move, filled with fear for Adrienne. Her cries of pain came louder, more intense. He shuddered, almost as though her pains were coursing through his own body. Then she let out a long, terrible wail and he couldn't restrain himself; he raised his eyes over the sill. But all he saw was the back of Claudette Cormier's dress. He lowered himself to his haunches again and said a prayer to the close, cold snow. It was a prayer like the ones he used to say in the trenches.

Suddenly, the snow started to radiate with a green incandescence. The corner of the Cormier barn, formerly lost in the murk, shone dully. The fence next to it revealed itself in an eerie luminosity. He heard a faint sizzle like the sound of saltwater along a hull—the sound of the Northern Lights. Jérôme turned his gaze to the horizon in the northwest.

Slightly above the horizon he saw a growing green effulgence. It seemed to pulsate. He watched, awestruck, as the spherical light slid across the sky. Rays of light shot down as shimmering bands of red and violet, some bluish-red like birth blood.

All at once, he heard a cry. It was pitched higher than Adrienne's, thinner. It was a baby's cry.

"It's a girl, Madame Cormier," said Doctor Tréguy. "A healthy, beautiful girl."

Adrienne stared at him from a tear-stained, sweat-drenched face. Her breathing was short, rasping. A new lightness of being settled around her. She had the sensation of floating slightly above the bed. "A girl?" she asked. She gave out a short laugh of amazement.

"A healthy girl. Here, see for yourself."

Doctor Tréguy held the tiny, wrinkled infant out to her. She felt its eggshell weight on her chest, felt its tiny wriggling movements, heard its fragile cry, and she wept. Her eyes grew wide and radiant; a broad smile fixed itself on her relaxed face.

She scarcely heard her mother-in-law whisper, "Doctor Tréguy, there's a prowler outside the window."

When he heard the baby's cry, Jérôme was filled with a strange warmth. It was a foreign feeling that at first he didn't recognize as joy. He ached to know what the baby looked like, how Adrienne appeared. Was she well? Was the baby well?

He risked another peek above the windowsill. Claudette Cormier was still in the way. He lowered himself.

Would Adrienne name the baby Antoine as he had pleaded, or else Antoinette if it was a girl? Above his head, ribbons of light shot out in all directions radiating a spectral glow over the countryside.

There was a movement to his left. Alarmed, he started to rise, but he was too late; Doctor Tréguy stood beside him, looking up into the sky. "The aurora corona," he said.

"Yes."

"Spectacular."

Jérôme gazed up at the doctor, unsure what to say.

Doctor Tréguy turned to look down on him. It was a long, questioning gaze. "What are you doing here, Jérôme?"

"I … I saw you go by. I thought I could help."

"By crouching under the window? In the snow?"

Jérôme shrugged.

"You thought you could help by watching the Northern Lights?"

"I …." But Jérôme could find nothing to explain himself. Instead, he asked, "How is Madame Cormier?"

"She's doing just fine. But I still want to know what you're doing here."

"And the baby?"

"Fine, too."

"Boy? Girl?"

"Girl," replied Doctor Tréguy. "Why is it important to you? What are you doing here?"

Jérôme stared at the doctor, searching for words. Refracted light from the blazing aurora corona danced on his face. *A girl. Antoinette?* He shook his head and said, "That's wonderful. About them, I mean. You're a good doctor."

"It wasn't my doing." Doctor Tréguy continued to stare at Jérôme with a quizzical expression.

"We were ... are ... friends. The war ...."

"The war? What does that have to do with it?" Doctor Tréguy rubbed his hands vigorously together. In his haste to find the prowler, he hadn't put his coat or gloves on.

"Not this war, the last one," said Jérôme. He would never have said this to anyone if he hadn't been caught in such an unexplainable predicament. "She ... Madame Cormier ... is the only person I could ever talk with about it ... the war."

"She talked with you about the war?"

"She understood. We became friends."

"I see."

"I ... I care for her."

Doctor Tréguy said nothing. He continued to stare.

"That's all ... just friends. She ... listened ...."

"She listened?"

"Yes, she listened."

The doctor rested a hand on Jérôme's shoulder. He smiled. "Go home. They're both doing well. I'll tell Madame Cormier you were asking for her."

"No! Her husband would never understand."

Doctor Tréguy nodded, his smile broadening. "No, I suppose he wouldn't. Men like him don't understand how a woman can befriend a man. They end up imagining all sorts of things."

"Yes, that's it. They imagine ...."

"But I'm sure there's nothing to imagine, is there?"

"No. No, nothing."

Doctor Tréguy nodded. "I won't say a thing."

Jérôme let out a breath. "Thank you, Doctor."

"Go home and rest"

"I will."

"I'll keep you informed about Madame Cormier and the baby."

"You wont mention this to others, will you?"

"No, of course not."

"Not for my sake. For hers."

"Of course."

"Has she named it—the baby?"

Doctor Tréguy shook his head. "No, not that I know of. When I hear, I'll let you know."

Jérôme nodded, gave a sheepish smile, and turned for his house. The snow-mantled countryside still glowed with a ghostly green light.

Doctor Tréguy said, "Wait."

Jérôme turned back to the doctor. "Yes?"

Doctor Tréguy put a hand on Jérôme's shoulder. "Drop by my office. As you know, I also was in the Great War. Perhaps we can talk about it together. I'd like that. Speaking for myself, I mean."

"Yes, yes, I'll do that," replied Jérôme.

When he returned to his house, Jérôme checked the calendar. November twenty-fifth. Claude Cormier was due to be released in five days.

Jérôme spent the rest of the morning talking excitedly to Antoine's coat.

Lafitte's Revolt

S ITTING AT HIS CUSTOMARY TABLE in the Café Joinville, Jérôme wished he could talk about the baby to the others; he swelled with pride for his dear friend, Adrienne. But, of course, he couldn't. Instead, he listened patiently to their talk of Le Celte. Pierre Pichot was bemoaning the bare shelves in his shop again and saying that surely, somehow, Le Celte would make it through. "It must, it has to," he said, his voice cracking.

"Why do you keep speaking of *Le Celte*? Jérôme asked. "You know damn well she ain't coming this year."

"We can't give up hope," Pichot muttered, dragging on his cigarette.

"It's November," Jérôme said as he signaled to Madame Imatz, the proprietress, for another pernod.

"Ships have made it through as late as November."

Jérôme lit his own cigarette from the end of Pichot's. He wrinkled his nostrils at the acrid smoke. "Never *Le Celte,* and never ships who had to pass through the German submarines." He let a stream of smoke drift from his lips, sucked it into his nostrils, and exhaled it in two thin jets that coiled around his empty pernod glass.

"All the same …." Pierre Pichot stubbed out his cigarette and twisted his beret in his small, delicate hands. Jérôme was startled to see the man's eyes had become moist.

"Monsieur Pichot is right," said Gabriel. "There's always a chance *Le Celte* will make it through. I pray for it all the time."

"Oh, Gabriel, I'm sure you do, but have you seen the trawlers out on the quay? Ice all over their rigging and topsides. She ain't coming, I tell you." Jérôme paused, then in a lower voice touched with sadness, said, "Nobody's coming." Though he couldn't say it to the others, he was not upset at the continued absence of *Le Celte*. He was never happy when the little freighter arrived in Saint Pierre with news from France.

But his friend Chrétien Bastarache was another matter. Not a word from the man in more than two months. And now the weather was beginning to close the ring around them. Chrétien had always been the most reliable man he knew. But now? It seemed everything was different because of the war.

"General de Gaulle will liberate us," said Gabriel. "Then he will send *Le Celte* with everything we need."

Jérôme said nothing. After hearing Marie-Lisette describe her encounter with de Gaulle, he had decided the general would never come to the aid of Saint Pierre. Of course, for Marie-Lisette's safety, he could say nothing of this to the others.

Madame Imatz arrived with Jérôme's drink. She was a round woman with white hair that had come loose from her bobby pins. "If *Le Celte* doesn't come," she said, placing the pernod on the table, "we'll start to run out of this stuff so enjoy it while you can. I may have to ration it like everything else." This was met with howls of protest.

Jérôme lifted the pernod and took a sip. "We've been hearing the rumor about liberation for months now. De Gaulle has more on his mind than poor little Saint Pierre, I can assure you of that."

"You're wrong, Monsieur Sabot," said Raymond Pineau. "Soon we'll see a whole fleet of troop carriers coming over the horizon and right into the harbor."

"Troop carriers?"

"How else would they invade the islands?"

"Even if one troop carrier came, where would we put them all? This is a tiny place. Would we book the soldiers at the Hotel Lalanne?"

This drew laughter from everyone present except Raymond Pineau, who said, "Well, maybe a corvette or two. It wouldn't take much. Who would resist them?"

"You know," said Pierre Pichot, "he's right. There may be a dozen Vichy supporters in all of Saint Pierre and Miquelon. What would they do, fire the *Béarn's* cannon at them?"

"If they did that, they'd have only one shot because it would rip the deck off the old tub."

"Well, all I say is the Free French can't leave us here to rot under a Vichy government," said Monsieur Bernitz, the milk deliverer. "And I'll bet that General de Gaulle is thinking that right now. He's saying, 'I can't let those poor people of Saint Pierre rot,' that's what he's saying."

"You're all crazy," snapped Jérôme. "De Gaulle is concerned with liberating France, not Saint Pierre." He heard the distress in his voice and said to himself that he had to stop thinking about Adrienne and the baby; it was ruining his disposition. He'd learned from Doctor Tréguy that Adrienne had named the little girl Antoinette and the news had thrilled him. But at the same time, it had made him more desperate than ever to see the two of them.

Suddenly, a commotion at the door made him turn. Auguste Lafitte, in his ancient uniform, marched in followed by a half dozen other men. "We're going to march on the *Béarn*," Lafitte proclaimed. "Who's with us?"

A buzz went around the room as men exchanged glances. Some laughed. Lafitte scowled at them.

Gabriel pushed his chair back and stood ramrod stiff. "Me. I'm with you."

"And me," said Pierre Pichot, also standing.

"What are you going to do when you get there?" asked Jérôme.

"Demonstrate that we won't live under Vichy rule," replied Lafitte, his head thrust forward as though to emphasize his point. He smiled, showing his decayed, yellow teeth. Apparently he, like Jérôme, had given up hope that de Gaulle would respond to their plea.

"How?" asked Doctor Tréguy.

"We'll get the men from the trawlers, too."

"But that doesn't answer my question," said Doctor Tréguy. "How will you make this demonstration?"

"Don't worry, Doctor Tréguy. No one will be hurt. We won't need your services."

"So you plan a peaceful revolution," Jérôme said with a smile. "This is not to be the Bastille, then?"

Many of the men laughed. Nervously.

"All the same," said Doctor Tréguy, "I'd better go with them in case someone gets too excited and hurts himself."

Jérôme extended an arm in a show of politeness. "After you. We've had enough pernods for now anyway. Like Madame Imatz says, we need to save the stuff for the coming winter."

As Lafitte turned for the door, he saw Boullot. He stopped, bared his yellow teeth, and pointed. "Remember, Boullot, my dying words will be for you. 'Fuck you!' is what I'll say." With a smile, he strolled out the door.

In all, two dozen men marched down the Rue Maître Georges Lefèvre, their footfalls muffled by the layer of packed snow filling the street. They crossed the Rue de 11 Novembre onto the quay.

Jérôme felt a tug at his arm. He turned to see Marie-Lisette who started buttoning her coat. "What's happening?" she asked. Then, in a whisper, "Is it General de Gaulle?"

"It's a revolution. We're marching on the Bastille."

"The Bastille?"

"Well, since there's no Bastille, Colonel Lafitte has decided that we'll take over the *Béarn* instead."

"Is he crazy?"

"What do you think?"

The trawlers along the quay were bearded with salt rime and fishermen were busy hacking at it with hatchets and crowbars to clear the topsides and rigging. Even in harbor a boat that became too heavily encased in ice risked capsizing. But as the marchers stepped onto the quay, Auguste Lafitte marching stiffly in the lead, the red of his Franco-Prussian War trousers startling against the white of the snow, the men stopped and stared.

Lafitte held out an arm and the column came to an abrupt halt. He cupped his hands around his mouth and called, in his dry, thin voice, "We are marching for Free France against the Vichy oppressors. Are you with us?"

The fishermen looked at each other in amazement. After a moment's hesitation, first one, then another, then in groups, they climbed down from their boats onto the quay. "For France!" they shouted. Laughing like children who had discovered a new diversion from the boredom of their long confinement. With a shuffling of feet, they mocked a troop of soldiers forming up for an attack.

Lafitte, immune to their mockery, surveyed them as would a general then led them from the quay with a quick, marching step. They followed, mimicking his halting stride. Suddenly, he faltered and began to sway.

Doctor Tréguy caught him. "Are you alright, Colonel?" he asked.

Lafitte didn't answer. His eyes were glazed.

"Colonel?"

At last Lafitte, seeming to recover himself, said, "I'm alright, just a little dizzy spell."

"Have you been getting them often?"

Lafitte shook his head. "No, no. It's just the excitement."

"You should take it easy."

Lafitte gave a dismissive wave. "I'm alright I tell you." He started to march again. The others followed.

The crowd of hundreds of people marched onto the Boulevard Constant Colmay toward the Quai de Pêche where the *Béarn* was moored. As they marched, others joined from the Rue de l'Anse and the Rue Borsaint and the Rue Raymond Poincaré. The atmosphere was festive—men, women, and children singing and laughing and chatting excitedly. Some of the people had begun to sing the *Marseillaise*. They were led by Gabriel's sweet, pulpy baritone. It had been a long time since the people had something to cheer and it appeared they were going to take full advantage of the opportunity. When they arrived at the quay, Lafitte led them straight to the *Béarn*.

The men aboard the *Béarn*—all five of them—stared at the huge crowd, their eyes round and their mouths open.

"We demand that you turn over the *Béarn* to us," Auguste Lafitte called out, "in the name of Free France and General de Gaulle."

The men stood frozen. They looked at each other. Then the one who seemed to be in charge shrugged his shoulders and said, "Okay."

For a moment, Lafitte seemed unsure what to do next, He turned to Doctor Tréguy and said, "It could be a trick."

"I doubt it," replied the doctor with a laugh. "There are five of them and hundreds of us. Besides, I know them all. They're just making a living; they're not Vichy."

Emboldened, Lafitte started up the ice-encrusted gangplank. But after only two steps, he faltered and would have fallen into the water had not

Jérôme and Doctor Tréguy caught him. They helped him the rest of the way until the three of them stood on the deck of the *Béarn* facing the five men. A cold wind, which until then had been blocked by the *Béarn's* superstructure, clawed at their faces.

"You should rest, Colonel Lafitte," said Doctor Tréguy.

"No, I have a revolution to lead. I'll be alright."

Doctor Tréguy gazed at him for a long moment, shrugged, turned his collar up and said to the leader, "Georges, how are you today?"

"Fine, Doctor. My cold's better."

"Good. Make sure you keep yourself bundled up. It's awful cold these days." He hugged his arms across his chest, emphasizing the point. Then he said, "Colonel Lafitte, here, wishes to take over the *Béarn* for the Free French."

"Certainly, why not?"

"You won't resist?"

"Why should we? It's too damn cold to be out here anyway." He turned to Auguste Lafitte, snapped his heels together, and saluted. "She's all yours, my colonel." His four companions, following his lead, saluted smartly.

Lafitte squared his shoulders, returned the salutes with a stiff arm, then reached inside his greatcoat. He pulled out a folded flag and handed it to Georges. "In that case, you will please lower the Vichy flag and raise this."

"Of course, my colonel."

"It is the flag of the Free French."

"Certainly. Why not?"

A few minutes later, when Georges and his men had lowered the Vichy tri-color and raised the tri-color with the red Cross of Lorraine sewn in the center of the white band, a great shout rose up from the crowd.

"*Viva la France!*" someone shouted.

The call was taken up by many in the crowd.

"Will that be all, Sir?" asked Georges.

Lafitte nodded. Tears in his eyes, he saluted the flag. His small voice cracking, he started to sing the Marseillaise. "*Alons enfants de la Patrie, le jour de gloire et arrivé ....*"

All at once, the shouting and laughing ceased and the crowd fell silent for a moment. Only Lafitte's tiny, cracked voice could be heard. Then, at the chorus, first Gabriel then hundreds of other voices joined him, a wave rolling toward the back of the crowd. They sang with growing fervor, drowning out Lafitte's voice. Everyone's gaze was fixed on the flag snapping in the breeze.

They had nearly reached the end of a second singing of the Marseillaise—at least those few stanzas that people knew—when gradually a silence rolled from the back of the crowd to the front like a reflected wave. In the end, Auguste Lafitte was the only person still singing. He was on the seventh verse of the song, one that few people knew. *"Liberté, Liberté chérie ...."* He had failed to see Count de Bournat walking in long strides up the gangplank.

The count waited for him to finish singing, then said, "You're in fine voice today, Colonel Lafitte. But please do tell me what is happening here."

Lafitte, startled, hesitated for a moment. Finally, he said, "We have brought about a great revolution. These islands now belong to Free France."

"Are you drunk?"

Lafitte snapped his heels together. "I am drunk with joy."

"Better that you were drunk with pernod. Then I would understand."

"We are all drunk with joy for Free France."

"If you don't stop it, I'll have to arrest you."

"The day of glory has arrived," replied Lafitte, waving his arm towards the new flag flapping in the cold breeze.

De Bournat looked up. "Who sewed the Cross of Lorraine on one of our sacred flags?"

"I did."

"Well done. It looks very neat." Count de Bournat said.

Lafitte saluted smartly. "Thank you."

The count turned to Doctor Tréguy and Jérôme. "Will one of you please persuade Colonel Lafitte to give up this silliness. I don't wish to arrest him."

Doctor Tréguy and Jérôme, smiling, shrugged their shoulders.

"Let us keep our flag," someone shouted from the crowd.

"I can't do that. We would starve without the subsidies from the Vichy government. How many times must I explain?"

"Then we shall starve," said Lafitte.

Count de Bournat shook his head sadly. "You are all peaceful people.

Have I ever had my police raise a gun to stop your displays of patriotism? We have two machine guns. Have they ever been fired? No. And do you know why? Because we are all Saint Pierrais."

"We are Free French."

Count de Bournat rolled his eyes heavenward. "*Mon Dieu!* We are Saint Pierrais. We have no business being at odds with each other. Our home is far too small for that." He paused, surveyed the crowd, and continued. "You've had a happy time today and that is good. Heaven knows we haven't had much to shout about since France was overrun by the Nazis. Now I don't want to be a spoilsport, so here's what I will do. My official report will say that all this happened tomorrow rather than today and that I put an immediate end to it and that you all went home peacefully. Until then, if the flag of the Free French happens to be flying over Saint Pierre, well then, I don't even know about it. The flag can stay for today. And I declare today an unofficial holiday."

A hesitant cheer rose up from the crowd.

"We all need it," he continued. "So it shall be. I, too, you know, would like to sing the Marseillaise with you."

"If you take the flag down tomorrow, we will raise it up again," said Colonel Lafitte, his chin thrust forward.

"Damn it, Auguste, will you please cooperate?"

"Not while France is under the yoke of the barbarian Nazis ... and the Vichy."

"You pompous old fart! Be practical for God's sake. Keeping a low profile is our only hope."

"I will raise the flag of the Free French tomorrow ...."

"You'll do nothing of the kind."

"And I will raise it every day after that."

"No, you won't."

"You may take it down as often as you wish, but always I will be there to raise it up again." He elevated his voice at the end, bringing cheers from the crowd.

"Then I shall have to arrest you. Claude Cormier could use some company anyway."

"I will not stay in the same jail as that man."

Count de Bournat nodded. "No, no … neither would I. So here's what I'll do: I'll place you under house arrest … and I'll send over some good whiskey. What do you think of that?"

Lafitte stiffened, threw his shoulders back. "Are you trying to bribe me?"

"*Mon Dieu!*" de Bournat cried, slapping the side of his head. "Of course I'm trying to bribe you. What does it sound like?"

Lafitte stared at the administrator at a loss for words. His shoulders sagged.

The crowd was hushed, waiting to see what Colonel Lafitte would do.

Doctor Tréguy placed a hand on Lafitte's shoulder, but said nothing.

Suddenly, Gabriel shouted "*Le Celte*! I see *Le Celte*!"

A hush fell over the crowd. Everyone peered out to sea where Gabriel was pointing. Jérôme squinted into the dazzling light, millions of flashes as the sun played vibrato upon the water. His eyes burned with the effort. "Where, Gabriel? I see nothing."

"Coming over the horizon. There." Gabriel placed his hands on Jérôme's shoulders and turned him slightly to the right.

Jérôme held a gloved hand over his eyebrows and all at once, he saw it—a tiny speck barely visible where the limitless sky and the vast sea met. "It's a ship alright," he said. "No telling from here if it's *Le Celte*."

"It must be *Le Celte*. Who else would it be?" someone asked.

"It's *Le Celte*," said Gabriel. "I prayed for it."

"It's General de Gaulle! He's come to liberate us," said Marie-Lisette.

"With one ship?"

"Could be the Germans," someone else said.

"They also wouldn't come with just one ship. There would be a fleet. Otherwise, the Americans and Canadians would have them for lunch."

"It's *Le Celte*, I tell you. It has to be," cried Gabriel.

"Maybe it's a Vichy ship from Martinique," said Auguste Lafitte. "There's a whole fleet there. Maybe Count de Bournat has called for reinforcements." He turned an accusing gaze on the administrator.

"I called for no ships, I promise you," said the count. "And if it was a Vichy ship, don't you think the government would have informed me. If it were a warship of any kind I would know. If it were German or

Vichy, our government would have told us. And if it were American, British, or Canadian, the Americans, at least, would have told us. They are still trying to cultivate the government of Marshal Pétain."

"Then it must be *Le Celte*."

"I tell you, it is," said Gabriel. "It's *Le Celte*."

The crowd grew silent again. Everyone's focus was on the tiny speck on the horizon. Jérôme heard some people start to pray, some even falling to their knees in the packed snow.

He prayed, too. But he prayed that it was not *Le Celte*. He'd always known the ship would appear one day and there'd be a book or a magazine article about Verdun and his infamy would be known to everyone.

A sergeant approaches them, crouching low in the trench. He says that as soon as the shelling stops they'll be going over the top. He tells them to check their weapons and to fix bayonets, then he moves on down the trench.

Jérôme's hands are so cold, his fingers puckered and numb from the wet, that he has difficulty fixing the bayonet. Antoine helps him and they work together to fix Antoine's bayonet. Raindrops slither down the barrels of their bolt-action Berthiers. The horrific shelling has been going on for so long that they no longer react to the ear-shattering blasts and the heaving of the earth. The detonations seem to be coming from within Jérôme's bones and he no longer cares. He hears Antoine saying the Hail Mary. He is saying it rote fast and it comes out as one very long word, one long plea for mercy. Jérôme crosses himself and starts to pray also. How much of this can they take? How much shelling? How many charges? For a moment, Jérôme fantasizes about falling on his own bayonet. Then, at least, there would be peace. But instead, he prays.

Beside him, he heard Marie-Lisette murmuring, "Hail Mary, full of grace, the Lord is with thee ...." She was saying it in unison with many others. Monsignor Bernard was leading them. They were praying that the ship is *Le Celte* or the Free French. Those who were not praying were peering through the glare at the speck that slowly grew larger. Jérôme looked out to sea again but had difficulty focusing because of the millions of tiny sun explosions on the water.

More than an hour passes before, at last, the shelling stops. Jérôme has lost count of how many times he's said the Hail Mary. He and Antoine look at each other but neither of them says anything. He watches Antoine place the rosary beads into the pocket of his trench coat. It strikes him as a gesture full of meaning but he is at a loss to understand it. Then he notices that Antoine is breathing hard and it seems odd to him until he realizes that he, too, is breathing hard. Beyond the trench, no-man's-land is littered with bodies—boys who died obedient, bewildered, baffled, reduced, mystified, stumped ... bloodied, whose last words, "Mama, Mama," floated on the drifts of their last breaths like feathers in a stream; the boy-men lying there as though dropped only an instant before from the pelvic embrace of their mothers' wombs, from their own birth waters into the muck of the battlefield. Born for this. Very flares, mustard colored, suspended from parachutes, illumined the jaundiced landscape to make the earth itself seem nauseous. The light from the bogus suns is a ghostly radiance on the broken bodies of the boys. And on the other side of no-man's-land, there is laughter in the German trenches. Schadenfreude! A cloud of sulfur hangs over the land.

Suddenly, the order comes. Over the top! Sucking in one last breath, they haul themselves over the lip of the trench and begin to run. Side by side, they run blindly into withering fire. Men are falling on every side of them. The air is filled with shrieks of terror and pain. It seems they have been running only a short time when, suddenly, they confront men running back toward them. The attack has been turned back. No one will blame them if they, too, turn back. Who would expect them to continue the charge when everyone else is scrambling madly for the trenches? Jérôme turns and starts to run. A man fifty yards in front of him disappears into an eruption of earth and flame and smoke. Pieces of flesh are raining down on Jérôme. A drizzle of blood that he inadvertently in-sucks. A ghastly sharing, a macabre form of sex. His own blood feels like sludge. Then the man's head plops into the mud not twenty paces before him. It is still pumping blood. Jérôme feels he's going to be sick. He retches as he runs crouched over. At last he reaches the trench and falls into it, vomiting as he falls. When he is finished, he realizes that Antoine is not with him.

Antoine!

A bloodied feather spirals lazily into the trench.

He peers over the lip of the trench to see Antoine lying on the ground in no-man's-land. Antoine is waving his hand weakly. He is calling his name. Jérôme … Jérôme … Jérôme …

"There's no column of smoke."

Jérôme was jerked back to the present. He turned to see who had spoken. It was Doctor Tréguy.

"What?" asks Jérôme.

"No smoke."

The remark was picked up by others in the crowd. "No column of smoke."

"There's no column of smoke." It passed through the crowd like a shiver.

"Then it's not a ship," said Count de Bournat. "It can't be *Le Celte*."

The praying stopped while everyone strained to see what it was that was coming toward them.

"Maybe it's a trawler," said Doctor Tréguy.

"What would a trawler be doing coming into Saint Pierre in November. It's at least six months until the fishing season."

"None of our boats have left the quay," said Jean-Luc Lavedan. "I don't know who the hell it could be."

But a half hour later they were able to positively identify it as a trawler. As it neared, they could make out the distinctive rigging of a boat designed for deep sea fishing.

"It's not French or Spanish … or Basque," said Jean-Luc. "I'd recognize the superstructure and the rigging."

"American?"

"Could be. But what would an American trawler be doing this far north?"

"Maybe he got lost off the Grand Banks … or became disabled."

As the trawler started to pass the darkened lighthouse at Cap Noir and enter the outer harbor of Saint Pierre, Jérôme saw a man standing on the bow deck waving. For a moment, Jérôme was afraid the trawler would attempt to approach the inner harbor between Cap Noir and Île aux Marins, a course that would have driven her on the rocks.

However, the trawler continued on a north-by-northeast course and soon disappeared behind the Île aux Marins, a direction that would take it to the harbor channel.

As the crowd waited for the trawler to reappear, there were a hundred conversations speculating about the identity of the trawler and the man who had been waving at them. Everyone's gaze was fixed on the Île aux Pigeons where they expected to next see the boat.

Finally, after almost half an hour, she emerged from behind the tiny island, worked out into the Passe du Nord-Est, then turned for the quay. Riding a flood current, she made quick progress down the passage and was soon approaching the quay where the huge crowd had now started to cheer. Despite the disappointment that it was not *Le Celte*, the people were determined to celebrate any visit, no matter who might appear at the quay.

The trawler slowed, preparing to dock. Suddenly, it was Marie-Lisette who recognized the man standing and waving from the bow. "It's Monsieur Bastarache!"

"Chrétien?" asked Jérôme.

Doctor Tréguy laughed. "Your friend picks very dramatic ways to come to Saint Pierre. First it was an airplane out of the fog, now this."

The trawler shuddered to a stop alongside the quay. Chrétien leaped from the bow and stood staring at the mass of people. He shook his head in bewilderment. Finally, he turned to Jérôme and said, "I figured I would be popular, but such a welcome! So many people!"

"Well, it seems you came in the middle of a revolution, Monsieur Bastarache," said Doctor Tréguy with a smile. "We have become Free French."

"Free French? You've been liberated?"

"Yes, but only for today. Tomorrow, we go back to being Vichy."

Chrétien gazed at him.

"We'll explain later," Doctor Tréguy said with a laugh.

Chrétien turned to Jérôme and frowned. "My dear friend. You don't seem happy to see me."

"No, no …. It's not that. I just …. Oh, hell, I'm overjoyed to see you!" Jérôme held his arms out to embrace Chrétien.

"Ah, that's better," said Chrétien. "Well, here I am. I told you I would return. And wait until you see what I've brought for you." He turned to the crowd, raised his voice. "The boat is stuffed with goods. I will be making arrangements with Monsieur Pichot and in the next few days you can go to his shop and acquire what you need."

"*Viva Monsieur Bastarache!*" The cry was repeated throughout the crowd.

Chrétien bowed gallantly. Then he turned to Jérôme and Marie-Lisette and said, "And for you two, I have some very special things."

Antoine in the Killing Field

S LAPPING HIS HANDS against his upper arms as he entered Jérôme's kitchen, Chrétien said, "Mon Dieu, it's cold in here!" He placed the satchel he was carrying on the table with a thud.

"May I light a fire for you, Monsieur Sabot?" asked Marie-Lisette.

Jérôme nodded absently and took the chair furthest from the stove.

Chrétien zipped open the satchel and pulled out three bottles of whiskey. "First, for my friend Jérôme, some fine American whiskey. Jack Daniels. Sorry I couldn't get single malt from Scotland; there was rationing and I didn't have time to work the black market. But this is a whole lot better than Miquelon. Maybe this will cheer you up a little because I still believe you're unhappy to see me."

"No, no, Chrétien. I'm thrilled to see you. It's just—"

Chrétien held up a hand. "No need to explain. As far as I can see, everyone on Saint Pierre is depressed; I can see it in their eyes. I wasn't fooled by that wonderful reception. The war is weighing heavily on all of you. Anyway, there's plenty more whiskey on the trawler to help people forget the war or this ship you all keep waiting for, this *Le Celte*. All I need to do is strike a modest deal with Monsieur Pichot." He reached into the satchel and pulled out a phonograph record which he handed to Gabriel.

"For me?" cried Gabriel.

"I'm told you like opera. The shopkeeper in Bangor recommended this." He handed Gabriel the record. It was a collection of arias sung by Ferruccio Tagliavini.

Gabriel's eyes brightened. "Who told you?"

"Jérôme told me," Chrétien replied. He looked at Jérôme who smiled. "I was also able to get the records you said Doctor Tréguy wanted so badly." He showed the others the labels: Arthur Rubinstein playing the Chopin Concertos. "Don't tell him; I want to surprise him." He reached back into the satchel and pulled out several books that he showed to Marie-Lisette. "I hope you like these. I wasn't sure what to get you; I don't read much."

Marie-Lisette looked from the stove to read the titles. The fire she had just lit dazzled her eyeglasses. Her eyes grew round with excitement: *The Keys of the Kingdom, The Yearling, How Green Was My Valley, A Farewell to Arms.*

"The lady at the book store said all of them are very popular nowadays," said Chrétien.

"They're wonderful! And they'll certainly improve my English. I can't wait to show Madame Leclair. Of course, we've heard of this Hemingway."

"And this tiny book I got you on my last trip but I didn't give it to you because it was empty. Tomorrow I'll put something in it," said Chrétien handing her a bank passbook with the title Banque des Iles.

"I ... I don't understand."

"It's a savings account."

"But ... why?"

"Tomorrow, you and I will go to the bank and make the first deposit. Then you can put a portion of your earnings into the account each month or so and, considering what we'll put into it tomorrow, by the time the war is over, you should have enough to go to school in France."

"But, Monsieur Bastarache ... this is too generous." Tears welled in Marie-Lisette's eyes.

"It's a couple of good horses that you have to thank. I pick them well; it's a talent of mine."

"What do you mean?"

"I mean, young lady, I bet on horse races."

"I don't know what to say."

Chrétien placed an arm around her shoulders. "Then say only that you will study hard."

Marie-Lisette turned and threw her arms around him. "But I did nothing to deserve this."

Chrétien smiled. "No ... nothing except save my life when we couldn't find the landing strip. Many people told me how if it wasn't for you they wouldn't have thought to line the airstrip with their cars and trucks. And I can honestly say that if it were not for you I wouldn't have been around to bet on those horses. So, you see, ultimately it's you who is responsible."

"But it only made sense. It required no courage."

"There are all kinds of courage. For a young woman to demand that a bunch of men do as she says certainly does require courage. In the war, I saw lots of courageous acts, but, all the same, courage isn't something that happens only in war, isn't that true, Jérôme?"

Jérôme didn't answer. He stared blankly at Antoine's coat.

Many times, Antoine calls his name. "Jérôme! Jérôme! Help me!" But Jérôme can't bring himself to go out there again. The Germans are raking no-man's-land with machine gun fire. It's a killing field.

It's a killing field.

"Jérôme?"

Jérôme stared straight ahead, expressionless.

"Monsieur Sabot, are you ill?" asked Marie-Lisette.

Finally, he turned listlessly to gaze at her, the same blank expression on is face. "No... no, I'm not ill." There was a snap as a pocket of coal gas exploded in the stove.

Jérôme flinched.

The fire roared.

Chrétien raised his eyebrows, studied Jérôme for a moment. "No, Marie-Lisette, I believe I caused it when I mentioned the war. Those of us who were in it don't like to think about it. Is that the problem, Jérôme?"

Jérôme didn't answer him. Instead, he turned to Marie-Lisette. "What will your father say about you going to France to study?" His voice was flat.

"That will be a problem. I still haven't heard the end of it when he thought I had flown to Maine with you."

Another pocket of gas exploded. Jérôme flinched again. Warmth began to radiate into the room.

Still gazing at Jérôme, Chrétien addressed himself to Marie-Lisette. "Why should that be a problem? You're already a young woman. By the time the war is over, the way things are going, you'll be well past the age when you can decide such things for yourself."

"He's decided I should marry Raymond Pineau and live on Saint Pierre the rest of my life."

"That's absurd! Doesn't he realize that would destroy you?"

"He doesn't care."

"Well, we'll just have to find a way to make him care."

"How?"

Chrétien pursed his lips and gazed intently at her. "You'll just have to stand up to him. Tell him you're going to France. Don't ask his permission."

"I … I'm not sure."

"Because you've never stood up to him before? Because you only confronted him with your supposed trip to Maine after it was a *fait accompli*?"

"Yes. I don't know how."

"Just use the same courage you used to order all those men around when I was trying to land."

"That's easy to say."

"Yes, it is. And much harder to do; I'll admit that. But you must do it."

"Not even my mother stands up to him."

"Maybe you can inspire her. Maybe she's just been waiting for the right thing to take a stand on. Maybe she's been waiting for a chance all these years to put him in his place. Think what you'll be doing for her."

Marie-Lisette shook her head slowly. "I don't know … . She's never shown a lot of courage when it comes to him."

Chrétien laughed. "Oh you may be surprised. Often you find courage where you least expect it."

Marie-Lisette gave him a determined look. "You're right. I'll have to stand up to him. But at least I can wait; the war won't be over for good long while."

Chrétien shook his head. "If you wait, you'll find all sorts of reasons not to do it. Eventually, your dream will die for lack of effort. It'll die like a plant you neglect to water. You must do it now."

"But that would make life unbearable between now and the time I could leave for France … whenever that would be."

"Are you so sure? Perhaps it will make things a lot better."

"Monsieur Bastarache, I'm afraid."

"Of course you are. But what is courage without fear?"

A block of ice in the ice chest cracked, sounding like a gunshot. Jérôme flinched.

Chrétien gazed at Jérôme for a few moments, then turned back to Marie-Lisette. "So, will you tell your father about going to France?"

Marie-Lisette gave him a nervous smile. "Alright, I'll do it. But if he shoots me, you'll be responsible," she said with an uncertain laugh. She glanced at Jérôme.

Later that night, as Marie-Lisette strolled along the street toward the hotel, she glanced up in the sky and saw the Northern Lights—dancing swirls of green, sheets of orange, shimmering bands of red and purple—and she felt a new lightness. Perhaps because of that, she seemed more attuned to the people around her and what she saw made her sad.

Monsieur Bastarache had been right. She sensed the mood of the people had changed overnight, gone back to what it had been.

After the excitement of Colonel Lafitte's short-lived revolution and the gaiety surrounding Chrétien's arrival—which many had said was almost as good as seeing *Le Celte* pull into the harbor—the people seemed to have slipped back into a dark pessimism. Little of the joy and camaraderie that usually characterized the Saint Pierrais as they approached Christmas was evident on their faces. Instead, she saw in their eyes a despair that the war would go on and on, a hopelessness, a profound sadness at the fate of their homeland. The depth of their ongoing unhappiness had been demonstrated by how brightly their eyes had shone when Auguste Lafitte led them through the streets and raised the Free French flag. Now, it seemed, they were caught in that phenomenon by which despair deepens even further after a glimmer of hope is dashed.

Before stepping into the hotel, she turned to gaze out at the water. What everyone needed, what she needed, so desperately, was to see Free French warships coming to liberate them. But winter was on them and she knew now with certainty that her mission to de Gaulle had failed.

She muttered a little prayer for herself and the people of Saint Pierre, sighed, and entered the hotel.

When Chrétien left to go to his hotel room, Jérôme didn't know whether to be relieved or despondent. He liked being with his friend whose good spirits had always lifted his own, but on this day he was so troubled by the war memories that not even Chrétien's company could calm him. Just having Chrétien around, especially if he was going to make references to the war, sharpened his agony. On the other hand, he knew that when Chrétien left him alone the memories would come flooding back. And he sensed this time it would be different. In the past, he'd been able to stop the story before the ending. Maybe that was the role Antoine's coat had always played. But now he knew the ending of the story would play itself out and he would be powerless to stop it. He poured himself a large glass of whiskey to prepare himself. He sat down at the table and buried his face in his hands. When he finished the whiskey, he poured another. "I'm sorry, Antoine," he murmured in the direction of Antoine's coat. "I'm so sorry. I wish it had been me."

As he cowers in the trench he hears Antoine's cries for help. They are becoming weaker. During a lull in the machine-gun fire Jérôme forces himself out of the trench and starts to crawl toward his friend. The mud has a rich, fermenting smell that mixes with the lingering odor of cordite and corpses. Suddenly, there is a burst of machine-gun fire, then another. Bullets plop into the mud on all sides of him; thud, thud, thud, thud.

He can bear it no longer.

He scrambles back and rolls over the lip of the trench even as he hears Antoine call out his name again. "Jérôme! Jérôme!"

But Jérôme is sobbing in the loneliness of the trench. Over the next hours, as darkness settles over the land, Antoine calls his name over and over again. Yet the calls are becoming weaker. Several times Jérôme almost screws up the courage to try again, to drag himself over the lip of the trench to rescue his friend. But each time, a trembling runs through his body and he sinks down into the mud muttering, "I'm so afraid." He sits back against the wall of the trench and gazes at the sky. The clouds that have hovered over the battlefield for days, bringing interminable rain, are dissipating. He can see some stars. They seem indifferent, isolated in a vast, cold sky that is like the sea. A milk-white moonlight puddles no-man's-land, laying its eerie radiance on the faces of hundreds of corpses. The moon itself, shining through a gauze of clouds appears to be dissolving like a tablet in water. Jérôme hugs himself. He shivers with an overwhelming sense of cold.

Antoine's voice has grown weak, barely audible.

Then, sometime in the middle of the night, it ceases altogether. The next day, there is another charge and they gain a hundred yards of blood and bones and mud. As he moves forward to a new trench, Jérôme removes the trench coat from Antoine's body and slips into it. But he feels no added warmth, no consolation.

Clasping the drained whiskey glass in his white-knuckled hand, Jérôme looked over to Antoine's coat and said, "I'm sorry, Antoine. It should have been me who died." He paused, then said, "It *was* me who died … along with you."

"Mama, when this war is over, I'm going to France to study."

Sylvie Morel flipped the cod she was preparing on the cutting board and looked over her shoulder at Marie-Lisette. "What a silly idea. Where would we get the money?"

Marie-Lisette told her of Chrétien's generosity. "So, you see, money won't be a worry."

Sylvie frowned. "What business has a man his age giving money to a young woman? Is something going on between you two? Did something happen on that silly trip to Maine?"

Marie-Lisette gave a high-pitched laugh. "Mama, he's an old man! That's absurd. He says it's because I saved his life that time his plane was trying to land in the fog."

Sylvie sprinkled flour on the fish then wiped her hands on her apron. A drift of flour fell to the floor. "Your father would never give his permission."

"I don't plan to ask for his permission. I plan to just tell him." Marie-Lisette felt her heart begin to race.

"Marie-Lisette, you can't! He'll explode, just like he did when he learned of your little trip to Maine."

"Why are you making fish again? I thought you said you were sick of it."

"I am, but your father likes it. He can't get enough of it." Sylvie pulled a frying pan down from the cupboard and placed it on the coal stove. "There won't be a minute's peace in this house if you defy him like that. Think of me and Gabriel," she said. "Would you get me the butter, please?"

"I do, believe me. But I refuse to bow to his will any longer. Why do you always have to cook exactly what he wants?" asked Marie-Lisette as she removed the butter from the ice chest and handed it to her mother.

"Because he'll be furious if I don't."

"So, you see, that's how he does it to us. His temper is like a whip that he uses to keep us all in our place."

"Don't be silly. That's just the way he is."

"Only because we let him get away with it. *You* let him get away with it. What would happen if you stood up to him for once?"

Sylvie laughed nervously. "You know very well what would happen." The butter started to melt. Sylvie spread it around the skillet with a basting brush.

"Would he kill you?"

"No, of course not. He ain't like Claude Cormier."

"Then …."

"My responsibility is to maintain a peaceful household."

"You sound like Marshal Pétain with Hitler."

"Marie-Lisette! Take that back this instant! And don't you ever let your father hear you talking like that, him and the way he supports the Vichy."

At that moment, Gabriel entered the kitchen. "What are you talking about?"

"Nothing that concerns you," said Sylvie. "Wash your hands. Supper will be ready soon."

Gabriel walked to the stove, screwed up his face, and said, "Fish again?"

"Mama, it does concern Gabriel. Haven't you seen the way Papa beats him? If we could only put him in his place, maybe he'd stop."

Sylvie dropped the fish into the skillet. It started to sizzle.

"Why do we always have to have fish?" asked Gabriel.

"Quiet, Gabriel!" snapped Sylvie. She turned to Marie-Lisette. "If you insist on doing this, can't you at least wait till after Christmas?"

"No. If I wait, I may lose courage."

Sylvie raised her eyebrows and lifted her eyes to the ceiling. She crossed herself and muttered a prayer.

Marie-Lisette was about to say something when Marcel walked into the house. He removed his coat, walked to the stove and nodded his approval when he peeked over Sylvie's shoulder and saw the fish. He planted a kiss of Sylvie's cheek.

Marie-Lisette's heart started to race faster. She noticed her hands were shaking, so she hid them under the table. Fearing she would lose her courage if she didn't act immediately, she said, "Papa?" Her mouth was dry and her tongue felt swollen.

"Eh?"

"I've got something to tell you."

"Well, what is it?" His voice, as usual, was gruff.

Marie-Lisette took a deep breath and, trying not to let a waver enter her voice, said, "I've decided to go to France to study ... when the war is over, I mean."

Marcel gazed at her for a moment, then laughed. "Of course," he said with a dismissive tone. He turned to Sylvie. "When will supper be ready?"

Marie-Lisette felt a flush of anger. She stood, placed herself between Marcel and Sylvie, and looked her father squarely in the eye. "Don't laugh at me! I'm not making a joke. It's been my dream for as long as I can remember."

Marcel narrowed his eyes and glared at her. "Don't you dare take that tone with me."

"I'll take any tone that will make you listen." Realizing she had now taken the irrevocable step and there was no turning back, Marie-Lisette felt her confidence growing. It was like the first time she'd gone swimming in deep water.

Marcel seemed speechless. He gazed at her, then at Sylvie, then back at Marie-Lisette again. Finally, he said, "I ain't paying for your crazy dreams."

"You don't have to." Marie-Lisette explained about the bank account that Chrétien Bastarache had set up.

"Who the hell does he think he is?" Marcel's voice rose until he was shouting. Then he stopped, glared at Marie-Lisette, and asked, "What have you been doing for him?"

"What do you mean?"

"I mean have you been sleeping with him, Daughter? Is that what you did in Maine?"

Marie-Lisette opened her mouth to speak, but nothing came. She just shook her head in amazement.

"Has that man been screwing our daughter," Marcel asked Sylvie. "Because if he has, I'll kill him."

"Marcel, don't ...." said Sylvie. She narrowed her eyes at Marie-Lisette.

Marie-Lisette finally found her voice. "You're problem is you think every man treats women like you do. But I have news for you; there are some decent men in this world."

"Marie-Lisette!" cried Sylvie.

Marcel's eyes bulged. The cords of his neck stood out as he advanced towards Marie-Lisette, his hand raised.

Marie-Lisette's hands and knees were shaking. All the same, she forced herself to stand stiffly, even offering her cheek to him. "If you hit me the way you hit Gabriel, I'll go to the police. That, on top of the library books you burned, will let everybody know what kind of man you are." From the corner of her eye, she saw her mother place her hands over her face. She saw Gabriel retreat to the far corner of the kitchen. "You can keep your friend Claude Cormier company."

Marcel stared at her, an incredulous look on his face. He lowered his hand.

Marie-Lisette, emboldened, said, "I haven't slept with Monsieur Bastarache. Don't be silly; he's even older than you. And I am going to France after the war, so you might as well get used to it."

Marcel continued to stare at her. He said nothing.

"I'll continue to work at the Hotel Lalanne and contribute to family expenses the way I have been," said Marie-Lisette. "But when the war is over ...." Her voice trailed off.

"And Raymond Pineau?" asked Marcel quietly. "What about him?"

"I don't love him, so I won't marry him."

"What's love got to do with it?"

"What?"

"I said, what's love got to do with anything?"

Marie-Lisette stared at him, speechless.

"Well?"

Finally, Marie-Lisette asked, "Don't you love Mama?"

Marcel looked at her. He looked at Gabriel. He looked at Sylvie. "Yes, of course," he said.

"And she loves you; she's told me. That's all I want, a man like you I can love. Not some Raymond Pineau."

Marcel gazed at her.

"I only want what you and Mama have."

Marcel gave a world-weary nod and raised his eyes to the ceiling as if begging for divine intervention. He spread his arms and said, "You've always been so damned stubborn."

Marie-Lisette gave a nervous laugh. "I take after you."

Marcel lit a cigarette. For a minute or two, he watched the smoke rise and fan out across the ceiling. He sat at the table and smoked in silence.

Marie-Lisette, unsure what to say, helped her mother set the plates and utensils. She laid them on the table quietly, somehow not wanting to make noise. Gabriel stood quietly in the corner.

Finally, after many minutes, Marcel said, "That Pineau kid has been getting on my nerves. Always moping after me." He curled his lower lip and made his eyes round to imitate a subservient child.

Marie-Lisette and Sylvie glanced at each other. There was an unaccustomed brightness in Sylvie's eyes. Gabriel also seemed dumbstruck. He returned to his chair and sat motionless, staring at his stepfather.

Sylvie smiled, an amused smile, the kind a person makes after discovering something wholly unexpected. She turned and flipped the fish, wiggled the skillet. A jet of smoke rose to the ceiling. She shook her head in wonderment.

Marcel asked, "Where in France?"

"I thought Toulouse," answered Marie-Lisette quickly, unable to believe her father's sudden change. She looked at him suspiciously.

"Not Paris?"

"No, Toulouse."

Marcel shrugged. "If it's still there after this war."

Later, when Sylvie placed the dishes of fried cod before them, she said, "We've been having fish too much lately. Tomorrow I'm going to make a nice casserole, or maybe some potato pancakes."

"But I hate casseroles," said Marcel.

"Oh, one now and then won't hurt you," said Sylvie, smiling at Marie-Lisette.

"*Merde!*" muttered Marcel. He turned to Marie-Lisette and said, "Don't pack your bags just yet. It's going to be a long war."

Jérôme and Chrétien appeared at the home of Auguste Lafitte. They had been summoned by Lafitte and Doctor Tréguy, who said it was very important, and they were told not to tell anyone of their visit. They were eager to learn what could be so important that it demanded such secrecy.

It was Doctor Tréguy who answered the door. He looked right and left along the deserted street and said, "Come in, gentlemen. Thanks for coming."

"What's this all about," asked Jérôme as he and Chrétien passed through the storm vestibule into Lafitte's living room. The room was crowded with old furniture, most of the seats draped with colorful afghan throws. A threadbare Persian carpet covered the floor. Jérôme couldn't tell if the nap was so short because it was worn down or if it had been short (and cheap) in the first place. Probably the latter.

"Have a seat and we'll tell you," said Lafitte who was ensconced on the sofa, an orange, brown, and green afghan over his lap and legs. It clashed alarmingly with his Prussian War uniform.

Jérôme and Chrétien sat themselves in chairs across the room from the sofa. Doctor Tréguy frowned and took a seat at the other end of the sofa. Lafitte had still not had his uniform cleaned.

Chrétien said, "That's a nice afghan you have, Colonel."

"Odette, my wife, made it. She was always making them. I think she wanted to keep all of Saint Pierre warm, bless her soul."

Jérôme asked, "So, what's so secret? Why did you—"

"—When I have it around me, I can feel her presence." Lafitte gazed at a framed photograph of his wife sitting on a bookcase across the room.

Jérôme glanced at the photograph. He remembered Odette Lafitte as a kindly woman, deeply involved in the social life of Saint Pierre. Everyone had loved her.

They remained silent, waiting for Lafitte to speak.

He gazed at the picture a moment longer, shook his head, then turned to Chrétien. "We want you to send a telegram to General de Gaulle for us. Apparently, he's decided to ignore our plea. We thought perhaps if we made another effort, then next spring …. You're going back to America in a few days; you can send it from there."

"But what makes you think he'll listen this time?"

It was Doctor Tréguy who answered. "I wondered the same thing. But I got to thinking; I put myself in de Gaulle's shoes. There I am sitting in England and there's not a thing I can do about France. All I am is a junior partner to Churchill and Roosevelt. Probably not even a partner; more a visitor, a refugee who's tolerated because I may be useful someday. So what do I need to do?"

"What?" asked Chrétien.

"I need to make myself relevant somehow."

"But how can de Gaulle do that?"

"By gaining the first allied victory, even if it's small. The thing is, there hasn't been a single allied win in this war, unless you want to count the fact that Britain held out against the German bombing. But that was a defensive victory. There's no place where the allies have taken the war to the enemy and won."

"Saint Pierre will be that place," said Lafitte, "if we have anything to say about it. Maybe if we make Doctor Tréguy's point clear to him, he'll hear us this time."

"But we are nothing to him—just a tiny little group of islands isolated across an ocean from France. He already demonstrated he doesn't care."

Doctor Tréguy leaned forward. "We'll point out that we're near the Atlantic convoy routes. If the Germans used Saint Pierre as a submarine base it would be a disaster for the allies. Our telegram will repeat the last message: he will encounter no resistance."

"It would be an easy victory," added Lafitte. "We're like a beautiful woman with loose knees; we are spread wide open for the great general."

"You mean weak knees."

"Same thing; we're here for the taking."

Jérôme glanced at Chrétien.

"It makes sense to me," said Chrétien. "I'll be happy to send your telegram. When will you write it?"

"We already have," said Doctor Tréguy. "The colonel and I spent all night at it."

"And drinking your whiskey," said Lafitte, baring his yellow teeth with a broad grin.

Doctor Tréguy stood, walked to the bookcase, and returned with a piece of paper. He handed it to Chrétien. "It's all there in Colonel Lafitte's elegant hand."

"Not from Count de Bournat this time?"

"No. We want to let him know it's the people of Saint Pierre who are pleading with him."

"I'll send it off first thing when I get back," said Chrétien.

"Excellent," said Lafitte, rising from the sofa. He crossed the room, poured four whiskeys and passed them around. He held his glass high in front of him. The amber liquid shook in his trembling hand. "Here's to our liberation."

Jérôme raised his glass. "Here's to our dream of liberation."

Little Toinon

16

THE FOLLOWING DAY—the day Claude Cormier was to be released from jail—a hesitant knock came on Jérôme's door. When he opened it, Adrienne was standing before him holding the baby. He gazed at the infant and a warmth came over him, a new tenderness. He was seeing something he had long ceased to believe existed—the miracle of new life. Innocent life. He was overwhelmed with an alien feeling, one he hadn't experienced in a long time. Was it joy? Awe?

"Well, won't you invite us in?' asked Adrienne with a shy laugh.

"Of course."

"My husband is being released today. It's the last chance I'll have to show you the baby. I thought it was … it was your right."

"Oh God," said Jérôme. He felt foolish. He could think of nothing else to say. "Please, please, sit here." He pulled a chair out from the table. "Is this alright? Do you need to put her in a bed? My God, she's beautiful."

"No, this is fine."

Jérôme continued to gaze at the baby. "You named her Antoinette like I asked."

Adrienne nodded. "I call her by her diminutive, Little Toinon."

"Little Toinon."

"Like you asked."

"Little Toinon." Jérôme let the name sound in the air, testing it, becoming familiar with it. "Antoine would have been so happy."

"You must forget Antoine. That was so many years ago."

"May I kiss her?" His heart was racing.

Adrienne stood and held Little Toinon before him so he could kiss the baby on the forehead. "She even looks like you," said Adrienne. "Who would have thought that just that one time …."

"One time," said Jérôme, his voice full of … what? Yearning? Sadness? All mingled with Joy? "One time only."

He recalled that cold day the previous March when, after two whiskeys, he had confessed to her how he had left Antoine to die in no-man's-land, and how she had taken him into her arms to console him, and then told him of her unhappy marriage, and how they had kissed and he had carried her to his bed, and he had been terrified by the intimacy of it, unnerved, threatened, and how they had made love with a passion filled with mutual self pity. He remembered the cool heat of her skin, her naked ankles pressing the backs of his thighs, and how, afterwards, she said it had been a mistake, a forgivable mistake between friends, and that it should never happen again, and he had agreed, even though he knew he was lying, even though he knew he had fallen in love with her, that she had helped him make an astonishing breakthrough, that she had shown him a new, light-filled possibility. But he had agreed with her because, along with the tenderness and the hope and the light, he had felt a rage roiling inside of him and he had been frightened of it. Perhaps, he had felt, he was, after all, truly unfit for love.

But now, with this child, none of that rage was present as he gazed at her. "I never thought I would have a child," Jérôme said. He touched Little Toinon's forehead lightly. The baby cooed. "She was born under the Northern Lights."

"The Northern Lights?"

"At the moment of its greatest flare."

"How do you know?"

He gave her a sheepish smile. "I was under your window."

"*You* were the prowler? Doctor Tréguy said he found nobody."

"He took pity on me."

"But why? Why were you there?"

He gazed at her without answering. Instead, he said, addressing the baby, "Imagine, to be born under the Northern Lights. It means you will live a good and happy life."

"That's superstition," said Adrienne with a laugh. "Would you like to hold her?"

"A life full of peace."

"You only say that because you want it to be so."

"No, no. I believe I've heard that before. Yes … it's an old legend … Inuit, I think." He held out his arms for the baby.

Adrienne said, "Keep her head supported." She handed him the baby.

Little Toinon felt light in his arms. Fragile. An assertion of life that was so delicate it had to be protected the way a hand shielded the guttering flame of a candle. And something flowed from the baby to him, a sense of purpose. The darkness he had for so long felt at the core of his being shifted a little. He felt a stirring of life in his soul, a hope.

He felt love.

"I'm afraid of what my husband will do when he sees Little Toinon," said Adrienne.

"If he touches either one of you, I'll kill him."

"And then your life would be ruined," Adrienne said, placing a hand on his forearm. The cool touch of her skin! "You mustn't let that happen. And you must never say anything about us."

He pressed his forearm against her hand. Cool, tender. Something else stirred inside him, a feeling he recognized instantly though it had been only that one time in March. Desire. "Where's your mother-in-law. Won't she be suspicious if she learns you've brought the baby to show me."

"She went with Monsieur Morel to meet Claude when he's released."

"You must leave Claude. There's no other way."

Adrienne nodded. "I plan to."

Jérôme's eyes brightened. "You'll live with me?"

Adrienne's eyes watered. "I can't. You know that, don't you?"

It was like a new weight falling on him. "But I love you. You've had my child."

"I have."

"Then?"

"What we did wasn't love. It was … compassion. It was just two human beings lost together."

"If you don't love me now, you'll grow to love me." His voice wavered. A sense of desperation swept over him.

Adrienne shook her head. "I can't stay in Saint Pierre. I would die. Besides, Claude would never accept it. He already hates you because of the zebra. If he came to know you were Little Toinon's father, he would kill you … or you would kill him."

"We'll go away."

"Where? You've already said you can't live in France. I don't think you could be anywhere except here. This place suits you."

"I'd do anything to be with you."

"This is your place."

"That can change."

Adrienne squeezed his forearm. "Don't you understand? What brought us together is the very thing that would keep us apart. You have your memories from the last war and I'm living through the hell of this one. I can't live two wars at once."

"The memories don't trouble me anymore."

"Tell that to your eyes. They say otherwise."

"I'll make an effort."

"It won't work, Jérôme. You should know that. You must stay and I—"

"—must go," he said bitterly. "Then you'll leave Saint Pierre?" Jérôme was afraid to say it lest the very sound of it in the air would make it true.

"You died in that war every bit as much as Antoine Douville. I can't live with a dead man … not after all these years with Claude."

"You haven't answered my question. Are you leaving Saint Pierre?" he asked. Her last words burned like a knife twisting in his chest. A familiar darkness came over him.

"I have to. Besides, if I stay, I'll only cause you pain and you've had enough pain for any man's lifetime."

"But Little Toinon …." He gazed at his baby, his tiny miracle.

"You must give her up." She said it quickly, with authority, as though she had been rehearsing it.

"I can't give her up. She's everything to me. Don't you understand? I can't give her up."

"You must. For her sake."

"But—"

"—And me. You must give me up, too."

Jérôme stared at her in astonishment. An unwelcome thought came to him, caused his heart to rise in his throat. "Is there another man?" he asked.

Adrienne lowered her eyes. She nodded.

Jérôme clenched his jaw. He ground his teeth together so hard that his cheek muscles spasmed. "Who?"

"One of the men from the trawlers. We'll sail for France as soon as it's safe."

A rusty nail driven through his brain, his soul. "But ...." Jérôme started to say. Yet he could find no words to express his devastation.

"You mustn't be bitter."

"You ask a lot."

"Bitterness will only make things worse."

"What else is left for me?"

Adrienne nodded sadly. "I know. But it can't be helped."

"What's his name?"

"Jérôme, please ..."

"What's his name?"

Adrienne sighed. "You might as well know. He's Jean-Luc Lavedan. He's from Bordeaux."

Jérôme remembered the man from the Bastille Day church service. He had sat right next to him. Handsome. Young.

A knock sounded on Jérôme's door.

Adrienne started. Her brow wrinkled. "Oh my God, who's that?" She started to rise from her chair.

"Monsieur Sabot?" a voice called.

"It's Gabriel," Jérôme said. He walked to the door and let Gabriel in. Wisps of snow entered with him.

Gabriel said, "I was just—" He stopped when he saw Adrienne and the baby. "Oh, Madame Cormier, it's you."

"Hello, Gabriel." Adrienne wiped the corner of her eye with the sleeve of her coat. She reached for the baby.

Reluctantly, Jérôme passed Little Toinon to Adrienne.

"And you have your little baby." Gabriel said with a broad smile. His eyes were flashing with excitement and pleasure.

"Would you like to see her?" Adrienne held Little Toinon before him and gazed at Jérôme as though to say, "What are we going to do?"

Jérôme said nothing.

Adrienne said to Gabriel, "I'm going to place Little Toinon on the bed. Will you watch her for a few minutes?"

Gabriel's eyes brightened even more. He nodded his head vigorously, removed his coat and hung it in the storm vestibule next to Antoine's trench coat.

Adrienne carried the baby into the next room and Gabriel followed her. When she returned, Jérôme whispered, "We're not finished talking." There was an unwelcome edge of anger in his voice.

She nodded but held her hands to the side as though to ask what could be done. There was a slight tremble to them. Her face was flushed.

Jérôme glanced through the doorway at Gabriel who was bent over the baby, stroking the baby's chin and patting the soft fuzz on the baby's head. Little Toinon almost disappeared in the folds of the duvet. Gabriel made little cooing sounds. The baby gurgled.

Jérôme said, "Leave Little Toinon with him for a few minutes while we talk outside where he won't hear us."

Adrienne bit her lower lip. "I can't. I ...."

"He's trustworthy. It'll only be for a short time."

"But she's only an infant."

"It'll be alright."

"She's never been out of my sight."

"It'll be alright. Don't you think I care for her as much as you do? Don't you think she means everything to me? I'm her father. I would rather die than expose her to danger."

Adrienne replied in a hesitant voice, "Well … if you say it's alright."

Jérôme went into the bedroom and asked Gabriel to watch the baby while he and Madame Cormier took a little walk. He slid the bed against the wall, moved a small bureau against it on the open side, forming a makeshift crib. He patted the duvet on all sides of the baby to form a recess surrounding her. He made sure her face was well clear of the duvet lest she suffocate. He gazed at Little Toinon. "She's sleeping," he said as though pronouncing a small miracle. He turned to Adrienne who had followed him into the room. "She's sleeping," he repeated. "Keep an eye on her," he said to Gabriel. "Make sure she doesn't bury her face in the duvet. Do you understand?"

Gabriel nodded.

"Don't take your eyes off her for a minute."

"I won't."

Moments later, as Jérôme led Adrienne up the slope of *The Mountain* behind his house toward a small stand of dwarf spruce where they would be shielded from prying eyes, she turned repeatedly to look over her shoulder at the house.

"She'll be alright," said Jérôme. "Like I told you; Gabriel can be trusted."

They climbed a slope of snow compacted by the dog sleds used to fetch firewood. The day was bright but the Saint Pierre winds, almost constant at this time of year, scraped at the snow. Skeins of cold snow-smoke skittered across the harder snow, whisking into eddies here and there—tiny, cold snow devils. Mounds and scallops of snow had been encrusted by the wind.

When they reached the stand of dwarf spruce, Adrienne turned and gazed out to sea, her shoulders hunched and her mittened hands stuffed into her coat pockets. A gust came and snow dust whisked across her face. Her cheeks were dry and red. Cracked. She was silent. The wind soughed through the spruce, it hissed against the surface of the snow.

"I got some facial cream for you," said Jérôme.

"What?"

"Chrétien Bastarache brought it."

"Oh."

"I asked him to."

"Thank you."

"There's lots. You'll never run out."

She looked at him for a moment, then turned to look out over the sea again.

"You're looking at France," said Jérôme.

"What?"

"The direction your looking; it's toward France."

"Yes, I suppose it is."

"I'm really going to lose you and Little Toinon," He said it flatly, his voice betraying the bitterness that lodged like a lump in his chest.

She turned, gazed at him with sorrowful eyes. "I don't want to hurt you, but I must go. I can't stay on Saint Pierre."

"So you've said."

She placed a hand on his cheek. "Please, Jérôme, try to understand."

He wanted to scream at her. He wanted to say something that would hurt her, would give her as much pain as he felt, but nothing came. He wanted to ask her about the man from the trawler—this Jean-Luc Lavedan from Bordeaux—but the questions that came to mind were ones he guessed would only yield answers he didn't want to hear. He turned his back to her.

"Jérôme …" she said.

"I thought you didn't want us to use our Christian names."

"Well, under the circumstances …."

He kept his back turned, remaining silent.

"I shouldn't have come," said Adrienne.

"No."

"But you had to see the baby. You had to see Little Toinon. It was your right."

He turned to say something but saw that Adrienne was crying openly now and he was ashamed that this gave him a small pleasure. At least she was suffering too.

Then he saw a movement out of the corner of his eye. He looked down the slope to see Gabriel climbing towards them. He was only twenty yards away. Small whorls of snow rose from his hurrying feet. "What the hell?" Jérôme cried.

Adrienne followed his gaze. "I thought you said he could be trusted?" she cried. There was anger and panic in her voice.

"Gabriel!" Jérôme called. "What are you doing? We asked you to stay with the baby."

"She's sleeping."

"But we asked you to watch her."

"I wanted to show Madame Cormier where we hid the wooden zebra."

"Damn it, Gabriel! I'm angry with you," said Jérôme.

Gabriel gave a hurt expression. "I … I …."

"Oh my God!" cried Adrienne. She brought her hands to her mouth.

"What is it?"

"Claude is at your house! He'll see that I brought Little Toinon to you. He'll know."

Jérôme looked down the slope through the streaks and coils of snow-smoke to see Claude Cormier standing before his front door for a few moments then turning and going into Jérôme's shed. He emerged a moment later, carrying a can. Jérôme recognized its shape even across the hundred yards that separated them. Turpentine! Claude run up to the house and emptied the can all over the front door.

"Jesus, he's going to set fire to the house!"

"Oh, dear God! Little Toinon!" cried Adrienne. She started to bolt down the slope, her feet turning up whirls of snow. "Claude, no! NO!"

Jérôme took off at a run down the slope. Several times, he slipped on the packed snow and went sprawling, plowing crusty snow before him. He passed Adrienne, who shouted, "Stop him! For God's sake, stop him!"

Jérôme fell again, tumbling head over heels twice before landing on his belly, his face scraping through the cold, packed snow. He felt a sharp pain in his right wrist when it became wedged under his body.

Snow snakes coiled up the slope, stinging his eyes. He pulled himself to his feet, holding his wrist with his other hand. With his good hand he brushed the snow from his eyes and was horrified to see a wall of flames suddenly erupt around his front door. Again, he started to run and slide down the slick slope. He saw Claude running from the house toward his own place. He stopped and cupped his hands around his mouth. "Claude, the baby's in there," he yelled. But Claude kept running. "My baby," Jérôme murmured to himself. He saw the curtains in the two windows erupt into flames. He covered the remaining yards as fast as his legs would allow. His lungs ached from the effort. By now, the entire house, its wood dried out by the constant winds, was burning. When he finally reached the house, he hesitated a moment.

The wall of flame has him surrounded. He can hear Antoine calling out to him, but he is disoriented. He doesn't know where the entrance is. "Save me!" he cries....

Then he heard, from inside the inferno, the baby's cry, the sweet, fragile life he had fathered. Shielding his face with his arms, he burst through the disintegrating front door.

Antoine's Trenchcoat

S
HE WAS STILL MORE THAN fifty yards away when Adrienne saw Jérôme pause before the burning house then lunge through the door. She felt as though she were running in slow motion, as though in some nightmare. Every time she tried to run faster, she fell and slid a few yards before coming to a stop. Tears of frustration and fear froze on her cheeks. Again, she picked herself up and started down the slope screaming, "My baby!"

Gabriel hurtled past her. He was moaning, "Oh, please, oh please," and running as fast as he could in the deeper snow to the side of the path.

Suddenly, there was a loud crack and a roar. Adrienne was horrified to see part of the roof collapsing into the house. She couldn't believe it was happening so fast. Was she being punished by God? That was the only possible explanation for the nightmare unfolding before her eyes. Hurriedly, she crossed herself and mumbled a prayer as she ran. "Please, Mother of God, save my baby." She said it over and over, her eyes wide with fright, as she stumbled toward the house and felt the intense heat emanating from it.

Walking now as if in a trance, she started to enter the house when she felt herself being pulled back by a strong pair of arms.

"No, Madame Cormier; there's nothing you can do," cried Gabriel. The house was engulfed in flames. "I'm sorry. I didn't mean it. I did a bad thing."

She struggled in his arms. "Let me go, Gabriel. I must go to my baby." Her voice was dull, lifeless, as though weighed down by an overpowering sense of futility. "I must go to my baby .... my Little Toinon."

Gabriel held her close to him and forced her face into his chest. She felt his chest heaving with his sobs. "I did a bad thing," he snuffled. "I did a very bad thing."

Weakly, she tried to pull herself away, but it was no use. He was too strong. He was holding her too tightly.

"I'm bad! I'm just an idiot!"

Adrienne couldn't move. Everything started to swim before her eyes and she felt faint. It was as though a monster was strangling her, sucking the life from her. And the monster was guilt. In that moment she knew, as she had never known before, the enormous, crushing weight of it. Then all of a sudden Gabriel released her and he was running toward the house. She turned to watch him and saw that he was running toward Jérôme who had just appeared at the opening where the door used to be. He had a bundle cradled in his arms. A rush of new energy flowed into her like wind. She ran.

Jérôme emerged staggering from the flames. His clothes were aflame. Adrienne ran up to him.

His face was blackened and he had no eyebrows. He looked at her, a dazed expression in his eyes, terror. But there was something else in them. An accusation? Then he started to fall backward still cradling the baby in his arms. His head hit the frozen ground with a sickening crack. His body cushioned the baby.

Gabriel fell to his knees beside Jérôme and smeared snow over Jérôme's burning clothes. When the flames were extinguished, he took the baby, who was completely wrapped in a trench coat, and handed it to Adrienne. Then he threw himself beside Jérôme's motionless body and cried, "Monsieur Sabot, wake up! Oh, oh, I did a bad thing! I'm an idiot! Wake up Monsieur Sabot! Please wake up!"

Adrienne pulled back the trench coat. Little Toinon was shrieking. She hurriedly examined the baby's body, probing, prodding, until she was satisfied the baby was unharmed.

Then she turned her attention to Jérôme.

His face appeared badly burned and his body lay stiffly on the ground. Adrienne thought he must be dead. Holding the baby in one arm, she knelt and felt for a pulse. A strip of skin came away in her hand and she felt a retching come to her throat. She jerked her hand away. She saw Jérôme's chest move. "He's breathing, Gabriel!"

Gabriel cried, "Wake up Monsieur Sabot!"

Someone came up from behind Adrienne. "What happened?" It was Claudette, a dishcloth still in her hand.

"Mama, call an ambulance," said Adrienne.

"How did this happen?"

"I did a bad thing!" Gabriel looked up at Claudette with pitiful eyes. His entire body was trembling. "I'm an idiot!"

"Call an ambulance, please," shouted Adrienne.

"I told you something bad was going to happen. I told you God would punish you. I told you."

"Madame Cormier, call a goddamned ambulance!" screamed Gabriel, his eyes round with fury. He charged at her, waving his arms wildly.

Claudette gaped at him, backed away, and said, "Yes ... yes, of course." She ran toward her house.

"Gabriel, go with her. Make sure she calls," said Adrienne.

Gabriel looked from her to Jérôme. His eyes were like those of a frightened animal.

"Go. I'll watch over him."

The ambulance arrived trailing a small convoy that included a fire engine and a police car. They left a trail of spiraling snow clouds. Seconds later, Doctor Tréguy in his battered, salt-encrusted, Peugeot appeared through the swirling snow. One of the firemen knelt over Jérôme while the rest turned their attention to pumping water on the burning house. Columns of hissing steam and smoke started to rise up from the flames.

Doctor Tréguy slid his car to a stop, scrambled across the snow toward Jérôme's prostrate form. "Thank God you're here, Doctor; he looks bad," The fireman said.

Doctor Tréguy knelt beside Adrienne at Jérôme's side, felt for a pulse on the wrist that was not charred. "His pulse is rapid and weak, but he's alive," he said after a moment. His eyes rapidly scanned Jérôme's body. "He's in a bad way. Mostly second-degree burns that I can see, some third-degree. No doubt, he's in shock. We'll need to get some fluids into him."

"He hit his head hard when he fainted," said Adrienne who was still holding and comforting Little Toinon. The baby was wailing.

"Did he fall backward, hit the back of his head?"

"Yes."

Doctor Tréguy carefully examined Jérôme's head and neck. He nodded. "It's safe to transport him. Let's get him to the hospital quickly."

With the help of the ambulance men, Doctor Tréguy maneuvered Jérôme onto a stretcher and carried him into the ambulance. He turned to Gabriel who was shaking violently. "Are you alright?"

Gabriel nodded. "I did a bad thing."

"Yes, yes, but are you alright?"

"I'm alright."

"Are you sure?"

"I'm an idiot."

"Gabriel, listen to me! I need to know if you're alright, able to help."

Gabriel nodded again, his eyes begging for forgiveness.

"Can you drive a car?"

"Yes."

"Then take my car and follow us. I'll go in the ambulance."

"I'm going, too," said Adrienne.

Doctor Tréguy gazed at her for a moment. "Alright, you go with Gabriel. Watch him."

"Hold on," said one of the policemen. "We have a few questions for Madame Cormier."

"Then you can drive her in," said Doctor Tréguy. "We've got to be going!"

"I can't go in the same car as my husband."

"Was he the one that did this?" asked the policeman.

Adrienne nodded.

"I guess I'm not surprised."

She saw the man's look of disapproval and she was certain it was meant for her.

Doctor Tréguy, who had already scrambled into the ambulance, said. "Gabriel, drive Madame Cormier into the hospital after she's finished here." Then he shouted for the ambulance driver to move it. The rear wheel squealed before gripping the snow and the ambulance soon disappeared toward Saint Pierre.

Jérôme's house was a tangled mass of charred wood. The water poured on it had already started to turn to bearded ice. Tendrils of smoke coiled into the air.

After spending five minutes explaining to the police what had happened, Adrienne climbed into Doctor Tréguy's car with Little Toinon. Gabriel said, "If I didn't leave the house, none of this would have happened."

"If all of us didn't do certain things, this wouldn't have happened," replied Adrienne.

Gabriel was confused by the one-way streets and he had to make several attempts before finally finding the Rue Maître Georges Lefèvre. He parked in front of the hospital and he and Adrienne rushed through the main door. They were ushered to a waiting area where Adrienne sat in a chair cradling Little Toinon. Gabriel paced back and forth, mumbling incoherently to himself.

Over the next half hour, several nurses passed through the waiting area, but none of them could, or would, answer Adrienne's worried questions, saying only that the doctor would meet with them as soon as he was free.

Gabriel moved to a corner and stood facing it, rigid, still mumbling.

After twenty minutes, Marie-Lisette appeared. "What happened? How is he?" she asked, her voice edged with anxiety.

Adrienne shook her head. "We know nothing. He was unconscious when they took him in. Doctor Tréguy says he was in shock."

"How did it happen?"

Adrienne averted her eyes and just shook her head.

Marie-Lisette turned to Gabriel. "What happened? Why are you standing in the corner like that?"

Gabriel turned to look at her over his shoulder. His face was streaked with glistening lines where tears had tracked. He said, "I didn't do what I was supposed to do and Monsieur Sabot's house burned down .... The baby was almost killed .... Monsieur Sabot saved it. Now he may die ... I'm as bad as can be!"

"Stop blaming yourself, Gabriel," said Adrienne. "If anyone's at fault, it's me for arousing my husband's jealousy."

"Your husband?" asked Marie-Lisette.

Adrienne nodded. "He set the fire."

Marie-Lisette stared at her and made the sign of the cross. "Oh, my God! But the baby ... Jean-Luc ... Why Monsieur Sabot's house?"

"Please," said Adrienne. "No more. Leave it be. Let's just say that Monsieur Cormier was mistaken." Her eyes begged Marie-Lisette to understand.

At that moment, Doctor Tréguy entered the room, removing a pair of rubber gloves.

Adrienne stood. "How is he, Doctor Tréguy?"

Doctor Tréguy shook his head. "It's too early to tell. He's receiving intravenous fluids. Burn victims lose a lot of body fluids. We're also dressing his burns. Fortunately, what we saw on his head and arms was most of it."

"Will he recover?"

Doctor Tréguy took a deep breath, stuffed the gloves in his side pocket. "Let's get the fluids into him, then see what happens."

"Oh, God," said Adrienne. "We must pray for him."

"That wouldn't be a bad idea," said Doctor Tréguy.

Gabriel returned to the corner, buried his face in his hands. His shoulders heaved.

Doctor Tréguy placed a hand on Adrienne's shoulder and said, "Yes, by all means." He looked over to Gabriel and frowned.

"He feels responsible," said Marie-Lisette.

Doctor Tréguy nodded. "I'll keep you informed. It may be a while."

"We'll wait," said Adrienne.

"Yes, we'll wait," said Marie-Lisette.

Fifteen minutes later, Claudette entered the room. She had a dazed expression. She walked over to Adrienne. "They say Claude did this. Is it true?"

Adrienne nodded.

Claudette's shoulders slumped. She started to sway. Marie-Lisette caught her and guided her to a chair. "My poor boy," murmured Claudette. She looked up at Adrienne and, in a resigned voice, asked, "Is the baby his?"

"Claude's?" Adrienne asked, her brow furrowed.

"Monsieur Sabot's. Is it his? Is Little Toinon his?"

"No," said Adrienne. She snatched a quick glance at Marie-Lisette.

"I don't believe you. Why else would my son do such a thing? It's a crime of passion; they'll understand."

"Monsieur Sabot is not the father. The father is one of the fishermen from the trawlers." As she said it, Adrienne gazed at Marie-Lisette with pleading eyes.

Marie-Lisette stared at her. It was obvious from her expression that the truth had just dawned on her. She shook her head slowly in amazement. Then, taking a deep breath, she turned to Claudette and said. "It's true, Madame Cormier. I must confess that I helped them arrange meetings."

Claudette gazed at her, disbelief written on her face. "No, no, it must be Monsieur Sabot. It was a forgivable crime of passion. Claude was driven insane by Monsieur Sabot's and Adrienne's adultery."

"Believe me, Madame Cormier," said Marie-Lisette. "It was one of the foreign fishermen. His name is Jean-Luc Lavedan."

Adrienne sucked in her breath and shook her head at Marie-Lisette.

But Marie-Lisette ignored her. "You see, it's true. He has a name. Why would I say it if it were not true?"

Claudette stared at her for a long moment then buried her face in her hands, weeping. "My poor son. His life is ruined." She raised her head, took a long, shuddering breath … and fainted. Her body slid from the chair and sprawled on the floor.

While Marie-Lisette ran out of the room to fetch help, Adrienne knelt over Claudette's prone body. "I'm sorry, Mama, I never meant for all this to happen. I should have tried harder to make it work with Claude."

Gabriel stared over his shoulder at them.

Adrienne hugged her baby close to her and knelt gazing at Claudette and mumbling that she was sorry.

Moments later, Marie-Lisette returned with a nurse. By this time, Claudette had regained consciousness and was struggling to sit up. The nurse, however, commanded her to lie down again. "Wait five or ten minutes before trying to get up." She felt for Claudette's pulse.

Doctor Tréguy burst into the room. "What happened?"

"She fainted," said the nurse. "But she seems alright."

Doctor Tréguy knelt to examine Claudette, nodded his agreement with the nurse, and stood. "What caused her to faint?"

Adrienne looked at him without answering.

"The baby doesn't belong to Monsieur Cormier," said Gabriel. "It belongs to Monsieur Sabot and also to a fisherman named Jean-Luc. They are the fathers."

"What?" Doctor Tréguy looked from Marie-Lisette to Adrienne. "What is he saying?"

"The father is one of the fishermen," Adrienne said. But she could tell from the disapproving, suspicious look he gave her that he didn't believe her. After all, he had seen Jérôme under her window when she was giving birth.

"I'm going to check on Monsieur Sabot," he said. "I'll let you all know when there's a change."

But by evening, there was no change and they left for the night, promising to return first thing in the morning.

Because Claudette had told Adrienne she was not welcome in her house, Marie-Lisette prevailed on Monsieur and Madame Freneau to permit Adrienne and the baby to live at the Hotel Lalanne temporarily since it was half vacant. Though they resisted at first, they finally relented, saying they would do it as a favor to Marie-Lisette for her years of excellent service. But as to Adrienne, they made clear their disapproval and that they would not tolerate a situation in which the foreign fisherman was permitted to live at the hotel with her.

Word of what had happened spread quickly throughout Saint Pierre and Adrienne felt that everyone was staring at her every time she left the hotel. For the most part, she stayed in her room, waiting for the few times that Marie-Lisette, in the owners' absence, was able to smuggle Jean-Luc into the hotel by the back door.

She heard from Marie-Lisette that Claude would stand trial for arson and attempted murder at minimum—murder, if it came to that. And though the news left her feeling protected from his violence, it also plunged her into a sea of guilt. Just because Claude was a difficult man to live with and a man who was unable to give her pleasure, just because she had felt lonely for years, she had set things in motion that had led to this. But didn't every woman on Saint Pierre feel lonely at least some of the time? And why should it be any different in France?

Claudette was right: Claude's life was ruined and Adrienne was largely to blame for it. Then there was Jérôme. She had hurt him terribly and for what? He had been a wonderful friend and, that one time, a sweet, tender lover. Now, his life was in the balance and she was planning to take his child from him. If he recovered, perhaps she should make an effort to love him as a husband. She would have to give up Jean-Luc and France, but why should she be afraid of sacrifice after what Jérôme did?

Of course, they couldn't stay in Saint Pierre, but there were other places: Prince Edward Island, Martinique. And every time she thought about it, and about losing Jean-Luc, she collapsed in tears. But what else could she do after causing all that had happened? What she'd said earlier to Jérôme, that he had suffered too much pain to be forced to suffer more was true. But what would give him more pain—her staying with him when she really didn't love him, or her leaving?

And would any of it matter if he died?

The following day, a vicious wind lashed the island. The windowpanes in the hospital rattled in their frames.

Marie-Lisette and Adrienne had been at the hospital only a short while when Marie-Lisette's mother burst into the waiting room. "Gabriel is missing!" she cried.

"What? How?"

"He was crying in his room all morning, then when I went to get him for lunch, he wasn't there."

"But there must be some explanation," said Marie-Lisette.

Sylvie shook her head. "We looked all over, your father and me. Then we went down to the beach where he sometimes likes to go. Your father's dory was missing."

"Oh, God, in this weather?"

"A man on the beach said he saw a boat heading north a few hours before."

"Toward Newfoundland?"

Sylvie nodded. "Your father borrowed a motor dory and headed out after him."

"But the sea is so big. How will he ever find Gabriel?"

Sylvie's lips quivered. She started to sob. Marie-Lisette put her arms around her mother, held her close.

"Marie-Lisette, you must go to Jean-Luc," said Adrienne. "He can help with his trawler. I can't go because of Little Toinon."

"Will he take his trawler out in this weather?"

"Of course he will. Tell him I sent you."

When Marie-Lisette arrived at the quay, there was little activity. On several of the trawlers, men were clearing the topsides of ice, but otherwise the quay was deserted. She assumed most of the men were at the Café Joinville. A bitter, cold wind whipped the slushy water into white caps, sending jets of spume into the air.

She prayed Jean-Luc was on his trawler.

She rushed along the quay.

The footing was treacherous and she had to go slowly lest she slip and fall into the water. She would have little chance of surviving in the icy conditions. The thought made her concern for Gabriel swell to near panic.

When she arrived at *La Petite Fleur* she called his name. "Monsieur Lavedan!" At first there was no answer. She called again, more loudly.

At last, Jean-Luc appeared on deck, rubbing his eyes. "Marie-Lisette, what's the matter? Is there something wrong with Adrienne?"

"No, she's fine. It's my stepbrother." She gazed at Jean-Luc, the angular face, the strong nose, the deep, piercing eyes.

"Gabriel? The—"

"—Please don't say that. He's sweet and intelligent in his own way."

"I was going to say the singer."

"Oh."

"What's wrong?"

Breathlessly, she explained. She had to shout because of the roar and moan of the wind through the rigging of the trawlers.

"A small motor dory in these conditions? It's a near gale out there." He flipped his cigarette over the side. The wind caught it and sent it sailing to leeward.

"Adrienne said you would help."

"Of course," he said, extending a hand. "Come aboard."

She grabbed his hand and levered herself onto the deck. "My father went out after him. He's in a small dory, too."

Jean-Luc shook his head in disbelief. He called his crew topside and guided Marie-Lisette into the pilothouse. "We have no time to waste," he said as he turned the ignition and the trawler's engines rumbled into life. He looked out at the salt rime encrusting the sides of the bow deck. "We should have cleared the ice earlier. But who was to know?"

When two men appeared in the pilothouse, confused expressions on their faces, Jean-Luc explained the situation and ordered them to start clearing as much ice from the rigging as possible while he headed the boat out of the harbor. "Start aloft first," he said. "That's the most dangerous ice."

"Who don't know that?"

Jean-Luc eased the trawler away from the others and steered it towards the mouth of the Passe du Nord-Est. The water in the harbor was relatively calm, protected by the Île aux Marins and the Île aux Pigeons. It was made sluggish by a slush of ice. But as soon as they left the lee of the islands, they were buffeted by steep waves with breaking crests. *La Petite Fleur* reared as if startled, then plunged into the trough between waves, spewing spray to the sides. Marie-Lisette had to grip a railing in the pilothouse to avoid being thrown off her feet.

Gabriel's Flight

18

THE TRAWLER TEETERED MOMENTARILY on the crest of a wave, then plunged into the following trough with a giant spray of seawater. "The sea is even worse than I thought," shouted Jean-Luc. "This is no place to be out in a little motor dory."

"Do you think we'll find them?"

Jean-Luc shrugged. "It's a big ocean and it's hard to see with the waves. All of ten feet, I'd say. They can hide a small boat."

They took a few more big seas over the bow. Already, Marie-Lisette saw rime forming again where Jean-Luc's men had minutes before hacked it away. "Is the ice going to be a problem?"

"Eh?"

She repeated the question, shouting it this time over the shrieking wind.

He nodded. "Changes the balance. Be a problem for those little dories, too. And they don't have nobody to hack at it." As he said it, Marie-Lisette saw the two crewmen stagger forward, holding on to the lifelines, and start to work again at the building ice.

"Your stepbrother," Jean-Luc called. "Does he know much about these waters?"

"As much as anyone on Saint Pierre who grew up the stepson of a fisherman. He went out often with my father."

"Any smuggling?"

"What?" She had heard the question, but it was so odd that she wanted him to repeat it.

"Any smuggling to Newfoundland, like lots of folks here?"

Yes, some," she replied, gazing at him with a baffled expression. "With Monsieur Sabot."

Jean-Luc pressed his lips together and nodded. "Then he probably knows enough to stay away from Little Green Island and Guinare Bank. In that case, I'll make his course to be fifty degrees, true. I guess that's what your father would figure, too." He turned the wheel to starboard and watched the bobbing compass card until they were settled on the proper course.

At her new angle to the waves, *La Petite Fleur* yawed and pitched violently. Marie-Lisette felt a knot of nausea swell in her stomach. She tried to concentrate on the horizon, but it kept being obscured by the heaping waves. Once, she went out on deck, thinking that if she got out of the pilothouse and the smell of fuel she would feel better. But she only lasted a minute or two. The howling wind whipped spume, filled with salt and ice crystals, that stung her face. When she returned to the pilothouse, her cheeks were raw and her eyes were watery.

"I didn't think you'd last long," shouted Jean-Luc with a laugh.

"No."

"Besides, you can't open your eyes long enough out there to be of much use searching."

She took his mild reproach to heart and willed herself to peer out the window despite the growing nausea. Several times she asked, "Do you see anything?"

Jean-Luc only shook his head.

They lurched and plunged into the seas. Marie-Lisette's arms ached from gripping the rail that ran across the pilothouse waist high under the windshield. After a while, she learned to anticipate the violent rhythm and to ease her grip the moment the trawler paused on a crest before crashing into the next wave. Her breathing was quick and shallow, trying to hold down the building nausea.

A half hour later, one of the other men, who had spelled Jean-Luc at the helm, said, "Something off the port bow. Two points."

Jean-Luc rushed forward.

Marie-Lisette said, "Where? What's two points?"

Jean-Luc took her by the shoulders and turned her slightly to the left. "Look just off the bow at about eleven o'clock."

Marie-Lisette opened her eyes wide to gather in more light. But she saw nothing except heaving waves and spume.

Then suddenly Jean-Luc shouted, "Got it! That's them. At least one of them." He took the wheel from the other man and turned *La Petite Fleur* to port. He jammed the throttle forward, the propeller gripped the water, and the trawler shuddered momentarily, then lurched ahead.

After a few minutes, Marie-Lisette saw there were two dories. They were being tossed about violently in the waves. As the trawler approached closer still, she saw that the dories were riding alarmingly low in the water, weighed down with ice.

"They haven't got much time left by the looks of it," shouted Jean-Luc.

One of the dories was completely at the mercy of the sea. The other appeared to make several passes at the first. Marie-Lisette assumed her father was steering the second dory and Gabriel was in the first one. Each time her father approached Gabriel's dory, however, he was driven away by the waves and had to make a long, difficult loop to steer back into position.

La Petite Fleur slowed as Jean-Luc nudged her in close to the dories. Marie-Lisette saw that Gabriel was lying prone on the floorboards of the first dory.

"Your father will never make it in these seas," said Jean-Luc. "As soon as he's out of the way, we'll go in."

"Can you give him another chance?" A sudden thought had come to Marie-Lisette as she watched her father trying so valiantly to save Gabriel.

"What, are you crazy? Look at them. They're so low in the water that they'll go under any minute."

"If there's a way ... it's important."

"What do you mean?"

"It's important that it be him who gets to Gabriel, not us."

Jean-Luc shook his head in bewilderment. He pressed his lips together as though coming to some resolve and yanked a chord to give a blast with *La Petite Fleur's* horn.

Marie-Lisette saw her father look up at them.

Jean-Luc maneuvered *La Petite Fleur* so that she was directly upwind of Marcel and heading slowly toward Gabriel's dory. Marcel nodded his understanding and steered his dory into the lee of the trawler. Close under the starboard beam of *La Petite Fleur*, Marcel's dory rode much easier.

Soon, they were at Gabriel's dory. Jean-Luc played with the gear shift, slipping it into forward and reverse repeatedly in rapid succession to maintain a stationary position to windward of the two dories, calming the waters. Marie-Lisette watched her father lash the dories together and adroitly climb from the one to the other. He bent over Gabriel's inert form for a few minutes then looked up and made a signal to Jean-Luc.

"Swing the crane to starboard," Jean-Luc called to his men. "Lower the tackle to him."

As the men positioned the crane, Marcel untied the two dories and let the one he had been in drift away with the waves. In a matter of moments, the men had lowered the tackle to Marcel. The huge iron hook at its end swayed wildly just above his head. He made several grabs for it, but it was whipping back and forth so violently that he kept missing.

Marie-Lisette muttered a prayer.

Finally, with a lunge that almost propelled him overboard, Marcel caught the hook. His action, however, brought more water into Gabriel's dory. It was swamping. Working quickly, Marcel fashioned a bridle and slipped it under his armpits. Then he gathered Gabriel's body into his arms and waved to Jean-Luc.

"Haul them aboard," shouted Jean-Luc.

Marcel grimaced as the combined weight of his own body and his stepson was taken up by the sling. They were only half way up when a wave lifted *La Petite Fleur* and she lurched. Marcel was slammed hard against the hull. He gave a cry of pain.

"Haul them up quickly or we'll lose them," shouted Jean-Luc.

The crewmen gave a mighty heave on the lines. The pulleys squealed.

Marcel shrieked as the rope cut into the flesh of his armpits. With two more heaves they got Marcel and Gabriel up to the gunwale and hauled them aboard. Marcel fell to the deck hard, grimacing in pain.

Marie-Lisette ran out on deck. "Is he alive?" she cried.

Marcel, pulling himself up to examine Gabriel, said, "Yes, but he needs help. He's frozen stiff."

Marie-Lisette saw blood trickling down her father's wrists. "Papa, you're hurt." she cried.

"The rope cut into me. I'll be alright. Let's get Gabriel below."

It took all three men plus Marie-Lisette to lift Gabriel's body and carry him below where they arranged him on a crew berth. Marie-Lisette gazed at him, horrified. His face was covered with a thin layer of ice and his eyebrows and hair were crusted with salt rime. His legs and arms were stiff and when they positioned him on the berth, his pants and coat sleeves crackled.

"We need to get him warm," said Marcel.

One of the crewmen appeared with a stack of woolen blankets. Marie-Lisette started to carefully arrange them over Gabriel's body.

"No," the man said. "Take his clothes off first. Otherwise, they'll thaw, become wet, and that will keep the cold in."

They worked hurriedly to remove his clothes, struggling with the frozen, resisting material. At last he was naked and Marie-Lisette, once again, arranged the blankets. "Is there a hot cloth?"

"I'll get one," said the man. He went forward and returned moments later with a steaming cloth.

Marie-Lisette took it from him and tenderly applied it to Gabriel's face and hair. Gradually, the ice melted and she tried to catch the drips with a pillow in order to keep the bed dry. She felt *La Petite Fleur* surge forward and knew they were speeding back towards Saint Pierre. The trawler took on a new, even more uncomfortable rolling motion now that the waves were on the quarter.

After about ten minutes, Gabriel's eyes fluttered open.

"Gabriel," Marie-Lisette said. "Can you hear me?"

He moved his head.

Marcel said, "That man gave me this." He held out a bottle of whiskey. "Let's see if he'll take any."

"Can you sit up?" Marie-Lisette asked Gabriel.

He nodded. They lifted him, propped him against the bulkhead, and made him sip the whiskey.

The smell of the whiskey, combined with the close atmosphere below decks and the sickening motion of the boat finally got to Marie-Lisette.

She threw herself onto her hands and knees and started to retch. She heaved violently for several minutes, leaving a string of spittle between her lips and the floorboards, thin as a baby's drool.

"I guess you ain't no fisherman's wife after all," Marcel said with a chuckle. "Might as well read books and such, I guess."

Marie-Lisette looked over her shoulder, wiped her lips with a sleeve, and gave her father a weak smile.

It took almost an hour to return to the quay at Saint Pierre. When they arrived, Sylvie and Adrienne were waiting along with a dozen other people. An ambulance sat at the end of the quay, its motor idling.

By the time they tied up, Gabriel was able to walk with an arm draped over his father's shoulder for support. When they stepped down onto the quay, Sylvie ran up to put her arms around them. "Gabriel, Marcel, are you alright?"

"He's pretty shaken up," said Marcel. "We gotta get him to the hospital so Doc Tréguy can have a look at him."

"My poor boy."

Marcel said, "I'll tell you something, though. He's a hell of a seaman. He got that dory a pretty long ways in some mighty tough seas. I didn't know he had it in him. Make a good fisherman, he will."

The ambulance men came forward to help Gabriel, but Marcel insisted on taking Gabriel to the ambulance himself and then riding in the back with him to the hospital.

Several days passed with no change in Jérôme's condition. Adrienne visited his bedside daily, her only regular excursions outside the hotel. Each time, she was accompanied by Marie-Lisette who hoped in this way to shield her from the reproachful townspeople. Marie-Lisette also visited many other times, often insisting on helping the nurses change his dressings. Indeed, Marie-Lisette was with Jérôme more than anybody, including the medical people.

Doctor Tréguy was at Jérôme's bedside one day when Marie-Lisette and Adrienne visited. He said that Jérôme's vital signs were steadily improving and that he expected his body to recover fully from his burns.

"But what about his mind?" asked Adrienne. "When will he come out of the coma?"

"Ah, that's more difficult to predict. It's hard to say how much of the coma is due to the shock from the burns and how much is due to the severe blow to the head he received. More the latter, I suspect. A coma induced by the shock of burns shouldn't last nearly this long. All we can do is wait ... and keep testing his responses."

"How do you do that?" asked Adrienne. "Can we help?"

Doctor Tréguy nodded. "Talk to him. Touch him. But don't get your hopes up if he does things like yawn or blink or move his eyes about. Those are just automatic responses indicating that the lower brain stem is functioning. The key will be when he recognizes people."

"So he'll recover?"

Doctor Tréguy frowned. "I must be frank. I should have said *if* he recognizes people."

Adrienne and Marie-Lisette exchanged crestfallen looks.

In the days that followed, they took turns talking to Jérôme and touching him, being careful not to touch areas of his skin that had been severely burned. Marie-Lisette read Saint-Exupéry's *Southern Mail* to him, cover to cover. Adrienne told him of Little Toinon's development, her feeding and her sleep patterns. But as each day passed and there was no response, they all started to fear that he might never come out of it.

Two days later, while Marie-Lisette was alone with Jérôme, one of the nurses came into the room and said, "Madame Cormier would like to know if it's alright if she comes in."

"Of course," said Marie-Lisette with a bemused laugh. "She's been here every day, although this would be her second visit today."

"No, no, not that Madame Cormier. Her mother-in-law."

"Oh. Well, yes ... of course she can come in."

"She wanted to be sure that ... that the other Madame Cormier was not here."

"Tell her it's safe. Adrienne left an hour ago."

Moments later, Claudette Cormier walked hesitantly into the room. She seemed tired, drained of emotion. Her hair was unkempt and there were deep shadows under her moist eyes. "How is he?" she asked in a voice entirely stripped of its former acerbic quality. It was an almost fearful voice.

"Physically, he's improving wonderfully. Doctor Tréguy says he should make a full recovery from his burns. It's this coma ... he hasn't responded since the day of the fire."

Claudette gazed down at Jérôme.

Marie-Lisette was certain she detected a look of sympathy in the woman's expression.

"I ain't got nothing against him, you know," said Claudette. "He was always a good neighbor ... except for the stupid zebra thing that is. But that don't amount to nothing compared to ... to this."

Marie-Lisette wondered if Claudette only wanted to know that Jérôme was alive so her son wouldn't be charged with murder. But something in the woman's manner told her otherwise; she seemed genuinely remorseful about the affair.

"Claude asked me to come," said Claudette.

"He did?"

"He's very ... sorrowful ... for what he did. He's always had a terrible temper. He's been praying for Monsieur Sabot. He had a long talk with Monsignor Bernard and I think it did him good. I was there. He made confession."

Marie-Lisette didn't know what to say.

"You can't blame him entirely," Madame Cormier continued. "His father left when he was just a kid. Maybe if I ... if I ...." Claudette waved an arm as if to say it was all so futile. "I don't know."

"Would you like a seat, Madame Cormier?"

"No, I must be going." She paused, then said, "I'll pray for him. I've given Monsignor Bernard money to say a special Mass for his recovery." Then, with a last, sorrowful glance at Jérôme, she left.

The next day, Jérôme regained consciousness. It happened on a day when Adrienne had brought Little Toinon with her and the baby had cried throughout the visit. Perhaps it was the baby's crying, perhaps it was the way Adrienne touched his forehead lightly, or perhaps it was the Mass that Madame Cormier had purchased; whatever it was, Jérôme's eyes flickered open. He seemed to be trying to focus them for several moments, staring blankly at the ceiling.

"His eyes are open," gasped Adrienne.

Marie-Lisette bounded out of her chair to the bedside. "Are you sure it's not just the automatic eye movement that Doctor Tréguy told us about?"

Adrienne didn't answer her. Instead, she leaned closer to Jérôme and asked, "Jérôme, can you here me?"

He blinked his eyes several times, but otherwise gave no response.

"Can you hear me, Jérôme?"

This time, he rolled his head toward her and murmured, "Adrienne."

"Dear God, he's come back," whispered Adrienne. "Yes, it's me." She saw that his arms were shaking and the muscles of his face were twitching. Because of the burn scars, it was difficult to read his expression, but his eyes seemed to betray some kind of terror.

"Oh, my God!" said Adrienne. "Something's wrong!"

"What?"

"I don't know."

"I'll get Doctor Tréguy," said Marie-Lisette as she made for the door.

"Please hurry!"

Silent Night

Octor Tréguy burst through the door, rushed to the bed, took one look at Jérôme, and said, "I think he's in pain." He spoke to Jérôme. "Jérôme, blink twice for 'yes' and three times for 'no' Do you understand?"

Jérôme blinked twice.

"Are you in pain?"

Two blinks.

"Is it severe?"

Jérôme gave two rapid blinks and uttered a garbled "Yes."

"Don't talk." Doctor Tréguy turned to the nurse. "Prepare a morphine injection—a quarter ... no, make that a half grain."

The nurse left the room and returned moments later with a syringe. Adrienne and Marie-Lisette stood against the wall, watching. Adrienne had her hands on Marie-Lisette's shoulders. "How long will it take?" asked Marie-Lisette.

"A few minutes," replied Doctor Tréguy as he probed for the brachial artery in Jérôme's right arm and injected the morphine.

Jérôme squeezed his eyes shut. His breathing was rapid and beads of sweat had formed on his forehead.

Doctor Tréguy said, "You'll feel a lot better soon, Jérôme. Just hang on a few minutes." He stood, handed the expended syringe to the nurse, and approached Adrienne and Marie-Lisette.

"He didn't feel that kind of pain when he was in a coma, did he?" asked Adrienne in a low voice.

"No. At least, I don't think so."

Adrienne raised her hand to her mouth in horror. "You mean it's possible?"

"I wish I knew. Medical science doesn't know everything. The problem is coma victims, when they recover, can't report something their unconscious mind didn't record as memory."

"You mean it's entirely possible he felt that pain all along but was unable to tell us?" asked Marie-Lisette.

"His unconscious mind might have felt the pain even if his conscious mind didn't," replied Doctor Tréguy. "But as to whether he felt the pain, that amounts to a philosophical question about the nature of consciousness and whether a person's identity is his consciousness. I'm afraid that's not my field."

Suddenly, they heard Jérôme make a sound.

They rushed to his side.

"Is the pain going away?" asked Doctor Tréguy.

"Uhh," said Jérôme with a slight nod of his head. Then he rolled his eyes to look at Adrienne. He said something in the form of a question, but she had difficulty understanding him. She gave him a confused look. He repeated his question and this time it came out more clearly. "Little Toinon?"

Adrienne smiled. "She's alright. You saved her."

Jérôme's face muscles twitched slightly in the expression of a smile. A tear formed in the corner of his eye, hung there for a moment, then slid down past his ear. "My baby," he murmured, then closed his eyes.

Doctor Tréguy said, "The morphine is going to make him very drowsy; that was a heavy initial dose I gave him. Before he fully wakes up, we'll give him a little booster, then I think we'll be on top of the pain and can manage things from there."

When Adrienne and Marie-Lisette visited the next day, Gabriel was with them. He had recovered from his ordeal with only a few frostbitten fingertips to show for it. They found Jérôme markedly improved. And each day after that saw him improve even more until Doctor Tréguy finally said, "He'll be able to leave before Christmas."

"But where will he live?" asked Adrienne. "His home was burned to the ground."

"That's already taken care of," said Marie-Lisette. "Monsieur and Madame Freneau have offered him a room at the hotel."

The following day, Gabriel came alone to visit. He approached the bed with his beret clutched against his belly, leaned down, and asked in a quiet voice, "Are you awake, Monsieur Sabot?"

Jérôme opened his eyes. "Gabriel. How are you feeling? They told me about your little escapade."

"I'm alright."

"Your fingers?" asked Jérôme, nodding to Gabriel's bandaged fingers.

"Alright."

Jérôme gazed at him for a few moments, then said, "Pull up a chair."

The chair scraped loudly on the floor as Gabriel dragged it across the room. He sat.

"You know, Gabriel, none of us are saints. Not me, not you, not Adrienne, not nobody. Do you see a halo around my head?"

That made Gabriel laugh. "No."

"There, see?"

"But I did a bad thing."

"Sure, but we all do bad things. It doesn't make us bad people, just like doing good things doesn't make us saints. I guess it's because here, where we live, we have that damned sea. It may look like it's outside of us, but in reality it's inside of us; it affects everything we do."

"But—"

"—Don't 'but' me. I know what I'm talking about. This guilt stuff can get you into real trouble, know what I mean?"

"It was bad out there on the sea."

"That's what I mean."

"I guess."

"I wouldn't want you to be good all the time. It'd be boring."

"Boring?"

"Having to squint my eyes to look at you because of the shining halo."

Gabriel laughed. It was a hesitant laugh.

"Gabriel, do you know the trench coat I wrapped Little Toinon in?"

"Yes."

"Where is it?"

"Madame Cormier has it, I think."

"Find out. If she does, I want you to have it. It was your father's during the war."

Marie-Lisette was behind the desk at the hotel when Monsieur and Madame Freneau entered saying they wanted to talk with her. They wore grim expressions as they went into the small room behind the desk.

She followed them.

Monsieur and Madame Freneau glanced at each other.

Finally, it was Madame Freneau who spoke. "Marie-Lisette, we're very disappointed in you. We agreed against our better judgment to let Madame Cormier stay here with her baby, but it has since come to our attention that you have permitted the foreign fisherman to visit her, contrary to our explicit wishes. Is this true?"

Marie-Lisette felt a tightening in her chest. "Yes, I'm afraid it is."

"We're surprised at you."

"I'm sorry. I take full responsibility."

"That's good, but it doesn't remedy the situation. We're afraid that Madame Cormier must leave."

"But where will she and the baby go?"

"Regrettably, that can't be our concern. We have a respectable hotel to run. Please understand."

Marie-Lisette lowered her eyes. "I'll tell her."

"She can stay through tomorrow."

Marie-Lisette nodded. "Is that all, Monsieur and Madame Freneau?"

They glanced at each other again. This time, it was Monsieur Freneau who spoke. "I'm afraid not, Marie-Lisette. We can't afford to ignore your behavior. I'm afraid you'll have to leave our employ."

Marie-Lisette felt as though she had been punched in the stomach. In an instant, she saw her dreams of studying in France after the war vaporize to nothing. Jobs were extremely hard to come by on Saint Pierre, especially with the war, especially for a woman, and without a job she had no hope of saving enough money. "I understand," was all she could say.

Later that afternoon, when she was alone with Jérôme in his room, Marie-Lisette told him what had happened.

"But that's terrible. Something must be done."

"Yes, I know. But I have no idea where Madame Cormier and the baby can stay. The trawler is out of the question. There's not nearly enough heat for the baby."

Jérôme placed his hand on her arm. "We'll think of something for Adrienne and Little Toinon. But I also mean something must be done about your job."

"There's nothing to be done."

"I'll talk with Monsieur and Madame Freneau."

"It won't do any good."

"You leave that to me." Jérôme stared at the ceiling for a long time while Marie-Lisette sat silently. Finally, he said, "I've got an idea."

"You have? What?"

He gave her an impish smile. "Colonel Lafitte."

"What about him?"

"We can ask him to take in Adrienne and Little Toinon."

"Colonel Lafitte?"

"Of course. Why not? He's got a big house; it's in town; and he's alone. It's perfect."

"But why would he agree to such a thing?"

"For the chance to taste some cooking other than his own. Besides, he thinks I'm some kind of a hero now. He'll do it for me."

"I don't know ...."

"Leave it to me. All you have to do is ask him to visit me and I'll do the rest. Do it now. He'll be at the Café Joinville."

Late that afternoon, Auguste Lafitte appeared at the hospital in his Franco-Prussian War uniform.

Jérôme smelled the urine-impregnated cloth from across the room.

Lafitte informed Jérôme that as soon as he recovered the *Anciens Combattants* would be holding a dinner in his honor to celebrate his heroism. Then he asked if there was anything he could do for Jérôme. When Jérôme told him the situation with Adrienne and Little Toinon, he agreed even more readily than Jérôme had anticipated. He stood up and saluted smartly. "It will be an honor. No true Frenchman would refuse a woman and her baby in need. I will protect them."

"She's a special treasure, you know, that Little Toinon."

"Yes, I understand. Odette and me wanted children very much, but it never happened. I'll care for the child like it was my own."

"Thank you, Colonel. You're a good man. And you know what? I'm sure Madame Cormier will be so grateful that she'll launder your uniform for you."

"Oh, I wouldn't think of it. I wouldn't want to impose."

"No, no, I'm sure she'll want to. After all, you'll want to be at your best when the liberation comes, won't you?"

Lafitte's eyes brightened, he gave a salute. "Yes, of course. *Viva la France!*"

"And there's one other thing, my Colonel. It's true, is it not, that the Hotel Lalanne makes a good deal of money when you hold meetings there?"

"It's true."

"And equally the Café Joinville in which Monsieur and Madame Freneau also hold an interest?"

"Also true."

"Would you do me the favor, then, of asking Monsieur and Madame Freneau to be kind enough to pay me a visit?"

The following morning, Adrienne appeared at Auguste Lafitte's door carrying Little Toinon. His house, one of the larger clapboard residences in Saint Pierre, was on the Rue Louis Pasteur. Adrienne knocked shyly. Moments later, Lafitte opened the door. He was wearing a floral-patterned apron over his uniform.

He bowed graciously. "Madame Cormier. You must forgive me. I was cleaning the house. Please come in." He swayed, grabbed the doorframe.

"Are you alright, Colonel Lafitte?"

"Yes, yes. Just a little dizziness."

"You should let Doctor Tréguy look at you."

"Nonsense, I'll be alright." He waved her into the living room.

Adrienne entered through the storm vestibule into a living room crowded with old Empire furniture—three chairs, a sofa, several lamps, end tables stacked with books, and a sideboard with a couple of glasses and a crystal decanter. A fire was roaring in the stove. On a small table were several old sepia photographs of a woman, presumably his long-dead wife.

Lafitte guided her to one of the chairs. He struggled with the knot in the apron string, blushing, saying, "It belonged to my wife."

"It goes well with the uniform," said Adrienne with a smile.

Lafitte laughed. "But you are not to tell the others." He went to the sideboard, lifted the decanter and showed it to her. "A whiskey?"

"Isn't it early in the day for a whiskey, Colonel Lafitte?"

"I find it fortifying. Besides, we must talk, Madame Cormier, and I find it goes better with a little tipple." If it hadn't been for the yellowed and rotten teeth, his smile could have been that of a country gentleman in France. Rumor was that he had once been exactly that. People pointed to the formality of his speech as evidence.

"In that case, Colonel, I'll have just a sip," Adrienne said, trying to match his polite elocution.

"Good, good. You'll enjoy it; it's some of Monsieur Sabot's," he said with a mischievous wink.

Adrienne blushed. "What is it you would like to talk about, Colonel Lafitte?" She noticed that as he poured the whiskey there was a tremble to his hands that caused the decanter and the glass to clink together musically.

He crossed the room and handed the glass to her, sitting himself in the chair opposite with his own glass. He gazed at Little Toinon. "Well, when Monsieur Sabot approached me about having you and the baby live here for awhile—"

"Monsieur Sabot?"

"Yes."

"I thought it was Marie-Lisette Morel who approached you."

"No, it was Monsieur Sabot."

"I see."

"Yes. But as I was saying, when it became apparent to me that you and your child would be living here for a time, I asked myself how I could assure that the arrangements were most comfortable for both of us." Then, nodding toward Little Toinon, he added, "For all three of us."

"That's most kind. I don't wish to be a bother."

"Nonsense." He gave his dry, thin laugh. "It has been some time since I've enjoyed the company of a lovely woman." He snatched a glance at the sepia-toned photographs. "And, I must tell you, Madame Lafitte and I were never blessed with children. So you see, this will be a completely foreign, but I assure you, delightful experience for me."

"I hope Little Toinon doesn't cry too often and disturb your peace."

"Tut, tut!" He gazed at Little Toinon with soft eyes, then said, "I've seen to it that I have milk in the house for the little one."

Adrienne said, "Oh, that's very kind, but it's not necessary. I breast feed."

Lafitte's mouth dropped. Apparently, this was something he had not considered. "Oh, oh, oh … I see. Well, I … In that case I … I shall leave the room whenever it's necessary." He rose from his chair. "Shall I leave now?"

Adrienne laughed. "That's not necessary. She's already been fed."

"I see." Lafitte paused, at a loss for what to say. Finally, he said, "Well, there's extra milk should you want it." He lowered himself into the chair again.

When he didn't speak for a few moments, Adrienne said, "You wanted to talk with me about living arrangements?"

"Oh, yes," he said, jolted back to the moment. "Habits."

"Habits?"

"Yes, habits. A man of my advanced age has accumulated a lifetime's worth of habits. I thought it best to tell you what they are so that you may … may …."

"Accommodate to them? I assure you, I don't wish you to change your routine in any way."

"Yes, of course, something about old dogs and new tricks. You're quite right. That is, indeed, what I'm talking about, Madame Cormier."

"What are these habits, Colonel Lafitte?"

"Oh well, this is, how shall I say? Delicate?"

"If we are to live together, we mustn't be overly concerned about delicacies. Don't you agree, Colonel Lafitte?"

"Yes, of course." He paused, then said, "I'm regular, Madame Cormier."

"Regular?"

"Yes. Very. You see, I require the facilities at precisely the same time each morning." He smiled sheepishly. "The older I get, the greater the need for precise timing without even a moment's delay."

"I wouldn't dream of upsetting your timing."

"It's always very early in the morning. You'll probably be asleep. You see, I've made it my business to be down at the quay each morning before dawn. When the Free French come to liberate us, I intend to be the first to greet them. Invasions always occur at dawn."

"You believe we'll be liberated?" Adrienne's heart quickened at the prospect. She refused to dismiss the notion as an old man's fantasy.

"Without doubt. I, myself, have communicated with General de Gaulle." He gestured toward the photograph of de Gaulle he had cut from a magazine and framed.

"I pray that it will be soon," Adrienne replied.

"It will be, I assure you." He went on to tell her about other details of his daily routine, concluding with, "And I must say, I have difficulty from time to time clearing my nose. My wife used to say that I hacked."

"Hacked?"

"Yes. Quite ... forcefully."

"Oh, well, I have the same problem, Colonel Lafitte."

"It's this awful sea climate," he said.

Jérôme improved so rapidly that he was able to move into the hotel a week earlier than expected. Two days before Christmas he said he wanted to go out into the street for the carol singing. "It's been a long time since I've heard Gabriel's sweet voice. Will you help me, Marie-Lisette?"

"Of course. How could I refuse the man who persuaded Monsieur and Madame Freneau to give me back my job?"

Supported on one side by Marie-Lisette and on the other by the crutch lodged under his left armpit, Jérôme prepared to step outside onto the snow-covered street. Since he no longer required morphine, he asked Marie-Lisette to take him first to the Café Joinville for a drink. "To warm my insides before we sing carols."

"But Monsieur Sabot, women don't go into the café."

Jérôme laughed. "There's no law. I think the men will make an allowance this once. I am, after all, somewhat of a hero," he said with a chuckle.

They went out into the cold air.

All through that afternoon, Marie-Lisette had watched as the weather moved in leaving a featureless gray dome over the town. It was a snow sky and it reminded her of those toy globes that encase tiny village scenes and when you shook it, imitation snow descended on the village. It had seemed to her Saint Pierre needed only some giant child to shake its world and the snow would come tumbling down from the sky. Now, as they walked to the café, she felt the first snowflakes wet and warm on her nose and eyebrows. The ice-crusted old snow groaned under the crunch of their footfalls.

Jérôme's crutch left a sinuous trail in the snow.

They passed under Doctor Tréguy's window and faintly heard a snatch of one of the Chopin piano concertos. The doctor had been playing his new records incessantly since receiving them from Chrétien Bastarache.

At the café, Jérôme was greeted as a hero. So many men wanted to buy him a drink that he ended up having three before Marie-Lisette could drag him out of the place. "We'll miss the carol singing," she said, tugging him on the arm.

Out on the street, people were slowly converging on the Place de l'Eglise where the choral group, with Gabriel as their lead singer, was already warming up. The mood was one of longing. Everyone Jérôme met first asked about his recovery then made some comment about the course of the war. The plight of France was on everyone's mind.

Auguste Lafitte said, "As for me, I will not celebrate Christmas until our beloved France is saved just as you saved that lovely baby." He was breathing heavily, as though unable to catch his breath. He raised a hand to his chest.

Monsieur Pichot, who was standing with him, nodded his agreement. "The salvation of France is the only Christmas gift I want." He gazed at Lafitte with a furrowed brow.

"That may be a while coming," said Jérôme, who was also watching the colonel. "For the moment, I'd settle for our own little liberation."

"Yes," said Auguste Lafitte, "a permanent one."

"But you heard General de Gaulle today, didn't you?" asked Pichot.

"Of course. Who didn't?" replied Lafitte.

From London, de Gaulle had broadcast a Christmas message to the children of France in which he had said France was like a beautiful lady who had a brutal, cunning, and jealous neighbor.

"This neighbor, Germany, wanted to reduce all those who surrounded her to servitude and so she launched an attack in nineteen-fourteen. But Lady France stopped her at the Marne and at Verdun. Then the victorious allies had gone their separate ways and ignored Germany who took advantage of this naiveté and pounced again on Lady France. He said the enemy claimed it served France right to be beaten. But the French nation, he told them, is your fathers, your mothers, your brothers, and your sisters and that, as all the children of France knew well, they were not responsible for the defeat of France. The defeat was caused by a lack of planes and tanks. But now, the good and brave soldiers, sailors, and airmen of France will turn defeat into victory because she has allies who will help provide the materials necessary for victory. He concluded by saying, "My dear children of France, you are hungry because the enemy eats our bread and meat. You are cold because the enemy steals our wood and coal. You suffer because the enemy trumpets over you and tells you that you are the sons and daughters of a vanquished people. Hah! I myself am going to make you a Christmas promise. Dear children of France, you will soon receive a visit, the visit of victory. Ah, how beautiful she will be! You will see."

"This visit he promises," asked Pichot. "Can it be us who will be visited?"

"Why not?" asked Lafitte.

But Jérôme shook his head. "It would be a fine Christmas present, but you are dreamers. Why would de Gaulle bother with a tiny archipelago in the middle of a cold sea where German submarines roam?" Of course, he could say nothing to Pichot, but he exchanged a glance with Colonel Lafitte saying that just as de Gaulle ignored Marie-Lisette's plea, he would also ignore the latest telegram.

The others grumbled but could offer no satisfactory answer so they took their places with forlorn expressions in the church square.

Even the singing of the carols was subdued and melancholy as though people felt joy had to be put on hold until the allies won some victory—at least one.

A gentle snow fell, drifting down through the windless air. Lights spilling from the buildings daubed the snow a soft gray. It suited the somber spirit of the people of Saint Pierre.

With its edge of melancholy, Gabriel's voice was never so sweet. So much so, that when the choir finished singing the last carol, Silent Night, people begged him to sing it again, solo. And when he started singing, everyone fell silent and held hands under the slowly descending snow.

O nuit de paix, Sainte nuit
Dans le ciel L'astre luit
Dans les champs tout repose en paix …

When Gabriel's sweet voice faltered on the irony of the words that throughout the land all rest in peace, and when he repeated the phrase because he would settle for nothing less than perfection, and when his voice again failed him, it seemed to penetrate every heart.

When Marie-Lisette tightened her grip on Jérôme's hand and he saw she was crying, he reached out with arms still stiff with burn scars and half-hugged her. He looked to the edge of the crowd where he'd last seen Adrienne. She was still there, holding his Little Toinon close to her bosom. Jean-Luc Lavedan stood next to her, his hand on her shoulder. Colonel Lafitte stood behind them, fatherly. Jérôme marveled at the generous spirit of Lavedan who, upon learning the baby was not his, as he inevitably did, nevertheless professed his love for Adrienne and his desire to take her and the baby to France.

"I'm tired," Jérôme said to Marie-Lisette. "Perhaps it's time for me to go to bed."

"Yes," she replied. "Maybe tomorrow, and on Christmas Day itself, we can pretend just for a little time that there is no war."

"We can pretend."

As they started back toward the hotel, they were not alone. After Gabriel's singing of Silent Night, everyone seemed to feel it was time to go home and light some candles and say some prayers into the night and snuff out the candles and go to sleep. They walked through the softly falling snow mostly in silence, a people filled with fear and longing.

At first, Jérôme slept fitfully, thinking mostly of Adrienne and sweet Little Toinon. Only briefly did he think of Antoine and the war, but his memories no longer seemed to hold such a devastating power over him. Toward midnight, he slipped into a deep, peaceful sleep.

Liberation

T HE DAY BEFORE CHRISTMAS, Jérôme was up before dawn, feeling refreshed. When he entered the hotel lobby, Marie-Lisette said, "You're up early, Monsieur Sabot. Couldn't you sleep?"

"I slept well. Besides, I've slept far too much these last weeks. There are things I need to do."

"What could you possibly have to do on the morning of Christmas Eve?"

Jérôme looked out the window. Large snowflakes fell through the soft light that spilled from the hotel window. "I would like to go for a short walk before anyone else is up. I've always enjoyed the feeling of owning the world when everybody else is asleep. The solitude."

"Would it ruin the mood if I accompanied you?"

"On the contrary, in your case it would make it all the more special."

"Where shall we go?" asked Marie-Lisette as she slipped into her coat and gloves.

"I have a place in mind," answered Jérôme. He held the door for her. But he said nothing more.

In the fragile half-light that precedes dawn, a light as fragile as a new-born infant, they strolled through the snow-covered street, their boots crunching the newly fallen snow. Marie-Lisette didn't ask where they were going, but she saw from Jérôme's expression that he had a special purpose in mind.

They crossed the square and Jérôme, hobbling with deliberate steps, guided them towards the War Memorial, its stone surfaces softened by a mantle of snow.

Jérôme stopped, gazed at it for several moments before slowly mounting one of the two sets of stairs that reached out like welcoming arms to guide visitors to the obelisk. He placed the crutch on each step in succession, hauling himself up with difficulty.

He went to where the names of the dead were inscribed. He studied the names until he found the one he was looking for: Antoine Douville. He removed his beret and gloves and reached out with his bare right hand to touch the name. The marble was as cold as a block of ice. He allowed his fingers to explore the recessed letters for a long moment, feeling the coarse texture of the stone, before bowing once and turning to descend the stairs.

"My mother's first husband was a great friend of yours, wasn't he?"

"Yes, Marie-Lisette, a very great friend. What's more, I believe in my heart that he's a friend still."

They walked slowly back toward the hotel. Saint Pierre rested in almost total silence. There was no wind and even the seawater, without its usual waves, was silent.

As they crossed the foot of the quay, they came upon Auguste Lafitte, his red trousers shining dimly in the increasing light. His ancient uniform was modified by a pair of thick, pink woolen socks that clashed with the red of the trousers. He was gazing out to sea.

"Colonel Lafitte, what are you doing out so early?" asked Jérôme.

Lafitte started. "Oh, Jérôme … Mademoiselle Morel, you startled me. I'm out every morning at this time. It's my habit. Invasions always come at dawn and I want to be the first to greet our saviors."

"You're expecting to see General de Gaulle himself sailing up to the quay?" asked Jérôme with a broad smile.

"You're making sport with me."

"No, no. We all want liberation. But on Christmas Eve?"

"Can you think of a better time?"

"No, I guess I can't."

"There, you see?"

Jérôme and Marie-Lisette bid him a happy Christmas, then started across the square toward the hotel.

They'd gone no more than five steps when they heard Lafitte cry out, "*Mon Dieu!* Impossible!"

They turned. "What is it, Colonel?"

He pointed out to sea. "Look!"

A ship was emerging out of the murk of dawn. It ghosted toward them silently.

"*Mon Dieu!*"

As they watched in stunned silence, a second ship appeared, then a third. They appeared to materialize out of the gloom like apparitions in a dream, as though they were assembling themselves on the spot from moist molecules of atmosphere. They were followed by yet a fourth ship, a strange elongated tube low on the water that Jérôme recognized immediately as a submarine.

"It's the invasion," said Auguste Lafitte, his voice filled with awe. "At dawn on Christmas Eve."

"Are you sure they're Free French?"

"Who else would they be?"

"Germans … Americans … Canadians. Maybe even the Vichy fleet from Martinique."

Marie-Lisette squinted her eyes and said, "They're Free French," she said.

"How can you tell?"

"I see the flag. It has the Cross of Lorraine."

Lafitte gave a squeak of joy.

Jérôme peered at the lead ship. He could see a flag, but he couldn't make out what it was.

"I see no flag," said Lafitte, frowning.

But as the ships neared and turned to make for the inner harbor, the French tri-color with the Cross of Lorraine in the white band became clearly visible to them all.

"We're liberated!" cried Lafitte in a thin voice cracking with emotion. "We're liberated!" He started to dance a jig on the quay, then he stopped, out of breath. He put a hand to his chest.

"They're corvettes," said Jérôme. "And a submarine."

"The telegram worked!" cried Colonel Lafitte, amazement in his voice.

"No," said Jérôme. "Chrétien left only a short while ago. There hasn't been enough time for de Gaulle to receive the telegram and organize an expedition. It was Marie-Lisette who did it!"

Marie-Lisette gazed at him, accepted Colonel Lafitte's hug, and said, "I've got to tell the others," She took off for the hotel.

In moments, she burst into the lobby.

Several men, sleepy-eyed, looked up in bemusement.

"The quay," she said, breathless. "Ships! … Free French!"

The men stared at her, bewildered expressions on their faces. "Free French?"

She'd already started to bound up the stairs. She stopped, turned, and said, "Free French! General de Gaulle listened to me! Me, Marie-Lisette Morel!"

Then she took the stairs two at a time and began knocking on every door. When she'd aroused all the guests, she bounded down the stairs again.

The men who had been in the lobby were already gone. Several other guests appeared, rubbing sleep from their eyes. She shouted out the news to them as she dashed through the lobby and out into the street. She ran as fast as she could on the slippery streets until she came to Auguste Lafitte's house.

She pounded on the door. When no one answered, she pounded more vigorously.

Finally, Jean-Luc Lavedan came to the door. Marie-Lisette gazed at him and said, "You're not supposed to be here."

"It's alright. The colonel is always away in the morning."

Adrienne appeared, still tying her robe at the waist.

"Adrienne, we're saved!" cried Marie-Lisette. "Free French ships are entering the harbor right this very minute."

Adrienne gasped. "Can it be true?" She put her arms around Jean-Luc's waist.

"Get dressed. Come see for yourself," replied Marie-Lisette before turning and running out into the street again. To everyone she passed, she shouted out the news.

Already, a crowd of confused and sleepy people had started to gather, slowly walking toward the quay in awed silence. They emerged in small groups from the Rue Borda, the Rue General Leclerc, the Rue Paul Mazier, the Rue Maréchal Foch. Assembling from all directions, they quietly came together as if afraid to believe only to be disappointed once again.

Marie-Lisette ran through them to find Auguste Lafitte standing at erect attention, his right hand raised in salute.

Jérôme stood beside him.

"It really is them, isn't it?" Marie-Lisette said.

Jérôme nodded slowly, a look of exaltation on his face.

The ships glided silently on the still water, barely making headway. Two of them, plus the submarine, slowed to a stop a short distance from the quay. The lead ship, however, drifted slowly up to the quay, stopping alongside with a rumble of its engines. A gangplank was lowered with a clatter of chains and a dozen men, weapons ready, bounded down the gangplank. Holding their weapons on the crowd, they split into two groups, one heading for the bollard near the bow of the corvette, the other toward the one near the stern.

The people of Saint Pierre stood motionless and silent, eyes wide with amazement. While several men at each bollard stood facing the crowd with their weapons, several others accepted lines heaved to them from the bow and from the stern of the ship. Working quickly, they fastened the lines to the bollards then joined the other men facing the crowd, guns leveled.

An officer appeared at the top of the gangplank. He addressed the people of Saint Pierre. "I am Admiral Muselier of the Free French Navy. In the name of General de Gaulle I must warn you against resistance."

Several people in the crowd chuckled. "Resistance?"

Auguste Lafitte snapped his heels together. "I am Colonel Lafitte, veteran of the Franco-Prussian War and leader of the Gaullist forces on Saint Pierre. We welcome you." He saluted smartly, breathing heavily.

Admiral Muselier returned the salute with a smile. "We have come to liberate the people of Saint Pierre and Miquelon from the Vichy collaborationists. We have three corvettes and the *Sourcouf*."

Jérôme recognized the name. It was the largest submarine in the world. He thought it had gone over to the Vichy.

"Where is the Vichy administrator of these islands?" asked the admiral.

Count de Bournat, pushing his way to the front of the crowd, out of breath, apparently from running all the way from his residence, said, "I am here."

"Do you intend to resist?"

The count gave a sardonic smile. "We have two machine guns and a cannon which we are afraid to fire. I have already ordered my men not to shoot."

"We do not intend to impose liberation on you," said the admiral. "Tomorrow, on Christmas Day, we will hold a plebiscite. Each citizen will chose between the Free French forces of General de Gaulle, and the Vichy collaborationists of Pétain. It will be a secret vote, so no one need fear reprisals."

A great cheer rose up from the crowd. Some people started to dance. Others shouted Christmas greetings to the sailors aboard the corvette. Others sang the Marseillaise.

The next day almost everybody on Saint Pierre and Miquelon who had the vote showed up early at the city hall. Each was handed a ballot that offered two choices:

—Free French

—Collaboration with the axis powers.

As each person was handed a ballot, an official reminded them that it was a secret vote and they need not reveal their choice.

However, starting with Auguste Lafitte who had insisted on being first in line, most of the people walked up to the official after completing the ballot and proudly announced, "I have voted for Free France."

And, though he kept reminding them they need not announce their vote, they continued to do so. "I have voted for Free France."

After voting, nearly everybody milled about near the city hall, unwilling to leave, waiting for the official vote count. Even in the street, people went around to tell their friends they had voted for Free France. There was joy in their eyes as they chatted excitedly. Suddenly, despite all that had been happening, the war seemed far away. Only after seeing the happiness in their faces did Jérôme realize how truly sad they had been.

As he stood on the corner chatting with Auguste Lafitte and Marie-Lisette, Jérôme saw Adrienne at the edge of the crowd carrying Little Toinon in her arms. And in the midst of his own joy for Saint Pierre, he was suddenly hit with a deep sadness. Now that the Free French would be governing Saint Pierre, he realized he would have only until spring to persuade Adrienne to stay. If the trawlers sailed in May when conditions turned favorable for an Atlantic crossing, and she had not agreed to stay, he would lose her and Little Toinon.

Several hours later, an official emerged to announce the vote totals. Ninety-eight percent of the vote had gone to General de Gaulle and the Free French.

Auguste Lafitte started to sing the Marseillaise in his squeaky voice. But he managed to get only part way through the first verse when his eyes grew round, his chest heaved, and he gasped. He grabbed at his chest. His knees buckled and he collapsed to the ground, sprawled on his back and staring up into the sky. Snowflakes drifted onto his blanched face.

Jérôme fell to his knees. "Colonel Lafitte!"

Lafitte rolled his head to look at him. "I told you they would come at dawn."

"You did, Colonel."

Lafitte took several rapid breaths. He seemed to be having difficulty. He looked at Jérôme. "Where's Boullot?"

Jérôme looked over his shoulder at the crowd. He spotted the man. "Boullot, the colonel wants to see you."

Boullot stepped forward, gazed at Lafitte.

Lafitte bared his teeth in a broad smile. "Remember what I said?" He passed his left hand over his right biceps. His smile broadened. Then his eyes rolled. He murmured, "Odette." Then he died.

The following day, someone advanced the idea of firing the Béarn's cannon in celebration of the liberation and in honor of Colonel Lafitte. Several dozen people were gathered on the quay when the cannon was fired with a roar, ripping a gaping hole in the Béarn's deck through which it tumbled, plunging through the hull to the bottom of the harbor.

Within minutes, the Béarn followed.

Epilogue
May, 1942

Iceblink in a New Light

S PRING CAME AGAIN as it always did. The ice that had fringed the harbor disappeared and the waves became more sprightly. The rigging and topsides of the trawlers were at last free from rime and men in shirt-sleeves prepared their boats for departure.

Motor dories once again made out to sea for a day of fishing.

And in the streets of Saint Pierre snow melted and movement became easier. On *The Mountain* rivulets of melt water appeared and began to meander down the slope. Warmer winds blew and the trees shook themselves of snow.

Cracks appeared also in the despair that had frozen the souls of the Saint Pierrais. Admiral Muselier had appointed an aide to be the new Free French administrator of Saint Pierre and the Cross of Lorraine flew over the town. Britain, in her finest hour, had survived the blitz and the war was now being taken to Germany as Lancasters and B-17s began bombing Lubeck and Essen, Cologne and Kiel. America had entered the war and had begun a massive mobilization to prepare for the eventual liberation of Europe. Already, she had won several engagements in the Pacific and had even sent Doolittle to raid Tokyo.

More melodious voices appeared in the air to counter the constant grunts, rasps, and screeches of the sea birds. Chickadees sang their sweet whistle of a mating song. Nuthatches appeared, feeding as always upside down, and singing their seesaw series of high, thin notes. The northern mockingbirds filled the air with all manner of song matched, of course, by the babbling of the bobolink.

The bird songs accompanied the metallic *chip-chip-chip* as Colonel Auguste Lafitte's name was being carved onto the war memorial.

One day, Marcel Morel appeared at the hotel with Marie-Lisette and Gabriel. He said to Jérôme that he wanted to help him rebuild his house. He offered to recruit as many men as possible and even to provide some of the wood. Madame Imatz at the Café Joinville said she would set up a pernod bar at the building site in the back of Jérôme's truck and this helped inflate the workforce. Doctor Tréguy appointed himself building supervisor and insisted a Free French flag be raised at the building site in honor of Colonel Lafitte. It flew from a pole affixed above the door of Jérôme's shed.

By mid-May, building was already well along with a crew of carpenters working and singing traditional songs to Gabriel's lead. But even before the rebuilding of his house had started, Jérôme had assigned himself a special project.

Near the shed, he built a bird feeder.

Toward the end of May, Adrienne, feeling it was her responsibility before leaving for France, visited Claude at the jail. He seemed a changed man, quiet, sorrowful. The anger was gone from his eyes, replaced by a look of deep contrition.

"I've been talking with Monsignor Bernard," Claude said when she commented on his changed attitude. Then he startled her by begging that she not leave him. "I'll adopt the child," he said.

"No, Claude. It would never work. You know that."

"But I've reformed."

She shook her head sadly. "Sometimes, it's too late." Her knees trembled; she wanted to leave the place. "You'll find another woman."

"I don't want another woman."

"It's too late, Claude."

She stayed for only five minutes. As she left, Claude said, "I never had a father!"

It made her weep.

As the last of the supplies were being loaded aboard Jean-Luc's trawler, Adrienne said to him, "Before we leave, I must say goodbye to Monsieur Sabot who saved our Little Toinon."

"I'll go with you," replied Jean-Luc. "I owe him thanks, too."

"No, I must go alone."

"But …."

"You must trust me, Jean-Luc."

At last, Jean-Luc relented. She kissed him and gathered Little Toinon into her arms. "I won't be long," she said.

When Adrienne knocked on Jérôme's door at the hotel, Marie-Lisette answered. "I just brought him breakfast," she said, stepping aside so Adrienne could enter with Little Toinon.

Jérôme bolted out of his chair and rushed toward her. "You've come to show me Little Toinon," he said with the excitement of a child.

Adrienne turned to Marie-Lisette. "Can we talk alone?"

Marie-Lisette gave her a knowing smile. "Of course."

After Marie-Lisette left, Jérôme said, "She's grown." he tickled the baby under the chin, looked up at Adrienne, smiled, and said, "May I try one last time to persuade you to stay?"

Adrienne smiled, shook her head.

At least once a week since Christmas, Jérôme tried to persuade her to stay. At first, his pleadings had been impassioned, but gradually he'd appeared to be doing it only out of form. He seemed to have accepted the inevitable and with that acceptance a new peace had come to his countenance. It pained him to lose his child, but he knew she would have a far better life in France than she could possibly have on Saint Pierre. He had come to realize that wherever she was, he would always know that she was his child, that he had brought a life into the world. In the end, that was enough.

"When do you leave?" he asked.

"You should eat your breakfast," she said, nodding to the bowl of porridge that sat steaming on a side table.

Jérôme gave a dismissive wave. "I have years and years to eat breakfasts. When do you leave?"

"Today. In an hour."

"So soon?"

"It's almost June."

Jérôme nodded. He gave her a resigned smile. "May I hold her in my arms?"

Adrienne handed the baby to him. He gazed down at Little Toinon, his eyes aglow with love and awe. In a soft voice he said, "Grow up to be a fine woman, Little Toinon ... and always remember to have courage. You were born under the Northern Lights and that means you will have a good life. Someday, I'll visit you in France ...." he lifted his eyes to Adrienne. "If it's alright with your mother."

"It would please me greatly to see you in France," she said. "For my sake, for Little Toinon's sake ... and for your sake."

After Adrienne and Little Toinon left, Jérôme went down into the lobby. "They're leaving in an hour," he said to Marie-Lisette.

"I know. She told me."

"I'm going down to the quay to see them off," said Jérôme. "Would you like to join me?"

"Are you sure you want to?"

"I'm sure."

"And are you sure you want me there?"

"I would be very pleased to have you there."

Together, they walked down to the quay and stood at a distance while the trawlers made final preparations to leave in convoy. They would be escorted most of the way across the Atlantic by two of Admiral Muselier's corvettes. Each of the trawlers carried a Free French flag in its rigging, donated by the many friends of Auguste Lafitte. A gentle breeze fluttered the flags. Dozens of seagulls swooped and glided around the trawlers.

A small crowd of people stood with Jérôme and Marie-Lisette watching the preparations. There was little conversation.

When, at last, *La Petite Fleur* pulled away from the quay, Jérôme waved. He was pleased to see Adrienne answer his wave with a beaming smile. She held Little Toinon up above her shoulders for Jérôme to see. He watched as *La Petite Fleur* and the other trawlers formed themselves close alongside the two corvettes and headed out of the harbor.

Slowly they moved past Île aux Marins and then Île aux Pigeons, and then out onto the vast isolation of the sea under a benediction of sunlight, their hulls and rigging silhouetted against the glow of iceblink.

Marie-Lisette fingered the bank passbook that was never out of her possession and said, "It must be sad to see your child leave."

"She'll have a better life in France ... once the war is over."

"But you're her father."

Jérôme shook his head. "It's true, I gave her life. But it's the child who also gave me life. I couldn't be more happy."

"Will you ever see her again?"

"When the war is over, I'll go to France."

"Perhaps we'll go together."

"Perhaps."

Marie-Lisette took Jérôme's hand. They walked back along the quay, across the square, and into the hotel crowded with people talking about the possibility that *Le Celte* would make it through this year now that the warmer weather had arrived.

Please visit
www.normanggautreau.com
to see video trailers and descriptions
of the author's other books

www.ingramcontent.com/pod-product-compliance
Lightning Source LLC
Chambersburg PA
CBHW020550180626
46810CB00007B/2452